"I sup

Jennifer spoke quietly. "Thanks for coming to rescue us, and I'm sorry for knocking you into my flower bed." She raised her chin slightly. "Though I can't believe you were that upset just because the boys had dug a hole."

Jason suspected they'd be at odds again if they pursued that discussion. "Why don't we have breakfast before we talk about your petunias or your sons?"

"Do my sons annoy you, Roger Hollenbeck?"

He could see sparks igniting in her beautiful eyes. He mentally crossed his fingers. "It's Jason, and your sons are adorable." How could she argue with that one?

He was rewarded with an electric smile just as he noticed a big cloud of black smoke wafting from his kitchen.

"Good Lord!" he cried. "What have those kids done now!"

Dear Reader,

Get ready for a double dare from Superromance!

The popularity of our Women Who Dare titles has convinced us that Superromance readers enjoy the thrill of living on the edge. So be prepared for an entire *month of living dangerously!*

Leading off is this month's Women Who Dare title, *Windstorm,* in which author Connie Bennett pits woman against nature as Teddi O'Brien sets her sights on a tornado chaser! But our other three September heroines also battle both the elements and the enemy in a variety of exotic settings. *Wildfire,* by Lynn Erickson, is a real trial by fire, as Piper Hilyard learns to tell the good guys from the bad. In Marisa Carroll's *Hawk's Lair,* Sara Riley tracks subterranean treasure—and a pirate—in the Costa Rican rain forest. And we're delighted to welcome back to Superromance veteran romance author Sara Orwig. Her heroine, Jennifer Ruark, outruns a flood in the San Saba Valley in *The Mad, the Bad & the Dangerous.*

For October's Women Who Dare title, Lynn Leslie has created another trademark emotional drama in *Courage, My Love.* Diane Maxwell is fighting the fight of her life. To Brad Kingsley, she is a tremendously courageous woman of the nineties, and as his love for her grows, so does his commitment to her victory.

Evelyn A. Crowe's legion of fans will be delighted to learn that she has penned our Women Who Dare title for November. In *Reunited,* gutsy investigative reporter Sydney Tanner learns way more than she bargained for about rising young congressman J.D. Fowler. Generational family feuds, a long-ago murder and a touch of blackmail are only a few of the surprises in store for Sydney—and for you—as the significance of the heroine's discoveries begins to shape this riveting tale.

Popular Superromance author Sharon Brondos has contributed our final Woman Who Dare title for 1993. In *Doc Wyoming,* taciturn sheriff Hal Blane wants nothing to do with a citified female doctor, and the feeling is mutual. But Dixie Sheldon becomes involved with Blane's infamous family in spite of herself, and her "sentence" in Wyoming is commuted to a romance of the American West.

Please enjoy **A Month of Living Dangerously,** as well as our upcoming Women Who Dare titles and all the other fine Superromance novels we've lined up for your fall reading pleasure!

Marsha Zinberg,
Senior Editor

THE MAD, THE BAD & THE DANGEROUS

Sara Orwig

Harlequin Books

TORONTO • NEW YORK • LONDON
AMSTERDAM • PARIS • SYDNEY • HAMBURG
STOCKHOLM • ATHENS • TOKYO • MILAN
MADRID • WARSAW • BUDAPEST • AUCKLAND

With love to David

Published September 1993

ISBN 0-373-70563-8

THE MAD, THE BAD & THE DANGEROUS

ABOUT THE AUTHOR

Sara Orwig's fourth Superromance novel is set in the Sangre de Cristo mountains of New Mexico, one of her favorite locations. *The Mad, the Bad & the Dangerous* is also based on one of her favorite subjects—families and children—enlivened by her trademark touch of humor.

Sara was one of the first inductees into the Oklahoma Professional Writers' Hall of Fame. With six million copies of her books in print, Sara's Superromance novels have been translated into more than twelve languages.

Sara enjoys hearing from her readers. Letters can be sent to Sara Orwig, P.O. Box 780258, Oklahoma City, Oklahoma 73178.

Books by Sara Orwig

HARLEQUIN SUPERROMANCE
57–MAGIC OBSESSION
212–A CHANCE IN TIME
241–GYPSY FIRE

HARLEQUIN REGENCY ROMANCE
2–THE FAIRFAX BREW

CHAPTER ONE

"WHAT THE DEVIL?" Jason Hollenbeck scratched his head as he stared into the cool shadows beneath the tall pines. Dozens of cone-shaped mounds of dirt like oversize anthills were scattered along the slope of the mountain.

Curious, he bent down to study one more closely, poking his finger into the dry, crumbling dirt. No ants came scurrying out, nothing. Just a small pile of dirt. And another and another, everywhere he looked. He stood up, perplexed.

"Need to get over here more often," he said aloud. Trail thirteen was on an isolated mountainside in the San Saba National Park in the Sangre de Cristo Mountains, and he knew he was the only person who traveled the steep trail most of the year.

A flash of orange in the pine trees beyond him caught his attention. He started toward it, increasing his stride. It looked like a man in a white shirt and orange coveralls.

He hurried along the trail, trying to keep his eye trained on the elusive figure ahead. With no warning the ground suddenly gave way beneath him and he tumbled forward into some kind of pit, leaves and small branches spilling on top of him.

"What the hell—"

Jason landed unsteadily on his feet, then promptly toppled backward with a splash into the muddy water. Scrambling up again, he bumped a broad shoulder against the side of the pit, and dirt rained down on him. As he gazed at the sky, he heard the sound of children's laughter.

With a surge of red-hot anger, he lunged up the wall of the pit, clinging to the top in time to see a boy in orange coveralls racing away.

The wall of the pit crumbled and Jason fell back to the bottom, clods of dirt dropping on him. Now he knew where the cone-shaped mounds originated—the little piles of dirt were from this pit. And he could guess who wore the white shirt and orange coveralls—one of those Ruark kids waiting to lure him along the path. Those truant monsters had to have done this. He knew their names—Will, Brett and Kyle—because he had asked them a year ago.

Tossing his flat-brimmed Stetson out of the pit, he yanked his knife from its scabbard to gouge holes in the dirt walls so he could climb out. Two minutes later he scrambled over the edge and stood up, glancing down at himself. His crisp olive green park-ranger uniform was covered in mud. He raked his fingers through his wavy black hair, sending bits of leaves flying. "You hooligans," he yelled. "Fill this pit!"

His only answer was the soft rush of wind through pine boughs. Jason stormed down the mountain path. He hadn't talked to the boys' parents before, but he was going to now. He'd always tried talking directly to the kids. He'd told them to stop beating drums and practicing for band in the park, where they were scaring the wildlife. He made them stop skinny-dipping in the river. He tried to catch them when they shot off firecrackers.

The Ruark hooligans. He pictured the two younger roly-poly ones with their untied shoes, dirty T-shirts and grubby hands. The parents were probably slovenly people who lived off the land and the river and didn't care what their boys did. Thank the Lord the ruffians went to school. Otherwise he would have them on his hands the whole year.

They thought they were funny—digging the pit, watching him fall into it, then running for home. They thought they were safe from his wrath because the Ruark place was out of the park and therefore out of his jurisdiction. But not this time. With this stunt they had endangered the well-being of park visitors. Jason lengthened his stride, crunching through pine needles as he winded his way down to the valley. The steep mountain slope leveled out into a narrow valley cut by the cascading San Saba River. Only yards away water tumbled over rocks and drowned the sounds of his footsteps. He crossed the sturdy wooden bridge over the San Saba and turned east, leaving the gravel road and angling off toward the Ruark place. Steaming with anger, he strode into a clearing and vaulted the log fence at the boundary of the park, only yards away from the Ruark house.

Set back from the river, with a county gravel road running past, the house was on a prime piece of property, though it looked anything but at the moment. Two bicycles lay in the front yard next to an automobile tire, a bike tire and a football. Jason wondered if the same dirty plates he'd seen on his last visit were still in the yard. The house—a sizable two-story log cabin with flower beds bordering the front—had possibilities. Jason could imagine it an attractive place with new owners. If they could ever clean up after the Ruarks.

And then he saw a round, orange-clad rear bending over in the garden. Digging again. Probably the oldest Ruark kid, the orange coveralls he had glimpsed through the trees.

Jason moved with a stealth he had learned walking through woods. He didn't care which of the boys it was. He stepped through the pink petunias and locked his fingers in the boy's collar to yank him around.

"Try to get away now, you little hooligan!" he snapped. "You're in big trouble for that pit."

"What!" The "hooligan" twisted free, then turned, his face inches from the park ranger's.

Shocked, Jason had a momentary glimpse of green eyes and auburn hair pulled back in a ponytail. In that instant he released his hold and stepped backward.

"Who—"

The girl doubled her fists and shoved against his chest with all her might.

Caught by surprise, the retreating Jason lost his balance. His heel came down on a rock and he slipped, flailing his arms and falling into the petunias.

"Get off my petunias!" she shouted, picking up a hand shovel and waving it at him. "You're crushing all the flowers!"

Her face was smudged with dirt, and her ponytail bounced as she waved the small spade at him. Looking at the swaying ponytail, Jason decided she was too young to be their mother; the boys must have an older sister.

Trying to control his fury, he stood up, his hands on his hips. "Where are your parents?"

"My mother's dead and my father's not home!" she said, leaning forward with her hands on her hips to glare back at him.

"And who are you?" he asked.

"I'm Jennifer Ruark, and you're standing on my petunias! I thought park rangers were supposed to *protect* flora and fauna."

"I'm Ranger Jason Hollenbeck, and I'll be back to talk to your father," he said. This girl was as troublesome as the boys. And just about as disrespectful.

"Why did you grab me?" she demanded.

"I thought you were one of the boys. They dug a hole in the park."

"A *hole?* For heaven's sake! Don't you ever lay a hand on me again, you miserable man. You smashed half of my flowers!"

"Only because you knocked me into them! I'll be back!" He turned to stomp away.

"You stay off our property! This is private land. No trespassing! You have no jurisdiction here."

"I'll be back." He tossed the words over his shoulder, his rage growing.

"You'll get buckshot next time, mister!"

"Not if I bring the sheriff!" he warned, determined she wouldn't have the last word.

"He better bring a warrant if he comes on this property! At least I can trust the sheriff not to smash my flowers!"

"Tell your father to be here—that a park ranger wants to see him!"

"He'll have his shotgun!"

Disgusted, Jason ignored her and strode toward the park, turning to look back at her. She shook the shovel at him and turned away.

As if a few petunias mattered in a junkyard like that one! He rubbed his aching backside, where the Ruarks had dealt double damage today. The little witch had probably learned to defend herself from her brothers.

When he arrived back at trail thirteen, he glared at the mounds of dirt that would have to be shoveled back into the hole. He pulled out his radio to call the park maintenance office.

"Della, this is Hollenbeck. I have a problem here." He surveyed the mounds of dirt. They couldn't even use a Bobcat for this. The mounds were too small and scattered everywhere.

"Della, we need some men out here to fill in a pit. And some warning signs to keep visitors off the trail."

"I'll see if the Bobcat is available right away—"

"Della, we need men and shovels," Jason said. "The dirt is all over the mountainside."

"How big a pit?"

"Big enough to hold a man," Jason said evenly. "It's about seven feet deep and four feet wide."

"Who would dig a pit like that?"

"Vandals." Jason clutched the phone. How he would love to contact the sheriff, but there was nothing he could prove.

"Which trail?"

"Fortunately, it's one that isn't used much except by me. Trail thirteen."

"No one ever goes up there. How'd you find this pit?"

"I check this area every month," he said, his anger growing. "Get the men out here before someone el—er, someone falls into it!"

He switched off the radio and jammed it back into the case on his hip, glaring at the piles of dirt. Juvenile delinquents! He rubbed his back again. Worried about her petunias! He'd give them all something to worry about. He looked over his shoulder. He would go back tonight and talk to the father. All the time he'd been talking to the daughter, the rest of the Ruarks had probably been hiding in the house. Thunder rumbled and Jason glanced up, feeling a flicker of worry. More rain was the last thing this part of New Mexico needed.

Then he noticed dirt strewn across the ground on the far side of the pit. Some of the mounds were gone. He moved forward and peered into the hole.

"Son of a gun," he muttered, placing his hands on his hips and looking around. While he'd been lying in the petunias, the little devils had been shoving the dirt back into the pit. It wouldn't do any good to yell at them; they wouldn't come out now to finish the job.

Thirty minutes later, as he helped the crew get warning barriers in place, he noticed both men glancing at his muddy uniform. It wouldn't take the brains of a gnat to know that he'd fallen into the blasted pit, and now he would hear about it all summer.

The radio beeped and he flipped a switch. "Fire along trail three," came the deep voice of Harris Lowman, park supervisor. "Can you check it?"

"Right now." After replacing the radio, Jason left the two men to finish the job.

After putting out the smoldering campfire on trail three, he went to help a stranded camper at the river's edge. Then he had a call that a camper had reported sighting a bear. It turned out to be another camper's collie. At four o'clock he gave a nature talk to a troop of Scouts, and finally, at the end of the day, Jason climbed into his Jeep to drive to the Ruarks'.

The place was dark and he wondered whether they were all hiding or had closed up and gone back to town. As he knocked on the door, he looked at the drooping petunias. It had been too cool for petunias, anyway. Just then the first big drops of rain splattered on the roof, distracting him.

He studied the dark sky as lightning flashed. Already the northern part of New Mexico had had five inches above normal rainfall for the year, three inches this month. The Patrick Lambert Reservoir above the dam was high, and the floodgates had been opened twice in the past week to let water flow downriver.

The weather hadn't been warm enough to melt snow on the highest peaks of the Sangre de Cristo Mountains. When rain was added to the runoff from the snow, streams overflowed and the river and reservoir rose. This rain had been predicted, so this morning he had sent out flash-flood warnings to campers.

Jason pounded on the door again, but after his knock went unheeded he left to drive home in what had become a downpour. By the time he climbed the steps to his tower patrol cabin, high enough for a panoramic view of the park, he felt relieved to be home.

As he yanked off his boots, his smoldering fury vanished. In minutes, strains of Bach filled the room, and he looked around his haven of peace. The wooden floor of the cabin gleamed with polish, green plants were thriving. Unlike the Ruark home, here everything was in its place: fishing rods were lined in a rack near the door; his rifles and pistol were in a locked gun case; snowshoes were neatly hung on the wall; and weather gauges and thermometers were aligned outside. Jason knelt to light a fire in the freestanding metal fireplace, and as soon as it was crackling, he sorted through the mail he had picked up earlier.

Lightning flashed outside and drops of rain spattered against the floor-to-ceiling windows. As he looked through the latticed divider between the living area and the small kitchen, he again felt glad to be indoors. In stocking feet he crossed the living area to his tiny bedroom, where a bookcase lined one wall. In the adjoining bathroom, he peeled off his muddy clothes and carried them to the washing machine in the kitchen area, humming with the music as he did so.

As soon as he had showered, he broiled a chicken breast for dinner. At thirty-six, he was content with his life. He loved the park, the solitude and the outdoors. He would worry about the Ruarks tomorrow.

The next morning the Ruarks were gone. When no one was home the following day, Jason guessed the family had returned to town so the kids could attend school. The pit was filled in, the trail smoothed over, and he was more than happy to forget the incident.

Nevertheless, he couldn't forget the rain and the danger it posed for the park and campers over the next month. Rain continued to fall and by the middle of June the river was a raging torrent and San Saba National Park was closed to anyone wanting to boat or swim.

One morning in late June, Jason returned to his cabin to get another thermos of hot coffee. As he reached the door, his phone rang. Yanking off his wet boots, he hurried across the room to answer it.

"Jason, Terrell," came a familiar tenor voice, and he pictured his closest friend, Terrell Skinner, the ranger assigned to the northeastern section of the park.

"Harris just called and I said I'd get in touch with you. Engineers have discovered a crack in the San Saba dam."

"Lord, according to predictions it's supposed to rain most of the day."

"That's right. They want us to get all campers away from the river and all homeowners out of the valley. You're to warn everyone east of your cabin, until you reach Rimrock."

"There are about two dozen homes in the valley between here and Rimrock," Jason told his friend. "If the dam breaks, the water from the reservoir could wipe out the houses."

"They've alerted Sheriff Garcia at Rimrock, and he'll get the residents to higher ground. Engineers have worked all night, but as long as it keeps raining, it looks hopeless. What about campers along the river? Do you have many?"

"Only three groups in my part of the park. Two guys, one man and three couples."

"Well, get them out if they haven't left already—the weather service is running bulletins and warnings on the radio."

"Campers rarely see or hear any news. That's one of the reasons they come here. I'll find them and get them out. I hope the engineers can fix the crack, because no one can do anything about the rain."

"Amen. Keep in touch."

It took two hours to locate and warn the campers along the river. When he crossed the park boundary, Jason veered east, winding down along the gravel road to the Ruark house. The river was higher now, spilling over its banks and running only a few yards from the road. Much of the same litter was in the yard as the last time he'd been there, with some new additions: two metal lawn chairs and a badminton net and poles. Jason strode purposefully—and almost tripped over something sticking out of the ground. He lurched forward, managing to regain his balance. A croquet wicket. He stepped over another one and skirted two more, the curving bits of wire like land mines, traps for the unwary.

Annoyed, he crossed the porch and rapped on the door. It opened and a brown-haired, freckle-faced boy gazed at Jason. None other than William Ruark.

"Will, is your father home?"

"Nope."

The kid needed a lesson in courtesy. "Will, tell your father that everyone is to evacuate, to leave the valley. The San Saba dam has a crack, and if it gets worse or gives way, this valley will be under water."

"Is that right?" Will asked, feigning exaggerated concern.

Jason wanted to yank the kid up by the shirt and shake him. "That's right," he said evenly. "Will you relay the message?"

"Oh, sure, Ranger Hollenbeck. Anything you say." He was studying his fingernails, looking bored. Then he glanced up and smiled. "Someone told me that you fell in a hole. Too bad. I hope you weren't hurt."

The little smartass. "When will your father be home?" Jason asked, trying to keep his voice steady.

"It'll be a long time."

"You be sure and tell him about the dam. All of you need to leave this area."

"Yes, sir, Chief Hollenbeck. And you watch out for holes." Will Ruark closed the door. Miffed, Jason climbed into his Jeep, putting the Ruarks out of his mind as he headed to the next house, a mile farther east along the gravel road.

It took half the day to work his way to the tiny town of Rimrock. Main Street was six blocks long and wide enough for four lanes of traffic. His first stop was the grocery, where he talked to Juan Sanchez, the owner. When he had the Jeep loaded with sacks of food, Jason stopped to see Sheriff Garcia. Next he talked to Ted Jackson at the gas station, then went by the café for coffee and to see Barbie Watkins before he started back.

By now it was late afternoon. Radio announcements were coming every fifteen minutes, warning about flash floods and alerting campers and residents to evacuate the area. On the return route, tumbling river waters raced within a few feet of the road in some places. In low spots, the road disappeared beneath muddy pools. How long would the dam hold?

Friday morning, Jason scanned the park from the vantage point of his cabin. Impatiently he picked up his binoculars, focusing on the curl of gray smoke twisting into the air toward the east. He glared through the lenses at the rock chimney of the Ruark house. There always had to be someone who was stubborn, determined to fight nature, thinking the warnings were blown out of proportion. Jason shook his head in disgust.

He picked up the phone and punched out a number.

"Terrell Skinner, San Saba National Park," came his friend's voice—a voice that always seemed an octave too high for a man of Skinner's size.

"Terrell, what's the latest?"

"Another small crack has developed, and with the rain, there's flooding north of us. I've warned everyone in my part of the park and I think they all left yesterday. I'm going to double-check my campers."

"I'll check mine again, too. I can see smoke from the Ruarks' chimney so they haven't left yet."

"Who are the Ruarks?"

"The monster family, remember?"

"Oh. The pit kids. We'll alert you if anything happens, but you'll only have a few minutes before a wall of water pours down the valley. How long would it take you to get to them?"

"If I raced, ten minutes, but I have to cross bridge ten."

"Could you get them to higher ground?"

"If I can get them to leave. Their house is in the lowest place for miles. The river is already up within a few feet of the road."

"Why the hell won't people get out when you tell them to?"

"The only one I've talked to is a smartass kid who won't listen to anybody."

"You'd better convince someone over there to be ready to fly to their rescue."

"Yep. I'll try again."

"Pray for sunshine." The connection was broken, and Jason went to the window to peer out again. As the smoke drifted into the sky, he didn't need binoculars to know the Ruarks were still in the valley. Stubborn or stupid or both.

Clenching his jaw, he strode toward the door. How could an entire family be stubborn enough to run such idiotic risks? There was no point phoning them. He'd probably get one of the kids. He'd have to drive over again and hope the father was around this time.

He opened the door and his gaze swept over tall Mount Rainy in the distance. For a moment he felt a pang. He loved the park and the outdoors and he prayed the dam would hold. Jamming his hat on his head, he descended the stairs.

The rain was now a light, steady drizzle. Jason whipped the Jeep up the Ruarks' drive and climbed out.

This time when he pounded on the door, it opened and a passel of dogs—small terriers and a nondescript shaggy mutt—nearly bowled him over. Three of them growled at him and two jumped up, wagging their tails.

"Down, down," an elderly man ordered the dogs. "Naughty boys!"

Ignoring the dogs, Jason looked down at the old man. Tufts of white hair ringed the shiny bald spot at the top of his head and his skin was deeply lined. The kids' grandfather, no doubt.

"Mr. Ruark?"

"Eh?"

"I'm Jason Hollenbeck, a park ranger." Jason raised his voice, trying to be heard over one of the dogs, who was whining and making strange noises as if he wanted to enter the conversation, as well. "Are you Mr. Ruark?"

"This is the Ruarks'. I'm Osgood MacFee."

"Mr. MacFee, the San Saba dam has a crack in it."

"You got car trouble?" he asked, peering around Jason toward the Jeep in the drive.

"No, sir!" Jason said, raising his voice another notch and shaking away a terrier who was chewing on the toe of his boot. "The dam—the dam upriver—has a crack in it."

"Something upriver is cracked?"

"Yes, sir. The dam."

"Sorry to hear that. Won't you come in? Snort, naughty!" The older man scooped up the terrier and looked the dog in the eye. "Don't chew on Mr. Hobeneck."

"Hollenbeck. My name is Hollenbeck, Mr. MacFee."

"Sorry, Mr. Hollowneck."

Jason gave up and nodded. "Sir!" he shouted as a terrier continued to yap, rain drummed on the porch roof and thunder rumbled overhead. "You folks should get out and go back to town until the rain is over. Everyone needs to evacuate this area."

"River has a ways to go before it gets to the house, sonny."

"Yes, sir, but if the dam breaks, all the water in the Patrick Lambert Reservoir will come pouring down this river."

"If the dam breaks, Patrick Hammer will come downriver?"

"You're in danger of flooding, Mr. MacFee!" Jason yelled, and the terrier threw back his head and began to howl.

"Thanks for telling me. Who's Patrick Hammer?"

Exasperated, Jason shook his head. "He lives upriver!" At least Osgood MacFee had understood the part about the flood. He was wearing a hearing aid but must have turned the thing off. Jason strode off the porch, two dogs following him to the Jeep. A shrill whistle sounded and they spun around, racing back to the porch and disappearing inside the house with their master.

At least the family was warned now. Jason frowned. Will Ruark had kept the message to himself, all right. Jason drove through the gate to the park and swung down along the trail toward the river, pausing on the wide, wooden bridge that was one of nineteen throughout the park. Only five years old, bridge number ten looked capable of withstanding the torrent rushing against it.

The bridge was usually well above the river; now spray blew up from the tumbling water only a few feet

below. Jason climbed back into his Jeep and drove up
the winding path to his cabin. At least that would be
safe.

"RAIN, RAIN," Jennifer mumbled, gripping the steering wheel as the Bronco skidded to one side. The wip-
ers clacked with each swipe across the watery
windshield. The truck was loaded with groceries and the
boys had videos to watch, so they were all set even if it
rained for days. As long as she didn't slide off the
mountain getting home. Her headlights cut through the
darkness of the stormy afternoon.

Suddenly a figure darted into sight. Someone in a
long black raincoat loomed up in front of the Bronco,
and Jennifer swerved to avoid running the person down.
Dashing across the road, the dark figure disappeared
into the trees.

Jennifer's heart pounded like a wild thing. "What on
earth—" she exclaimed. Why would anyone be running around in the rain?

Peering through the shimmering glass, she tried to
keep the truck on the road, avoiding the deepest pools
of muddy water as she struggled to follow the twisting
road. At the same time, she found herself glancing in
the direction the person had run.

Feeling strangely nervous, she shivered and clutched
the steering wheel. "Don't be a goof," she said aloud,
but her own voice wasn't reassuring. She could have
sworn the person was a woman. The shadowy figure
had been wearing a long, flowing black raincoat that
didn't look like something a man would wear.

She made the turn from the road to their drive, noticing that the water was now at the edge of the road.
Should they go into town tonight? Two years ago when

the river had risen as high as the road, she had gathered the boys and left in a panic, but the evacuation had been unnecessary. The sun had come out the next day and they had missed a fun weekend. Her thoughts turned to that last winding half mile down the mountain and the person in the raincoat, and for a moment she forgot about the rising river.

Hitting the horn, Jennifer climbed out of the truck and picked up a box of groceries. The door swung open and ten-year-old Will came out, passing her to pick up another box. The two younger boys followed and gathered up sacks.

As Jennifer put away her purchases, she barely heard their conversation. Should she tell Dad what she thought she had seen along the side of the road? Should she take him back with her to look?

The road that ran in front of their property and into the park was seldom used. Usually she felt safe, with three boys, five dogs and her father, but now her skin prickled and she moved around the cabin making sure the locks were secure.

By six o'clock she had a pot of chili bubbling on the stove. She showered and changed into a warm green sweater and jeans. As thunder rattled windowpanes, she paused in her upstairs bedroom and scanned the mountainside. Beneath tall aspen, dark pines and spruce, streams of water poured down the slopes in silver rivulets. It was dark early, and she didn't want to leave tonight to go back to town unless there was real danger from high water. With no radio and the family tuned in to videos instead of television, her father and sons probably hadn't heard any weather predictions or warnings.

When she went downstairs, she glanced around the spacious, pine-paneled front room. The boys were playing Monopoly with their grandfather, all five dogs lying on the floor around them. She stirred the chili then removed a tossed green salad from the refrigerator. As she did so, a knock on one of the windows sent a stab of fear through her.

Jennifer set the salad down and turned around. The knocking came again. Moving hesitantly to the window, reassuring herself there was safety in numbers, she reached out and rubbed her palm over the cold glass.

Eyes peered in at her. Frightened, Jennifer jumped backward. Her heart pounded and a scream rose in her throat, but all that came out was a gasp. Then she noticed the upturned nose pressed against the glass.

"Goldie!" she cried.

CHAPTER TWO

SHOCKED, JENNIFER stared in amazement at her younger sister.

Fear vanished as she rushed for the door and yanked it open. No one was there. Puzzled, she stepped outside onto the narrow stoop as rain poured off the roof.

"Goldie? Where are you?"

"Shhh! Turn out the light and pull the curtains so no one can see me."

Drawing a deep breath, Jennifer hurried to do as her younger sister requested. Something must be terribly wrong for Goldie to come sneaking up at night in a violent rainstorm. Had Goldie been the person she'd seen dashing across the road earlier?

Jennifer switched off the lights and pulled the curtains across the kitchen windows.

"Hey!" Will said, coming into the room and flipping on the light switch. His blue eyes were round and he shook his long brown hair away from his face. "Whatcha doing, Mom? Something you don't want us to see? Putting vitamins in the chili?"

"No. What do you want?"

"You gonna stay in the dark while you cook?"

"No, Will, I'm not cooking in the dark," she said patiently, wishing he would go. Goldie was getting drenched.

"Well, what *are* you doing?" He tilted his head to study her while he went to the refrigerator.

She knew she should talk to Goldie before the family did, yet she wanted to be truthful with her son. "I thought I saw a face pressed against the window."

"In this rain? You've lost it, Mom."

She shrugged. "Please set the butter on the table and, let me see..." She knew the moment she gave him a job to do he would disappear with the speed of the next bolt of lightning.

"Sure," he said, and was gone in the next ten seconds.

Jennifer turned off the lights again and hurried to the door. Goldie swept in, sending a spray of water over her. The moment her sister was inside, Jennifer locked the door.

"Thank God I'm here," Goldie whispered, groping for Jennifer and giving her a sopping hug. As she squeezed back, Jennifer was surprised to discover that Goldie was bigger than she remembered. The bulky raincoat added to her girth, but she also must have put on weight.

Goldie clung to her, and Jennifer realized her sister was crying.

"What's wrong?" she asked, worried now. "What's happened? Are you all right?" Remembering the incident on the road, she studied Goldie's black raincoat.

"No! I'm not all right. I'm scared. And I'm so glad to be here."

Jennifer felt a familiar unease settle over her. At thirty she was only two years older than Goldie, but sometimes she felt as if her sister were still a child. And she didn't want to ask about the man in her sister's life. Rudolph Allen Tabor—Rat Tabor. She shivered. The name was unfortunately well suited. Could he be behind this? Undoubtedly. She disentangled herself from Goldie and held her by the shoulders.

"Goldie, Dad or the kids could come out at any minute. How will I explain you? And I'm amazed the dogs aren't out here yet."

As if on cue, a terrier raced into the room and began a frenzied barking.

"Hush, Snort! Down!" Jennifer whispered forcefully. A whistle came from the front of the house and the terrier ran away. "He'll be back," she warned.

"Why are you whispering?" Goldie asked. "Do you have company?"

"No! I'm whispering because you're whispering."

"Oh, well, I'm safe now," Goldie said in a normal voice. "Can we turn on the light?"

"Yes...I left it off because I thought you wanted darkness," Jennifer said, remembering how confusing it was to deal with Goldie, whose reasoning showed she marched to a different drummer. The barking grew louder again, and the black-and-white terrier returned to the room, followed by their father.

"Snort, hush!" Osgood ordered. The terrier sat down obediently and wagged a stubby tail. "Good grief, Goldie!"

"Dad!" Goldie exclaimed, turning to hug him and soak his clothes, as well. Jennifer set another place at the table and heard the boys coming down the hall.

"Aunt Goldie!" came the chorus, and the dogs began to bark again.

"Will Ruark!" Goldie exclaimed, hugging the boy. "Look how you've grown!" Will looked sheepish. At ten, he was the tallest of the three boys, and several inches taller than most of his friends.

She turned to Brett and Kyle. "Give me a hug, fellas," she said, clasping them to her and ruffling Brett's unruly red curls.

"Gee, Aunt Goldie," Brett protested, "I'm nine years old."

"That's not too old to hug. And neither is seven years old." Her eyes sparkled as she gave Kyle another squeeze.

Will had his father's height, but unfortunately, Brett and Kyle had inherited their grandfather MacFee's rotund shape.

Her wide blue eyes the essence of innocence, Goldie added her little girl's voice to the din of dogs and children. In spite of the strangeness of her arrival, Jennifer was glad to see her.

"How'd you get here?" Osgood asked.

"I have a little vacation time and I thought it would be so good to see all you guys! My, it's really raining."

Jennifer left the room to change into dry clothes and laid out jeans and a navy sweater for Goldie in the spare bedroom, hoping they would fit. It would be late tonight before she could ask Goldie any questions, so she might as well be patient.

As they sat around the table, Goldie's eyes sparkled and she told the boys about her latest job as a clerk in a pet store. Relieved, Jennifer wondered what had happened to her job as a hostess in the Blue Orchid nightclub. And Goldie certainly had gained weight, which was a shock to Jennifer, because her sister had always had a knockout figure. As Goldie talked, she slipped the sleek black terrier, Tuffy, a bite of beef from her chili.

"Dad," Jennifer said, raising her voice and tilting her head in the direction of the two dogs who sat beside her.

"Snort, Tuffy, General, Priss—out of the kitchen," Osgood ordered in a firm voice.

The three spotted terriers and the fuzzy mutt trotted across the threshold to join the toy terrier named Oats. The five dogs sat down in a line from one doorjamb to the other, and Snort offered his protest in a high-pitched howl that ended abruptly.

Goldie laughed, her eyes sparkling, and to look at her, no one would guess she had a care in the world.

"Dad, they're adorable! How's the dog act?"

"He was on television last month," Brett said promptly, beaming. "We have it on video."

"Good! I'll have to see it. Why didn't you let me know so I could have watched?"

"It was local in Santa Fe," Osgood answered. A clap of thunder rattled the panes again, and Jennifer felt a vibration in the air.

"When I was in the grocery, they said there are more cracks in the dam and we should evacuate," Jennifer said, speaking loudly for Osgood's benefit. "But every time they've asked us to leave, nothing has come of it. Has anyone seen the news this afternoon?"

She looked around the table at blank faces, four pairs of blue and one pair of green eyes gazing back at her. Only Kyle had inherited her green eyes.

"We watched videos," Will said. "Saw another *Rambo*."

"You ought to switch over to the news once in a while."

"Ranger Hollowneck was here today," Osgood said, reaching out to take more crackers while the boys snickered.

"It's Hollenbeck, Dad." Jennifer lowered her spoon. "What did he want?" she asked, feeling the trace of anger that came every time she thought about the man.

Osgood shrugged. "Talking about rain and saying we should go."

"He said to evacuate?" Now she felt annoyed that her father hadn't told her. "When did he come by?"

"While you were in town."

"You should have told me. It would have been easier to pack and go home then."

All the males at the table exchanged conspiratorial glances, and her annoyance increased. "Dad?"

"The man's a worrier. You know they have to warn people to get out at the first sign of trouble. You remember the last time we left because of flood warnings? Ruined a perfectly good weekend. I'll bet the sun will be out in the morning."

"Yeah, Mom."

She glanced at Will, who looked down at his bowl and took a spoonful of steaming chili. They might be right. Lord knows, she didn't see eye to eye with Ranger Hollenbeck. She still remembered the way he'd grabbed her collar, and it made her furious every time she thought about it. Yet the dam did have cracks in it.

"Dad, he hasn't come by here before to warn us to go. That means this is urgent. I think as soon as dinner is over we should pack and leave."

Her announcement was met by a mixture of groans and a chorus of howls from the doorway. Even Goldie gripped Jennifer's arm and shook her head. Her eyes were wide and filled with unmistakable fear.

"All right!" she shouted, clinking her spoon against her glass. The dogs became quiet first. She gave Will an angry glare and he closed his mouth. The minute he did, his younger brothers followed his lead.

"When dinner is over, we'll watch the news on television. And I'm going to phone Ranger Hollenbeck."

The boys groaned louder, and the excited dogs began to bark. Jennifer clinked her spoon against her glass again.

"Will all of you stop this?" She glared at the dogs, and Priss lay down, covering her nose with her furry paws. Looking each boy in the eye, Jennifer said, "As soon as we eat, I'm calling Ranger Hollenbeck while all of you watch the news. If he says to go, we go." This time she let them all groan and howl.

"May I talk to you as soon as we finish eating?" Goldie asked.

"Of course," Jennifer agreed, wondering what new complication was about to fall into her life. Nothing was simple with Goldie.

"Mom, we can't drive to town in all this rain," Brett said. "Listen to it come down."

"Jenny, we should wait until morning," Osgood said, raising his voice. "It's night, and if we had car trouble, we'd be stranded out in the rain."

"I can't hear! One at a time." She glanced at the dogs and whistled, then turned to the boys. "Wait until dinner is over and I talk to Ranger Hollenbeck. No more arguments."

"I can't wait to hear all of you play for me," Goldie said. "And I want to see the dogs perform."

"Our newest member is General, and he can walk a wire better than any dog I've had. I'm taking them to Albuquerque to perform at a mall opening for the Fourth of July," her father told her proudly.

Conversation moved from the dog act to the boys' activities. Jennifer listened absently, filled with a vague sense of foreboding. She didn't know if her apprehension was caused by the weather, Ranger Hollenbeck's warning or Goldie's unconventional arrival. When they finished eating and the boys began clearing the table, she turned to her father.

"Dad, please get some news on TV and tell me what they say about the dam. I'm going to call the ranger. Goldie, come up to my room with me."

When they were in the upstairs bedroom with the door closed, Jennifer turned to Goldie. "We need to talk as soon as I call Ranger Hollenbeck."

Goldie stared at her and wrung her hands, and Jennifer braced herself for bad news. Sitting on the four-poster mahogany bed, she listened to the drumming of rain on the roof while she called the patrol cabin in the San Saba park.

When the deep voice came on the line, she felt her irritation rise.

"This is—" she paused "—the Ruarks. I wanted to check on conditions at the San Saba dam and in the valley. Is more rain predicted?"

"Is this Jennifer?" came a terse question.

"Yes, it is," she said abruptly.

"Look, you tell your father that you folks should be out of there. I've warned you, the television has warned you—"

She didn't care to listen to his tirade. She had her answer and she replaced the receiver. "We need to go tonight."

Instantly Goldie's bright smile vanished. "No!" Moving with amazing swiftness, she grabbed Jennifer's arm and sat on the bed beside her. "We can't!" Tears brimmed in her eyes.

Jennifer drew in her breath sharply. "Goldie, what is it? You have to tell me." She studied her sister's changed shape and wondered if pregnancy was the cause, but it seemed unlikely. What was Goldie involved in now?

"Please, unless we're going to wash away, let's stay here. If the downstairs floods, we can move upstairs. We can move the furniture, and it would be better if we were here to save everything."

"That would be true, except right next door is the San Saba National Park with an earthen dam that has cracks in it. With all the rain we've been having, if the dam gives way, the whole house might be swept away. Before the dam was built, this entire valley was under water."

"Oh, no! Surely not!" Goldie said, beginning to cry again. "Jenny, I'm scared. I need to stay here where it's isolated and no one can find me. People know your Santa Fe address."

The last remark triggered a warning. "Has Rat threatened you? Has he hurt you?" Jennifer's worry changed to anger when she thought of Rat Tabor. His movie-star looks and superficial charm could always dupe Goldie, but the guy was a jerk.

"No, Rat wouldn't hurt me," Goldie said indignantly, but Jennifer wasn't sure. Though she dreaded learning the truth, she needed to find out exactly what kind of trouble her sister was in.

"Goldie, you have to tell me. Is it Rat? He *must* have done something."

Sobs came harder and Jennifer sighed. She loved Goldie, and Rudolph Allen Tabor was the worst thing that had ever happened to her. "Goldie, tell me."

Wiping her eyes, Goldie stood up, unfastened her borrowed jeans and let them fall to the floor. Jennifer stared in dismay at the leather money belts strapped to Goldie's body.

Around Goldie's waist was a wide belt with bulging pockets, and below her knees were two more leather pouches. Goldie pulled up Jennifer's navy sweater and unfastened a fourth money belt. She flung it onto the bed, unsnapped a pocket and began dumping out the money.

Jennifer picked up one of the bills and stared. All the bills spilling out were in one-hundred-dollar denominations.

"Goldie, what is this?" Jennifer asked in a whisper, growing cold with fear yet mesmerized by the money tumbling onto the bed. As she stared at the growing pile, her fear mushroomed. Men would kill without hesitation for that much money. Someone was bound to be after Goldie. Her mouth felt dry. They were all in terrible danger.

Jennifer caught Goldie's hands in a tight grip. "Stop! We have to get this money out of sight. One of the boys might come in." She stuffed some bills back into the pouch. While Goldie gathered up the rest, Jennifer sat back. "Goldie, when I drove home from town tonight, someone ran in front of me. Was that you?"

Goldie's eyes were wide. "Yes. I didn't know it was you or I would have stopped you."

"Where did you get all that money?"

Goldie bit her lip and Jennifer could guess what was coming.

"You're not going to like it."

"I know I'm not. What did Rat do? Rob a bank?"

"No! I'm scared. Some men are after him and now they're after me. I had to hide and this seemed the best place." The words tumbled out in a rush.

"You have men after you and you came *here,* where there are three small children?" Her worst fears confirmed, Jennifer felt a flash of anger that Goldie would involve the boys in something dangerous. But her anger was fleeting. Her sister would never deliberately cause harm to the boys.

Feeling as if a menace lurked outside in the dark, she moved to the window and closed the curtains, even though they were on the second floor in a blinding rainstorm. She had never felt isolated at the cabin, always loving the mountains, the quiet, the river, but tonight she felt cut off from help and frightened. The roads were almost impassable with mud slides, and the nearest authority was the sheriff in Rimrock or Ranger Hollenbeck. Fine help he would be. She'd knocked him flat on his rear.

"We're going to the police in Rimrock," she announced.

"No!" Goldie sprang up and threw herself in front of Jennifer. "Oh, no! Please, please, no!"

"Why not?" Jennifer said, feeling frustrated and angry. Goldie had to be protected and Jennifer couldn't do it herself.

"Because that will mean Rat will die. I promised him I wouldn't turn in the money!"

"Goldie, I have to think about the boys."

Goldie was shaking now, her words coming out between sobs. "Jenny, I promised him I'd keep the money, because he said they'd kill him. I didn't want to

endanger the boys or any of you, but they tried to kidnap me—''

"What? Who tried to?" Numbly, Jennifer sat down
beside her sister and put her arm around her shoulders.
She'd been dealing with Goldie's crises since they were
children. Their mother had always fallen to pieces,
leaving Jennifer to cope. "Goldie, calm down. We're
safe right now. It's pouring buckets outside and no one
can find you tonight."

She hoped they were all safe and the dam wouldn't
break and the river wouldn't flood. She patted Goldie's back. "Goldie, don't cry. Tell me what happened.
Who tried to kidnap you?" She reached over to the
night table to get a tissue for Goldie to wipe her eyes and
nose. "Start at the beginning. Where did the money
come from?"

"You'll get mad—"

"I'll get a lot angrier if you don't tell me now. You've
jeopardized all of us and I need to know what's going
on."

Tears continued to stream down Goldie's face. "I
didn't mean to put all of you in danger. I thought I'd be
safe here, and no one would find me." She wiped her
eyes. "No one followed me. I'm sure. But I have to hide
and this was the only place I could think of to go."

"Goldie, what did Rat do?" Jennifer asked again in
exasperation.

Goldie twisted her fingers together. "Rat and his
friend Bobby knew a bookie, Gator. Gator was dealing
drugs, too, and they knew when he had a big deal coming up. They robbed him."

"Oh, no! Goldie, that was stupid." Jennifer's
heart sank. How could Goldie be infatuated with the
likes of Rat Tabor? "What happened?"

"They knew Gator couldn't go to the police about the theft. That's where the money came from."

"So how did you get it?" Jennifer asked, feeling terrified now. This wasn't Rat's usual small-time scam.

"Rat and Bobby didn't know Gator very well. They didn't know that Gator wasn't acting on his own. He had mob connections."

"Oh Lord, Goldie. Not *mob* money? That *rat!* Why do you associate with a man like that?"

Goldie sobbed. "He's . . . good to me, and he promised this would be the last time he'd do anything illegal."

"Give me a break." Jennifer rubbed her forehead. "Goldie, from the first moment you met him, Rat's been trouble, hiring you as an exotic dancer in his uncle's nightclub—"

"I became a hostess, instead," she said, lifting her chin somewhat defiantly.

"Go on with your story."

Goldie wiped her eyes. "Gator was killed. He was found floating in the bay with several bullets in him. Rat said some men were after him and Bobby. That's when I found out what he had done. If I take the money to the police, they'll go after Rat. He just wants me to hide the money until the heat is off and then he'll give the money back to the mob and he'll never *ever* do anything dishonest again."

"Not under any circumstances, Goldie, can you convince me that Rat will give that money back!" Jennifer exclaimed. How could her sister be taken in by the man? Even as she asked the question Jennifer knew the answer: Goldie had always been gullible. "Any man who is a congenital liar and thief won't stop stealing. How can you imagine that you love him?"

"Most of the time Rat is a good person. You were lucky when you married a man like Mark."

For a moment Jennifer was distracted as an incredible pang of longing for Mark and his exuberant self-confidence filled her. He would have handled this situation without a qualm. At times the hurt she felt over his death came without warning, and now the old pain gripped her once again. The knowledge that he was never coming home to her had created an immense vacuum inside her. She remembered his laughing blue eyes, his quick smile, his cocky sureness, which had finally gotten him killed at the Albuquerque air show. It had been more than three years now, and she wondered if she would ever stop hurting. She looked at Goldie huddled on the side of the bed, crying.

"By giving you the money, Rat's placed you in terrible danger. There's only one thing to do—take the money straight to the police so we'll all be safe."

With a loud sob Goldie burst into tears. "Rat said you'd want to do that, and he said if I did, it would be his death warrant. Jennifer, please don't hurt Rat."

Jennifer tried to be patient. "Goldie, Rat Tabor is just that—a rat. Name one good thing he's done for you."

Goldie thrust out her lower lip. "He's fun—and he's so handsome!"

"Oh, for God's sake!" Jennifer exploded. "Look at the trouble you're in because of him! Now you're an accomplice to a crime. Have you thought of that?"

Goldie's eyes grew round. "I didn't do anything except keep the money for him."

"If you give up the money and agree to testify, the police might not press charges," Jennifer said, praying that's what would happen. "But you are an accomplice. We have to turn the money in as soon as possible. We have to for the boys' sake.''

Goldie let out a wail. "I couldn't bear it if anything happened to Rat.''

Jennifer drew a deep breath, torn between love for her sister and the need to protect her family. "Goldie, I can't endanger the boys. We'll go to the sheriff in Rimrock or take the money to the police in Santa Fe, but we have to get rid of it. You'll be safer that way.''

"Think it over, Jennifer. Please. No one will find me here.''

"Rat knows we have this house.''

"He won't lead anyone here. I haven't seen him for two months.''

Jennifer stared at her in shock. "Two months? You've had the money that long?''

"Yes. The first month nothing happened. The second month I realized someone was following me, and then three weeks ago these guys tried to grab me and shove me into a car. I fought them and two more guys drove past and heard me scream. They stopped and they all got in a fight and I woke up in a hospital emergency room. I knew then I had to get out of town.''

"Oh Lord, Goldie. We have to turn this money over to the police.'' Jennifer suddenly remembered that Goldie had arrived on foot. "How did you get here?''

"I bought and sold three cars on the way, and in Albuquerque I took a bus to San Jon. Then I rented a car and drove to Santa Fe, where I turned in the car. In Santa Fe I bought another car and drove until I turned off the road near here in the park.''

"You've been crisscrossing the state,'' Jennifer said. "Maybe that would have thrown someone off the trail.''

"I hid the last car in some trees in the park and walked the rest of the way. If someone finds the car, they can't trace it to me. The registration is in a fictitious name."

"Look, we have to get out of here," Jennifer said, casting a worried glance at the windows.

"But I feel safe *here*."

"Ranger Hollenbeck said to get out, so we're going into town. Do you need to get the car? Or did you intend to abandon it?"

"It doesn't matter. But we can't leave now. Not tonight when it's storming and we can't see. We wouldn't know if anyone was following us or not. Goldie's eyes swam with tears again, and Jennifer felt mean, yet at the same time she was frightened for their safety. They had to get out. And they had to get rid of the money. Rat Tabor would never return it to the mob. She glanced at the darkened window. Suppose they were already being watched?

"Please, can we stay here just tonight and not go back to town where someone can find me?"

Jennifer hesitated. It was a quarter past ten now, and she didn't relish leaving in the dark. A few hours shouldn't make much difference.

"All right, but at dawn we're going to the police and then we're going home to Santa Fe. I'll set the clock for five and we'll be out of here by six. We can eat breakfast on the highway. And you tell me if you see anyone suspicious." Should they give the money to Sheriff Garcia in Rimrock or take it all the way to Santa Fe police? Rimrock was closer, although it was in the opposite direction. She thought of Dan Garcia, a man who inspired confidence. They would take the money to Rimrock and get rid of it as quickly as possible.

Goldie threw her arms around Jennifer and hugged her. "Whatever we do, I'm the luckiest sister in the whole world. I'm trouble, and you're good to me, Jenny."

Jennifer hugged her sister in return, feeling the surge of love she had always felt for Goldie. They had been the best of friends—until Rat.

"I'm going down to tell the boys and Dad that we go home early in the morning."

Goldie nodded, her blue eyes teary. "Please think about keeping the money just a little while longer."

"I'll think about it, but right now my answer is no."

In the doorway of the living room, Jennifer paused, assailed by doubts. The boys lay on their stomachs on the floor, Osgood stretched out beside them, while the dogs sat on the chintz-covered chairs. Her gaze went to the wide picture window, streaked with drops of rain. Was she doing the right thing in waiting until dawn? She hurried to the window, seeing her wide-eyed reflection in the glass. Should they leave tonight? Had Goldie been followed?

The inky darkness was menacing. Jennifer yanked on the cord of the rose-colored drapes, feeling relieved as they swung shut. She would tell the family her decision and prepare for an early-morning start.

At half past midnight, she pulled on an old blue button-down dress shirt, one that had been Mark's, the cotton soft from frequent launderings. She went to the window again and waited for the next flash of lightning. When the silvery brilliance illuminated the land, Jennifer was startled to see water lapping over the graveled county road. She felt a ripple of panic. Had she made the wrong decision to wait until daylight? Shivering, she rubbed her arms, wishing now she had packed them all into the Bronco and headed for Santa Fe early in the evening.

If Dad had told her sooner about Ranger Hollenbeck's warning—but then they might have missed Goldie.

As long as the dam held a few more hours, they would be fine. It had stayed intact through years and years of rains, she reassured herself. By daylight everything would look better, and if the rain stopped, the water would go down swiftly.

Just let the dam hold, and they would be gone.

JASON REACHED FOR the phone. "Hollenbeck."

A buzzing sounded in his ear and he sat up, realizing someone was pounding on his door. Wide awake now, he slammed down the receiver and threw back a sheet. He hurriedly pulled on his jeans and went to the door. Rain beat against the windows and drummed on the roof relentlessly.

"Jason! Wake up! Jason!"

He recognized Terrell's voice and yanked open the door to face the tall blond ranger, whose broad-shouldered frame almost filled the entryway. A spray of cold rain swept over him.

"Get the hell up. The dam's going!"

CHAPTER THREE

TERRELL STEPPED INSIDE, water dripping from his broad-brimmed hat.

"They called me from the dam. The cracks are widening and they think it'll be half an hour at most before all that water pours through this valley."

"Oh, hell!" Jason ran to grab his shirt, Terrell following him.

"You got anyone still in the park or in the valley?"

"The Ruarks were still there about eight o'clock last night. I talked to the girl." Jason yanked on a navy T-shirt and his socks and boots. "Let's go."

He grabbed his rain slicker and followed Terrell out the door. Both men climbed into their patrol Jeeps with Jason leading the way, winding down the mountain as fast as he dared, the lights dipping and rising, showing the silvery glisten of puddles along the road.

He gripped the wheel, trying to race the river. They tore across the bridge, the water only a few feet below, then wound down to the floor of the valley, where the road was completely lost from sight. Tense, anxious to get the Ruarks and get out, Jason hunched forward over the wheel.

They might have only minutes, and he wasn't even sure they could drive out on this side of the river because the roads were too steep. It would be safer to cross the bridge and head for his cabin—if they could make it in time.

The Ruark place was dark, but their Bronco was in sight behind the house and smoke still spiraled from the chimney. He jumped out and ran to hammer on the door. Dogs barked, their yaps growing louder. He pounded again and Terrell ran up.

"You think they're here?"

"I know they're here. Listen to the dogs." He pounded again. "Open the door! Flood!"

"How can they sleep through this racket?"

"The old man is deaf. Lord, we can't wait." Jason stepped back, took a quick stride forward and kicked. When the door splintered and swung open, five dogs spilled out, and he stumbled over them. Hitting the light switch, he ran for the stairs. "You look down here," he called to Terrell.

A dog nipped at his heels and bit a patch out of his jeans as he raced up the stairs. "Flood! Everybody up!"

Will Ruark, dressed in red pajamas, appeared in a doorway, his eyes round. "Ranger Hollenbeck?"

"Get your brothers—we have to get out!"

Another door opened and two more boys appeared. In a third doorway stood a blonde whom Jason had never seen before. Her mouth was open, her eyes wide, and all color had drained from her face.

"Flood!" he shouted. She wore a frilly red nightgown and he almost forgot his purpose. "Flood," he repeated.

"There's a flood. Oh, thank heavens, a flood," she said, and slammed the door shut.

Disgruntled, Jason rapped on the door and she opened it a crack. "Everyone out," he ordered. "The house may be washed away."

"I know. I'm coming right now." She flashed him a blinding smile. He strode away, wondering who she was. Another daughter? Ruark's girlfriend? She sure was a looker.

"No one's downstairs," Terrell called up while the three Ruark boys ran back and forth between their two rooms.

"Get your drum!" Kyle yelled.

Carrying a snare drum and sticks, Will ran past Jason.

"Get your sister," Jason said.

"Sister? I'll get Granddad—he's slow." Will's face was ashen. Fleetingly, Jason wondered if the boy had regrets now that he hadn't given his father the warning.

One door was still closed and Jason yanked it open. Red hair curled over the pillow and he knew it was Jennifer. How the hell could she sleep through this racket?

He ran across the room and jostled her shoulder. "Get up!"

Turning over, she flung her arm over her eyes.

"Get out of bed," he said, bending down to shake her shoulder and pull her to her feet. She was warm, soft and tousled, her body full of pliant curves, her long legs bare. As he set her on her feet, he leaned close. "Wake up!"

She blinked and jerked upright. As she stepped back in fright, she lost her balance and fell across the bed, the nightshirt revealing luscious bare thighs. Jason's gaze roamed up to her green eyes, now narrowed with fire.

"What are you doing in here?" she cried. "Help! Dad!"

"Wait a minute! I'm here because the dam is going!"

She paused, her hand in midair. They stood facing each other.

Dad? A wedding ring glinted on her hand, and the blue nightshirt she wore was unbuttoned halfway down the front, revealing delectable curves that almost made Jason forget the flood.

This wasn't the Ruark daughter; this was the Ruark mother, and she was sleeping alone. Where was the father?

If a wall of water had hit the house at that moment, Jason couldn't have kept his gaze from wandering down the long shapely legs revealed beneath the skimpy nightshirt. His pulse pounded, and the chilled dampness he felt changed to a steamy heat.

"The dam!" she snapped, and his gaze flicked back up to her face. Her cheeks were pink, and she clutched the shirt tightly beneath her chin.

"You have to get out," he warned, his voice a notch lower. He hadn't really looked at her during their confrontation in the flower bed. He remembered the green eyes, but he didn't remember their thick fringe of dark red-brown lashes. He didn't remember her full red lips, and the silky mane of auburn hair that had been tied in a ponytail. "I couldn't wake you," he said, or hoped he said. Mrs. Jennifer Ruark was mind-blowing gorgeous.

She nodded. "I'll dress."

"You better grab something fast. We could be washed away anytime. We have to get out of this valley."

"Right."

He couldn't move. His gaze drifted over her once more.

"Ranger Hollenbeck!"

He blinked as he backed up and left the room. Wiping his brow, he became aware of Terrell trying to direct everyone to the Jeeps. Who was the blonde? he wondered. She was almost as pretty as the redhead.

The Ruark women must have gotten all the looks. He glanced back wistfully at the closed door then went downstairs to help Terrell. Dressed in jeans, T-shirts and sneakers, each kid carried an armload of clothes and toys. When Jason stepped outside, he stared in dismay. Terrell's Jeep was bulging with clutter—videos, a drum, a trumpet and loose clothing strewn over the seat. Will pitched another load into the Bronco and turned toward the house. Jason caught him and motioned him back to the truck.

"Get in now!" he ordered, signaling to the two younger Ruarks as they staggered out, their arms full. "Everyone get in!"

Terrell helped Blondie into his Jeep, and then Osgood MacFee and five dogs piled in with them. The two youngest Ruarks sat in Jason's vehicle while Will waited in the Bronco.

Jason glanced over his shoulder as Jennifer came down the stairs. Her hair was a mass of riotous auburn curls that bounced below her shoulders with each step. The blue sweater she wore bounced, as well. In one arm she carried a bag and a purse, and with the other she was trying to pull on a yellow rain slicker.

"Thanks!" She ran past Jason and climbed into the Bronco. Terrell led the way and Jason motioned for Jennifer to go next, while he brought up the rear. They roared away from the house.

Jason concentrated on his driving. All three vehicles sent up plumes of spray as they rolled through water that was becoming deeper by the minute. Terrell was

driving as fast as possible, a space widening between
him and Jennifer. Jason prayed they would make the
bridge, and then it loomed into sight and he blinked in
amazement. The river splashed up against it and a thin
stream of water poured across. The river was level with
the bridge, something he hadn't seen in his nine years as
a ranger at San Saba.

Jason's sense of urgency mushroomed. Terrell raced
onto the bridge, his vehicle sending a high fan of water
on either side as he tore across.

Jennifer started across more slowly. Jason stepped on
the gas and stayed on her bumper. He leaned forward,
his knuckles white. "Get going, get going—" he muttered, trying to will her to hurry across the span.

"Are you honking at my mother?" one of the little
Ruarks asked.

"You bet I am! Move it, move it." Halfway... they
were halfway across.

Jason heard Terrell's horn, and with the next flash of
lightning, he looked upriver. His breath stopped as he
stared at the wall of silvery water bearing down on
them.

"Go!" he hollered. He hit the horn, but the sound
was lost in the roar of river, rain and thunder. "Get off
the bridge!"

They wouldn't survive if the wave hit while they were
on the bridge. They might not survive even if they made
it across, because it was a quarter of a mile before the
road climbed out of the valley.

His stomach lurched. The dam had gone. Terrell was
across and raced ahead, turning to drive straight up the
mountainside. He gunned the engine and took off over
the rugged terrain, climbing higher.

Jennifer bounced off the bridge and turned sharply to follow Terrell. She hit a rock and the Bronco slammed into a tree, blocking the road. There wasn't room for Jason to drive past her.

As Jennifer and Will jumped out to run, he heard a giant roar. Looking over his shoulder, he felt his heart slam against his ribs. A mountain of water bore down on them, sweeping giant pines in its path.

Jason jumped from the Jeep and grabbed the boys.

"Run for high ground and hold hands!" he shouted, grabbing Kyle and Brett's hands and running toward Jennifer and Will, trying to reach them before the water did.

"Run!" he cried, lengthening his stride, charging toward them.

The sound of the water was deafening now, and Jason's heart pounded. He stretched out his legs, urging both boys along. Only yards behind them the water was sweeping everything in its path. At last they caught up with Will and Jennifer, who scooped Kyle up under her arm. Jason picked up Brett and began to run.

Terror seized Jennifer as she scrambled up the mountainside, trying to escape the thunderous water. Glancing back, she saw her truck pulled into the current and tossed like a toy. The tree it had struck was gone. With her next step the ground gave way beneath her and she fell, screaming as she lost her balance and tumbled into the icy water.

Flailing her arms against the current, she gagged and spun along in the raging river, bumping into trees and logs, water rolling over her as she tried to grasp something solid. Terrified that the boys might have fallen in, too, she fought wildly, to no avail.

A strong arm wrapped around her waist and caught her, dragging her up against a lean, hard body. She clung to Jason, and they were buffeted along until he managed to grab a tree and pull them onto it. She gasped for breath. Her lungs hurt, and she shook with fear and cold. "My boys!"

"They're all right," he said in a deep voice. She wiped her eyes and looked around but couldn't see them. Water swirled around her waist while Jason clung to the pine with one arm and held her with the other.

"You're sure about the boys?"

"They're farther up the mountain," he answered, his strong body a barrier against the raging current. Relief swamped her, until she had another thought. "Dad?"

"I don't know where the others are. I think they made it up the mountain before the water hit."

Water continued to rush around them. "This pine may go at any time," she said, watching a smaller tree strike theirs and float on downriver. How would they ever get to the bank?

She became aware of Jason Hollenbeck's arm around her. His body was warm, the only warmth in the cold, wet night. She'd lost her rain slicker in the flood, and the sweater molded wetly to her body. She clung to him, thankful for his strength. If he hadn't come...

"Thank you," she said solemnly. He turned his head. His face was only inches away. Lightning flashed and she gazed into distinctive eyes with irises the color of clear, blue marble.

The pine shook as another tree slammed against it. His arm tightened around her and she clung to his lean, hard body.

"We have to get out of here," he shouted as the tree shuddered and toppled over.

Icy water splashed over Jennifer and strong arms tightened around her. As both of them resurfaced, she held on. In seconds Jason had found solid ground and pulled her up against him. Gasping for breath, she grabbed him as he steadied her, then they waded together through the calf-deep water to higher ground.

"Come on," he urged, taking her hand. They rushed up the muddy, slippery mountain, heading west. At last she could see the others through the trees.

"Mom!" the boys yelled, racing toward her. Crying with relief, she caught them and hugged them.

Goldie stood near their father, who held two of the dogs in his arms. A third sat at his feet. Jennifer was relieved to see he was warmly dressed and still wearing his hearing aid. She felt a clutch in her heart as she looked at his face.

"Where are the other dogs?"

He shook his head and his eyes brimmed with tears. "I don't know. I've lost Priss and Oats."

"They may show up later, sir," a tall blond ranger told him, and her father nodded forlornly.

Jennifer glanced back down the mountain, feeling weak in the knees. Her truck was gone. Trees were gone. Maybe even their house was gone. Their home was in Santa Fe, but still there were pictures back at the cabin and things with sentimental value. She blinked back tears. If the rangers hadn't come to wake them . . . She shivered.

"Where's Priss?" Kyle's voice piped up.

"We don't know," she said, feeling a lump in her throat. The boys had never really gotten over the death of their father, and now they had to face another loss.

"I want Priss! I want our house!" Kyle yelled, tears spilling over and running down his cheeks.

"I want Oats!" Brett cried, kicking a rock in frustration.

"The Bronco washed away!" Kyle added. "I saw it."

While Osgood hugged Kyle, Goldie began to cry. Even Will, who stood with his fists clenched and his mouth clamped shut, had big tears streaming down his cheeks. At the sight of her oldest son crying, Jennifer could no longer control her own pain.

They all sobbed, and she was aware of someone patting her back, and then she heard Ranger Hollenbeck's deep voice. "I'm sorry, Jennifer...." She felt his arm wrap around her and she put her forehead against his chest.

Minutes later, she stepped back and wiped her eyes. The other ranger held Goldie, and Dad comforted the boys. The three dogs sat at his feet and howled while cold rain poured over all of them. She realized her knees were trembling from the ordeal.

"I'm sorry," she said, hiccuping, feeling idiotic and at the same time hurting for their losses.

"I understand," Ranger Hollenbeck said, patting her shoulder, but there was a hint of impatience in his voice. "Look, we ought to get your father and the boys out of this weather."

She nodded. "Dad!" she shouted, and walked over to hug him and the boys. "We need to get the kids indoors."

Osgood nodded, and they all piled into the remaining Jeep.

Goldie sat on Osgood's lap while the boys squeezed together in the back, clutching their musical instruments. Ranger Hollenbeck motioned for Jennifer to sit on his lap. She climbed in, feeling his hard thighs beneath her.

The Jeep lurched and slid and she fell back against him. "Sorry," she said, without turning. She stared ahead and didn't look around at him, but she was acutely aware of the warmth of his body.

"We're going to stay in a patrol cabin?" Will asked, leaning forward from the back seat.

"That's right, Will," Jason answered.

"Ranger Hollenbeck can show you everything he does," Jennifer added.

"It's Jason. You don't need to call me Ranger Hollenbeck. I'll introduce you to Terrell when we get inside."

The patrol cabin loomed up ahead, and minutes later they climbed out of the Jeep. Leading the way up the steps, Jason opened the door to allow the women to enter.

Jennifer walked into an immaculate room that glistened with lemony polish and felt as if she'd stepped into a motel room. For a moment, she wondered if anyone lived here or if the cabin was kept in readiness for occasions such as this. Then she noticed a picture on a table, and bending down, she saw a man who looked like Ranger Hollenbeck. *He* lived here. The boys tromped in, leaving muddy footprints across the floor. The dogs bounded onto the furniture, and Jennifer glanced around to see Ranger Hollenbeck standing with his hands on his hips, a fiery glint in his fascinating blue eyes. She suddenly felt as if they were intruding.

"First of all, we need to get everyone warm and dry," he said in clipped words. "Folks, this is Terrell Skinner, another San Saba ranger. Terrell, meet Jennifer Ruark, Osgood MacFee, Will Ruark, Brett Ruark and Kyle Ruark." He looked at Goldie.

Jennifer said, "This is Goldie MacFee, my sister."

"Terrell, report in and see if we're needed." Jason scratched his head, trying to think of the most orderly manner to handle everyone. "We'll give the ladies the bedroom and the men will bunk in here. Mr. MacFee can sleep on the sofa. Bedrolls and pallets for everyone else."

"Bunk?" Brett squawked. "Mom, are we staying here? I don't see a television. Where's the television, Mr. Ranger?"

"I don't own one."

Groans filled the room, and Will said, "It figures." He dropped an armload of videos he had salvaged in their flight and they crashed onto the floor, setting one of the terriers barking.

"Will," Jennifer said in a threatening tone.

"There's one bedroom, and I know everyone will want to dry off and get changed, so you'll just have to take turns. Your family may go first," he said to Jennifer.

"I'm hungry," Kyle said.

"How about breakfast?" Jason asked, feeling pangs of hunger himself and wanting to escape the sight of his once-neat living area. "I'll start breakfast. Does anyone need a change of clothes?"

"I do!" yelled all three boys.

Jennifer nodded. "Our things were in the Bronco."

"Dad and I had clothes in Terrell's Jeep, so we're all right," Goldie said.

"I'll see what I can find." Jason left to rummage through his things, getting changes of clothing for himself, trying to find something for the boys, knowing his clothes would never fit the two youngest. Terrell knocked on the door and entered the room.

He rubbed his forehead. "I've talked to the office. I'm stranded here, too. Della said three bridges are gone—four, seven and eight. All the others except one and eighteen are under water. So far, no one has been reported injured. I told them we'd be out as soon as we get the family settled. She'll call if we're needed before then. Jeff and Dan are placing barriers at all the park entrances. Della said they'll try to keep campers out until the river crests. I guess the advance warnings paid off. They think some houses are gone," he added in a low voice, rolling his eyes toward the other room. "Have you got enough food?"

"Plenty. Food is the least of our worries right now. Fortunately I was just in Rimrock and loaded up while I was there. It's clothes we need. What can I give them to wear?"

"Beats me. Let them wash and dry what they're wearing. They can wear your bathrobe or sheets while they wait."

"I don't own a robe and I don't own that many sheets. Terrell, get down on your knees and pray for sunshine."

He grinned. "Okay, but if the water goes down enough to get to my place, I get to invite Goldie to stay with me."

"Fine," Jason said, thinking of the boys and dogs. "I wonder where Mr. Ruark is."

"He's dead. Jennifer Ruark is a widow."

"How do you know that?"

"Goldie told me. I wanted to make sure we had everyone out of the house. Want me to start breakfast while you rummage for clothes?"

"That's a good idea. Maybe if they're full of food they'll fall asleep."

"Don't count on it. I grew up with brothers."

Jason opened a drawer and looked at the rows of neatly rolled T-shirts. He pulled out one for each of the Ruarks and closed the drawer to open another one. He removed two pairs of jeans and thought about the little Ruarks. The legs would be yards too long. He picked up some Hawaiian shorts with elastic waistbands, three pairs he had never worn, and placed them in the growing pile of clothing.

Another light rap came at the open door and Jennifer thrust her head into the room. "May I come in?"

"Sure."

She walked into the room and paused, her arms wrapped around her waist. "I'm sorry you have all of us on your hands," she said, and he became aware of her again. The damp clothes clung to her body, the blue sweater outlining her curves. How could he have ever thought she was a kid—and a boy, at that? She stared up at him with a worried look, lower lip caught between even white teeth. Suddenly his sympathy went out to her. She had had a bad fright at the river and in all likelihood her house had been washed away.

"It isn't forever, and we'll manage. When everyone is dry and fed, we'll work out a schedule. You and your sister take my bed."

"Really, we can all sleep in the front room, and you can have your bed."

"Nope. This is fine. I don't have much that will fit your boys. Here's a sweatshirt and a pair of my jeans if you want them."

"Thanks, but I can borrow something of Goldie's." He caught her hands.

"You're chilled, aren't you? I can give you a sweatshirt to wear for now."

"Thanks. I'll warm up in a few minutes. I suppose we should declare a truce," she said quietly. "Thanks for coming to rescue us, and I'm sorry for knocking you over the other day."

"When I grabbed you, I thought you were one of the boys."

She raised her chin. "You were that upset because they'd dug a hole?"

Jason suspected they'd be at odds again if they got into a discussion about her sons. "Why don't we get dry and eat breakfast before we talk about your petunias and your sons?"

"Do my sons annoy you?"

He could see sparks igniting in her beautiful eyes. How could she be related to those ruffians? "You're widowed?"

"Yes. You didn't answer my question, Ranger Hollenbeck."

"It's Jason, and your sons are adorable." How could she argue with that one? A bolt of lightning might strike him for the lie, but she should be mollified.

She studied him for a moment, then smiled. It was as effective as a bolt of lightning. She had dimples and a smile that took his chill away. "I'm sorry," she said. "I guess I'm on edge."

He smiled in return. "I'm sorry about the day in the petunias. The washer and dryer are in my kitchen. The bathroom is right here—" He turned and noticed a big cloud of black smoke wafting through the door behind her.

"Good Lord, what have they done *now!*"

CHAPTER FOUR

JASON RAN PAST HER to see flames shooting high from a fire in his iron skillet. Terrell dumped a canister of flour over the flames and a white cloud rose along with the last trail of smoke.

Jason glared at Terrell, then at Will, who stood beside the stove. Terrell shrugged.

"What happened in here?" Jason demanded.

"I caught the bacon on fire," Will said. "It was an accident, honest."

"And I forgot the toast and let it burn," Terrell said, his gaze going past Jason to Goldie, who smiled at him.

"If everyone will get out of the kitchen, I'll cook breakfast," Jason announced, annoyed at all of them.

"You need to get into dry clothes, Mr. Ranger," Kyle said, staring up at him. "You're dripping."

"All of you, *out,* and I'll cook," he repeated tersely.

Suddenly a wail filled the cabin, and Jason looked around as the three dogs began to howl. Brett sat in Osgood's lap and let out another loud wail, while Osgood wiped his eyes and the three dogs threw back their heads in a canine chorus.

"Dad, don't cry, maybe the dogs will show up," Goldie said, rushing to him. She hugged Brett and straightened, then looked at Terrell and burst into tears.

Jason glared down at Kyle Ruark, the last one left in the kitchen. He held out his arm and pointed his finger. "Out."

Kyle left as Terrell hurried to pat Goldie's shoulder. "Don't cry. Jason and I'll go back for the dogs as soon as we eat."

Jason stared at Terrell, who avoided his eyes. Shaking his head, Jason turned to the kitchen and felt a chill that he knew didn't come from being drenched. What had happened to his orderly life? In ten minutes they had destroyed the kitchen. Cabinet doors stood open. Eggshells cluttered the counter. The stove was blackened from smoke and the skillet was hidden beneath a mound of flour.

He crossed the room, trying to ignore his squishing boots and the puddles that followed him as he cleaned. When another skillet of bacon was frying, orange juice was poured and cups of hot chocolate were ready, he felt a tap on his shoulder and turned around.

Jennifer took the fork from his hand and looked up at him. "I'll finish cooking breakfast, and the bathroom is yours now."

The mass of red curls framed her face. She wore his sweatshirt over a pair of Goldie's jeans, and it had never looked better.

"You like my shirt?" she asked with amusement, and he realized he was staring.

"You look great," he said, and a twinkle came into her green eyes.

"Hey, guys," Kyle piped up in a loud, piercing voice, "Mr. Ranger thinks Mom looks *gr-ay-ate!*" he cried, drawing out the word.

"Kyle!" Jennifer admonished, and he turned away.

Jason glared at the back of Kyle's head as he crossed the room. The younger Ruark boys were in his Hawaiian shorts, and they both appeared as if a sneeze would pop the shorts right off. Even though she said she had salvaged some of her own clothes, Goldie wore a T-shirt and the third pair of his Hawaiian shorts. She looked as if she were ready to pose in before-and-after pictures with the boys. Yep, the looks in the family had definitely gone to the women. Will was in a pair of Jason's jeans and a T-shirt. Osgood had changed and wore his own fresh shirt and trousers and leather slippers. Terrell was barefoot and had a blanket wrapped around him, his broad shoulders bare. In the background both the washer and dryer swished and hummed.

Jason stepped over a drum and entered the bathroom, only to get hit in the face with the wet clothes that hadn't made it into the first load of laundry. He lifted down a wet T-shirt that had been draped over the door and knelt to mop up the puddle on the floor beneath it. Picking his way through the soggy apparel, he finally stepped beneath the shower, jumping as he was hit with a spray of cold water. With gritted teeth he bathed and shaved—and wished his field kit held a tranquilizer.

As he emerged from the bedroom in dry jeans and another T-shirt, Brett Ruark blasted his trumpet and the three dogs let out more howls.

"Come eat!" Jennifer said in a soft voice that was miraculously heard by all. Jason stared at the Ruarks as they moved to the kitchen. In seconds Jennifer had them in line while she served each plate.

He moved to the end of the line and Kyle gazed up at him. "How do you live here without a TV? Did you know there wouldn't be a TV when you took the job?"

"I knew there wouldn't be. I don't miss television. There are other things to do in life."

"Like what, except go to school?"

"Like fishing or listening to records."

"We saw your records," he said darkly, and turned his back on Jason.

"Can I play one of your CDs?" Will asked, his plate filled with a mound of golden scrambled eggs, toast, strips of bacon and slices of orange.

"Yes, you may."

Kyle held up his plate for his mother to serve him and then she turned to Jason.

"Go ahead," he said, motioning to her.

She smiled and served herself and he caught an enticing scent of roses over the smells of bacon and toast and smoke hovering in the air.

The boys were sprawled on the floor to eat, his Beatles album was playing, and Osgood, Goldie and Terrell were sitting at the small kitchen table, so Jason went with Jennifer to the living area. They set their mugs of hot coffee on the small round table between them.

"As soon as we eat, Terrell and I will go look for the dogs."

"I don't expect you to find them," she said sadly.

"If we don't, maybe you can get him two more."

"I don't know. They're trained. Dad has a dog act."

Jason glanced at the three dogs, who sat in a row beside Osgood and waited expectantly as if they hoped to get a morsel from breakfast.

"I don't have any dog food."

Jennifer caught her lower lip with her teeth and frowned, looking past him as if deep in thought. "We don't usually feed them scraps, but I guess that's what we'll have to do. They have a special balanced dog food.''

"They'll have to rough it until the water goes down.''

"We should have gone home yesterday, but everyone failed to tell me until after dark that you had given a warning.''

"I figured they didn't tell you.''

"How long before we can get back across the bridge?''

"I don't know. After we finish eating, Terrell and I will check the bridges.''

"Can I come?'' Will asked, looking up at them.

"If you'll do what I say,'' Jason said sternly, surprised Will wanted to go with him.

"Yes, sir!'' he said in a quick salute.

"Will,'' Jennifer warned.

"I said yes, sir,'' he answered in a voice filled with innocence. He rolled over to continue eating, and Jason returned his attention to Jennifer. She controlled them with a voice that was almost a whisper. Out of her presence, they were first-prize hooligans. His gaze roamed over his home and he felt his stomach knot.

"Maybe the sun will come out soon,'' she offered.

"I don't think it's going to come out today.'' He stretched out his arm and picked up a pad and pen. "I'll make out a schedule for us. Lunch is at twelve. I get up at six.''

"You go right ahead.''

"Tonight, would you and Goldie prefer the bathroom first?''

"You don't need a schedule. You and your ranger friend get up and do whatever rangers do.''

"Unfortunately, this place wasn't built with entertaining guests in mind. To get to the bathroom, you have to go through the bedroom."

"You won't bother us. With three boys and five dogs, I'm accustomed to noise, so just go right ahead. If I want privacy, I'll close the bedroom door. Otherwise, we'll leave it ajar. Do you have any oatmeal or cereal? I try to watch Dad's cholesterol."

"I usually eat an egg and toast for breakfast."

"Maybe you get enough exercise, but Dad doesn't. We'll manage." She gave him a smile. "I think the water will go down soon."

As if to contradict her, the air vibrated with thunder, and the electricity flickered.

"You don't stay here year-round, do you?" he asked.

She shook her head, picking up a piece of toast and biting into it. "No. We live in Santa Fe when the boys are in school. School has been out for two weeks now, but I suppose you know that from all the kids who come with their families to the park. I teach and I'm an artist."

"You're busy, then."

"It's getting busier all the time. I've thought about retiring from teaching and devoting all my time to art, but with three boys..."

He couldn't imagine how she could draw a line with the noise and confusion of the Ruark boys. "If that's what you really want to do and you can manage it financially, you ought to do it," he said. "If possible, people should choose careers they like," he added, knowing he sounded a bit defensive.

She tilted her head to look at him. "Aren't you doing what you like?"

"Very definitely." He laughed and shrugged his shoulders, surprised she had picked up on his tone. "But my father has tried for years—most of my life—to push me into his business, so I've had a personal crisis about choosing the career I like."

"What does your father want you to do?"

He was surprised she hadn't recognised the Hollenbeck name. "Hollenbeck Enterprises, Commercial Real Estate. His business is in Santa Fe."

"I know the company. Your father is Thad Hollenbeck, and he's done television commercials for his company. I've never had dealings with anyone in commercial real estate, but I have heard of the company. And you really don't want to be in the real estate business?"

"No, I don't, but it took a long time before I admitted that to myself. I majored in business and then had a double major when I went into forestry. My master's degree is in park management, but all that is a sore subject at home."

"I can't imagine what that would be like. Dad's always let me make my own decisions and he's never pushed me in one direction or another."

"Be thankful. The other way is terrible for everyone concerned. No one wins."

Her green eyes were filled with curiosity. "Don't you have brothers or sisters who could step into the family business?"

"Unfortunately, no. I'm the only child, so all of Dad's hopes are pinned on me and it was a painful decision when I changed to forestry. I'd been raised believing that I would grow up and go into the business."

"Your father's with the Santa Fe Chamber of Commerce, too, isn't he? I remember seeing his name in the paper."

"He's a great promoter of the city. And very protective of it. He doesn't want outsiders coming in and changing it." He started to laugh. "Listen to me going on about my family. I don't usually talk about this." Actually, he'd never talked to anyone this much about his problems with his parents. "You're a good listener."

"Thank you. But go ahead and talk. I don't know how you can bear to stay here months at a time by yourself. I'd think you'd be talking to the trees after a while."

He grinned and shrugged. "I grew up alone. I enjoy the solitude, and it isn't all that lonely. There's always the tourists and campers to deal with, and I give nature tours and sometimes serve as a park guide." He glanced across the room at Goldie. "Does your sister live with you, too?"

"No. Goldie just came to visit. She's from—" She looked at her sister and blinked. "Goldie's from California. Dad and the dogs live with us. Mom is no longer alive and Dad does well, but he needs someone to cook. The dogs keep him busy and he's good for the boys."

"Do you go out with men? I mean, do you date?" The question popped out before he could stop it. Why had he even asked? He certainly wasn't going to ask out the mother of the Ruark hooligans.

"Mom, date?" Will turned around and Jason glared at him.

"No, I don't," she replied, dimples appearing.

"Are you asking Mom out?" Will swung around and crossed his legs, facing them.

"Will!" came her soft admonishment.

He turned and whispered something to his brothers, who giggled.

Jennifer rose from the table and looked down at Jason, ignoring her sons. "You go ahead with whatever you have to do, and the boys and I will clean the kitchen."

"Ranger Hollenbeck said I could go with him," Will cried, jumping to his feet.

"Take your dishes to the kitchen first," Jennifer said, and he hurried to do so. In minutes, Jason, Terrell and Will were in raincoats and boots again.

As they went out the door, Jennifer called, "Will— you do exactly what the rangers tell you to do."

"Yes, ma'am," he said, and Jason felt suspicious now. The only cooperation he'd seen from Will Ruark was in the presence of his mother.

"Bring back Priss and Oats!" the younger brothers chorused.

"Oats always gets lost," Will said. "Grandpa doesn't let him out without the other dogs."

"We should find them," Jason told him. "Those dogs made it across the bridge before the water hit."

They drove down the mountainside in Terrell's Jeep. The river was swollen high above its banks, and the water still rushed by like treacherous rapids, sweeping along whole trees with its powerful current. Jason felt both a sense of awe and a certain sadness, wondering how much destruction the flooding had caused. Thank heavens they had gotten the Ruarks to safety.

"Awesome," Will said, peering ahead.

"Wow." Terrell spoke softly. "I didn't imagine it would be like this. I'm surprised we have a bridge left in this part of the park."

"Our house will be gone, won't it?" Will asked solemnly, gazing up at Jason.

Jason looked at the water and wondered if anything was left in the valley. "Your home sits back from the river. It may still be standing, but it'll be flooded inside."

He wondered if Will felt any remorse for not giving the warning to his mother. The boy had looked away and was chewing on his lower lip, a frown furrowing his brow. Jason suspected his conscience was causing him a bit of discomfort.

"Let's check it out," Terrell said, climbing out of the Jeep.

"I'll go east and you go west," Jason replied. He motioned to Will. "You come with me. And don't get within three feet of the edge of the river. The water may have carved out ground beneath the surface. Trees are still toppling in."

"Yes, Ranger Hollenbeck," Will said compliantly, but Jason wasn't convinced. Away from their mother these Ruark boys were hellions.

Rain came down in a steady drizzle, the roar of the river drowning out all other noise. Will roamed ahead of Jason, catching a snake once and then tossing it into the river. It swam back to shore and slithered away. Jason saw him place a frog in his raincoat pocket.

"Will, let that frog go. This is his home. You want your home and he wants his. We have a balanced ecosystem, and you need to help keep it that way."

Startled, Will returned the frog to the ground.

Jason was shocked at the size of the river, now more than seventy feet across. Along the muddy bank he found a rabbit caught between the branches of a fallen tree. He freed the animal and scooped it up a moment, feeling for injuries. Satisfied there were none, he set the rabbit on the ground and it hopped away.

Terrell caught up with Jason. "Find anything?"

"No. How far did you go?"

"Where Owl Creek dumps into the river. Changed things around here, that's for sure. Guess the river will never be back like it was. Found your Jeep, though. It's stuck in the mud just over that rise."

"The water'll go down, but I don't know if they'll rebuild the dam."

"Where's the kid?"

Jason glanced around at wet trees and rushing water. Two mule deer approached then bounded up the mountainside, but Will was nowhere in sight. "He was right here a few minutes ago."

"You told him to stay away from the river. He'll be all right."

"He's a Ruark. We better find him."

Jason shouted Will's name and whistled loudly, but no one appeared. Feeling uneasy, he strode ahead, Terrell falling in beside him.

"Oh, Lord." Terrell stopped and pointed ahead. Jason's heart plummeted.

Will lay stretched out on the branch of a cottonwood, the river's powerful currents roaring beneath him. Just beyond, a tall pine was being sucked into the muddy water, and Will was edging slowly toward it.

"What in the hell is he doing?" Terrell muttered.

"Will, get back!" Jason shouted, sprinting toward the boy. "Terrell, look." He waved his hand in the direction of the pine. "One of the dogs is stuck in the tree."

The fuzzy white dog was draped awkwardly over a pine bough and yapping wildly, her barks lost in the deafening rush of the river. The tree itself was almost horizontal now and in another minute would be claimed by the current. "The pine is going!" Jason hollered. "Will, look out!"

Ignoring him, Will reached out and plucked the dog from the pine just as it toppled into the water. Clutching a squirming, yapping terrier, he began inching backward when the cottonwood tilted and mud sprayed from its roots.

"It's falling!" Terrell cried.

Jason watched in horror, helpless to do anything. "Jump, Will!"

As the tree toppled, Will twisted and flung himself toward the ground. The cottonwood came crashing down, half in the water, half on the sloping bank, its branches landing on top of Will and smashing him into the mud.

"He's beneath it!" Jason yelled, running toward the tree. "Will!" He spotted a yellow slicker-covered arm. "Here, Terrell."

Jason knelt and frantically began to dig through the mud. "He's buried under here and part of the tree is on him."

"If we pushed it off into the river—"

"We might hurt him more or he might go with it. This ground is crumbling fast."

"I'll lift the trunk, and you try to get to him." Terrell spread his feet and Jason dug wildly. Suddenly a mudball shot past him, then turned to stare at him with big brown eyes. The mutt shook, flinging mud on Jason.

"Will!"

He heard a groan and then he saw the round shape of Will's head. He scooped away mud as the tree trunk eased up another inch and then another.

"This ground is washing away!" Terrell cried. "I can't hold the tree much longer or I'll be in the river."

The branch pinning Will down was the only thing preventing him from being swept away into the current. Water swirled below them and the tree shook. It was a matter of minutes until the tree and Will tumbled into the surging water. On his knees, Jason dug frantically.

Will turned his head and spit dirt out of his mouth.

"You okay?" Jason yelled, standing to help Terrell lift the tree free. "Hold it," he instructed his friend as Will struggled to wiggle out of the indentation he had made in the bank. Jason caught Will by the arm. The boy's legs were in the water and Jason saw he couldn't get enough leverage to stand.

"Are you okay?" Jason shouted at the two blue eyes peering through a mask of mud. "I'll pull you out. Is your back okay?"

Will gave a faint nod and gripped Jason's arm.

"Do it!" Terrell yelled.

Jason slipped his arms beneath Will and tugged, and they both fell back. Will rolled as Terrell released the tree and Jason scrambled up and pulled the boy to his feet. For just a moment he grabbed Jason and clung to him. The tree slid away into the river and floated downstream.

"You all right?" Jason asked Will. He placed his hands on Will's shoulders and felt the tremors shaking him. "Are you all right, son?" he repeated gently, fishing out a handkerchief to hand to Will, who nodded in reply.

Will wiped the muck from his eyes and face. Priss ran in frantic circles around them, barking and shaking mud on them.

"Thank you," Will said, looking up at Jason. "I had to get her. Granddad loves his dogs." He stared wide-eyed at the river. "I didn't think both trees would go. I was afraid the one Priss was in would fall—" He turned a frightened gaze on Jason. "You saved me from falling into the river."

"You're okay, now," Jason said, feeling touched. "That was quite a rescue. You did a good job, Will."

"I thought you'd be mad at me."

"You did a brave thing, Will, now let's get you up to the house."

Will stumbled and Jason steadied him, feeling the boy's thin shoulder through his slicker. At the Jeep Will turned to him. "I'm okay now."

"Get inside, Will, and hold the dog. My Jeep is grounded over there, and Terrell is going to pull it out."

Both men hitched the chain and half an hour later the two Jeeps were headed back to the cabin. As they all climbed out, Priss danced around them.

"Wait a minute." Jason took Will by the arm. "You're not going in my place like that. We're washing you off." He picked up the hose and turned it on.

"Hey! That'll be cold!" Will protested. "I'm not—"

Jason squirted him with the water as Will yelped and jumped.

"Now where's that barking mudball?" Jason asked, looking around while Terrell gathered an armload of Ruark belongings from Jason's Jeep.

"Will!" Jennifer rushed down the steps and stopped, her hands on her hips. "What did you do to him?" she cried, waving her hand at Jason. "He'll freeze! What are you doing?" she repeated. "Turn that hose off!"

Before Jason could say anything, Will reached out to touch her arm. "Mom, he saved my life."

Blinking, Jennifer looked at Will and then back at Jason. Will turned away and bounded up the steps.

"Mom! Priss is here!" Kyle yelled from the platform above.

She looked up at Kyle, who ran back inside. Jason turned off the hose and came toward her.

"I'm sorry," she said. "What happened?"

"The dog was in a tree in the river," Jason explained. "Will climbed out on a branch to reach him. He's all right now and he's safe. He was very brave."

She frowned and glanced beyond him. "He's learned that from his father. Mark always let them do anything they wanted. That's twice you've come to our rescue," she said, returning her attention to him.

"That's my job," Jason answered, momentarily not caring that they were both standing in the rain. "Do *you* let them do anything they want?" he asked, thinking this might be part of the reason they were so rambunctious and ornery.

"No, I don't, but it's difficult to handle them with Mark gone. They're older now and they miss him. Sometimes I think some of their misbehavior is because of their grief. Will and Brett in particular seem so angry over losing their father."

"Mom!"

She looked up again as Kyle motioned to her to come upstairs.

She glanced at Jason, and he waved his hand. "Let's get out of the rain."

"I'm sorry I yelled at you," she said as he took her arm and they climbed the stairs.

"Forget it. You have to protect your kids."

"Mom—" Kyle was nearly bursting as they went inside "—Priss is here! Will got her out of a tree—"

"Kyle," Jason said, kneeling down before the dog, "get your dog and get her washed off before everything I own has mud on it."

"Do what he says now," Jennifer added as Jason closed the door behind them. Priss had already circled the room, leaving a muddy trail on furniture, on Osgood's lap, on the floor.

"I'll get you some coffee," Jennifer said to Jason, and hurried toward the kitchen.

Jason went to his bedroom and looked at the mounds of towels and clothing and stacks of clean, dry clothes someone had folded. What had become of his peaceful life? The boys rushed out of the bathroom with Priss wrapped in a towel.

"She's clean now—see, Mr. Ranger," Kyle said, holding up the dripping dog.

"I see." They left and he closed the bedroom door, yanking off his slicker and boots, his hat and shirt. A knock sounded.

"Come in."

Jennifer entered and closed the door behind her, shutting out yells and frenzied barking. She carried a steaming cup of coffee and held it out to him.

"I thought you might like this."

"Thank you, I would," he said, noticing her damp curls. The blue sweater had been washed and dried, and she was wearing it again. He raised his cup. "I get to bathe after the dog."

"Oh, my goodness," she gasped, taking his hand in hers. "You're bleeding."

For the first time he noticed the cuts crisscrossing his hands. "It's all right. A tree fell over Will and Terrell lifted it up while I tried to dig Will out. I must have scraped my hands. It's nothing," he said, looking down at her pale fingers against his.

"You need a bandage." She picked up a clean dry handkerchief from the stack of laundry, placed it on the worst cut and released him.

"I thought Will was right with me. All of a sudden he was gone."

"You're not accustomed to keeping an eye on kids," she observed, as if forgiving him. She bit her lip and looked away. "Sometimes it's hard raising boys. They do so many physical things that are dangerous."

"You seem to cope pretty well," he said, feeling a stirring of sympathy for her. "And you have your dad."

"He's about as bad as they are. Oh, he doesn't climb trees and almost fall into rivers, but he eggs them on." She studied him. "I apologize for losing my temper with you," she said softly, and he wished his hands weren't muddy, because he wanted to touch her. Her eyes lowered to his chest, then flew back up to meet his gaze. "Sorry I yelled."

"I told you before, just forget it. He wanted to save the dog, and he did a brave thing."

"Like racing the river and coming to get us this morning?"

"Yes, only that's my job." Unable to resist, he reached out to touch her hand. "Now you have mud on your hands."

"I'll wash," she said without looking down.

"How long ago were you widowed?"

"It's been more than three years now. Mark was the Aztec Petroleum Company pilot. He had his own plane, too, and he was killed doing stunts at the Albuquerque air show."

"Sorry, that's rough."

"He liked to take risks," she said quietly, gazing beyond Jason, seemingly lost in memories. "I'm trying to manage with the boys, but they're full of energy. Mark and I probably spoiled them."

"I'm never around children except when I give lectures here in the park, so I don't know much about handling kids."

"Looks as if you did just fine with Will today." Her lips were curved and rosy. "We're really trouble to you."

"Not at all," he replied, realizing he was enjoying getting to know Jennifer, and even her sons. He remembered the moment Will had clung to him, shaking and frightened. Somehow in those few terrifying moments rescuing Will, Jason had felt a bond forge with the boy.

A trumpet blast shattered the moment, followed by a chorus of canine howls as one of the boys played the semblance of a tune Jason thought he should recognize, but couldn't. The snare drum began a sharp *rat-a-tat-tat*.

"Now what?" he groaned. "How do you have a life of your own?"

"Mostly it revolves around them," she answered.

"They are going to stop that infernal racket," he vowed, brushing past her and yanking open the bedroom door. "Stop that!" he shouted. Brett lowered the trumpet and Will stopped beating the drum. Even the dogs quieted—except Priss, who added two high yips.

"There'll be no more of that racket in this place!"

"They're practicing their music," Jennifer said behind him. "They're in the school band."

"And I'm into solitude and quiet, and when they play in the band, there aren't four dogs howling along with them."

"May I talk to you *alone?*"

They stepped back into his room and she closed the door, storm warnings flying from her angry stance. "They'll fail music next fall if they don't practice. This is something I've talked them into taking, because I think being in a band puts some discipline into their lives. They need this. Don't be such a persnickety ogre!"

Persnickety ogre? She looked adorable, sons or not.

"I'm sorry if this disturbs you," she added, "but they're cooped up in this tiny place and can't get outside. Music really doesn't hurt anything."

Music from the *1812* Overture came floating through the air, and the dogs began howling again. The boys had put on his CD. "We can't even carry on a conversation—"

"Of course we can. I can hear you and you can hear me just fine."

"Why didn't the dogs howl with the Beatles CD?"

"They only howl with instrumental music."

"For God's sake, how do you stand it?"

She smiled at him, pearly teeth, dimples, dancing lights in her big eyes. "You're very uptight, Mr. Hollenbeck. I noticed your spices are alphabetized."

"I'd say I'm normal," he said, thinking of a beautiful Venus's-flytrap he had seen once, a delicate flowering carnivore. Jennifer Ruark would tempt any man, but along with Jennifer came the tone-deaf boys and the dogs.

"They need to practice."

"I'll agree with that, but they can practice when the water goes down."

"It seems a waste of spare time when they can't watch television. Do you know how often they pick up instruments and practice without my telling them to? Couldn't we make you some earplugs?"

"Tell them to practice," he said, waving his hands in disgust.

He was rewarded by another smile with the warmth of a bonfire. "Thank you. We all appreciate your patience."

He watched her tight jeans and softly rounded bottom as she went through the door.

"Boys, Ranger Hollenbeck said you may practice now."

"Way to go, Mom!"

The door closed behind her. The din started again, and Jason turned to yank open his dresser drawer. Reaching past the neat rows of folded socks, stacked according to color, he retrieved a pair of earmuffs. Ogre. Flunk band. If they flunked band, all of them, including Jennifer, would blame him. They should blame four noisy mutts. He was exhausted, wounded, his peaceful existence but a distant memory—and the Ruarks had only been here a few hours. He had the rest of the day and night. "Lord, let the sun shine," he prayed aloud. He heard a knock on the door.

"Come in," he said, expecting Jennifer. Instead, he looked down at Kyle.

"I need to use the bathroom."

"Be my guest," Jason said as he sipped the hot coffee. Kyle glared at him. "Mom says you don't have any brothers and to be kind to you because you're warped."

"Oh, she does?"

"What's warped?"

"Warped means you don't like chaos. Warped means you're normal. Warped means you like quiet."

Kyle mulled this over, studying Jason. "Will said you're brave. He said you and Terrell saved him."

"Yes, we did." This one had his mother's green eyes. And maybe some of her stubbornness.

Kyle turned and went into the bathroom. When he came out he squinted at Jason. "Are your ears cold?"

Jason remembered the earmuffs and held one up. "No."

"Is that 'cause you're warped?"

"Yes."

Kyle left, and Jason stepped into the bathroom to take a hot shower.

When he was dry and dressed, he opened the door and walked over to Terrell. "I'm going out," he announced.

"I'll come with you. I talked to Della and told her we'd go back to check on the campers and trails."

When they were outside the cabin, Jason looked at his friend. "How do you stand the racket?"

"I grew up with that kind of noise. I have three brothers."

"How could you grow up in that and then come live out here where you don't hear a sound?"

Terrell grinned. "I was ready for this. Now I'm ready to get back to that. I love it. I've been away from a family too long. From women too long. And the two

Ruark women are the best-looking women I've seen in a long, long time.''

"Yeah," Jason said. Terrell had that right.

"Terrell!" came a high-pitched voice from behind and they turned to see Kyle in boots and a raincoat that must be Will's. The sleeves were rolled high and he wore a cap on his head.

"Terrell, if I'm real good, can I go with you?" he asked as he came down the stairs.

"Sure, Kyle."

"Are you sure that's all right?" Jennifer asked from the top of the steps, and Jason looked up at her. She ignored him as she watched Terrell.

The very best-looking women.

"Sure. I'll take care of him." She went inside without glancing at Jason.

Jennifer closed the door, looking at Will and feeling another pang of fright over his brush with the river. She had had one catastrophic loss; she couldn't bear another. Catching Goldie's eye, she motioned to her to go into the bedroom. She closed the door behind Goldie, who turned to her with wide, innocent eyes.

"Jennifer, those park rangers are the nicest men. Terrell wants to know all about my job and where I live and what I like. He seems interested in everything I do."

Jennifer suspected that was a first in Goldie's dealings with men. Conversation wasn't Rat's strong suit.

"That's nice, Goldie. Now where's the money? Did you leave it in your room?"

"Heavens, no! The money belts are under the bed," she said, pointing.

"You brought it all here?" Jennifer didn't know whether to be relieved or angry.

"I didn't want it to wash away in the flood."

"All right. Keep it hidden and when we can get to the sheriff in Rimrock, we're turning it in. I haven't changed my mind about that."

"I know," Goldie said, smiling, and Jennifer realized that Goldie was happy because she knew they couldn't do anything about the money today, and Goldie rarely thought any further in advance than that.

"With two big strong rangers, we're safe. I feel safer than I have since Rat gave me all that money. Terrell and Jason are cute, aren't they?"

Laughing, Jennifer turned toward the door. "I suppose," she said, thinking cute was the last thing that came to mind when she was with Jason Hollenbeck. She went to the kitchen to finish cleaning. She thought about him growing up an only child and then picking a career that let him remain solitary. No wonder the boys drove him berserk. She thought about Kyle and prayed the two men didn't lose sight of him. Neither of the rangers was accustomed to keeping track of children.

AT THE FIRST TURNOFF Terrell headed west while Jason turned east. After another mile, Jason cut the engine of the Jeep. He was farther east than he had been in the morning, and he climbed out to walk near the river. The gushing water was the only sound, and his jangled nerves relaxed.

After an hour of roaming along trails he headed back to the river. Finding the lower trail under water, he took a higher path that wound around and finally ended up at the park boundary near the Ruark's place. He peered through the trees and his first glimpse assured him the house had survived. He moved farther east where he could see better. The lower floor of the house was two feet underwater, and he felt a pang for Jennifer and her family. She had said she was an artist as well as a teacher. Had she left her paintings behind? Too bad they hadn't saved the artwork and left the drum and horn.

Thunder banged and sent a vibration through the air. Jason raised his face skyward, feeling a fine mist hit him. The sky was darkening and he wanted to swear. More rain. The Ruarks would never leave.

He squared his shoulders and lengthened his stride. Terrell's Jeep was already beside the cabin when Jason parked his and climbed out. He could hear the banging of the drum and the clear notes of the trumpet. The horn player had improved in a few hours' time because he recognized a Sousa march.

As he put his hand out to open the door, he braced himself for the chaos that he knew would greet him.

CHAPTER FIVE

ABOVE THE DIN, Jennifer heard Priss yapping as the front door opened and closed. She peered through the latticed divider in the kitchen and saw Jason shrugging out of his raincoat.

When he stretched out his arms to hang up the slicker, her gaze ran across his broad shoulders and down over his long legs, and she remembered the moments in the storm when she had been pressed tightly against him. It had felt good to have him hold her.

Laughing at herself, she stirred steaming spaghetti sauce. It had been too long since she'd dated and she was vulnerable, but even if Ranger Jason Hollenbeck was the most attractive man on earth, he wasn't the man for her. She glanced at the alphabetized spice rack. The man was neat and solitary and didn't conceal his dislike of her family. She had to admit there were moments when something electrifying happened between the two of them, but that didn't matter because nothing would come of it. It was obvious he couldn't wait to get rid of them.

She looked at the schedule written on a sheet of paper by the phone. All over the cabin were schedules— schedules of appointments and duties, the time for the next trip to town, the time to stop at the San Saba office. She shook her head. She and Jason Hollenbeck had little in common.

"Hi. It smells good in here."

At the sound of his deep voice she turned around. He stood with his hands on his narrow hips, and she noticed that his gaze was drifting over her.

"Hi, I'm glad you're back," Jennifer greeted him. "We'll be ready to eat soon."

"It's thundering out and it's going to rain some more. I heard the weather report and talked to headquarters. We're due another inch tonight." He sounded grim.

"Oh, no!" They would have to stay with him longer if it rained. Jennifer placed the lid on the iron skillet. "Did you see the Bronco?"

"No, I didn't. I saw a yellow car, but no Bronco. It'll turn up somewhere along the river. It sure smells good in here."

"I've been waiting for you. We can eat now if you're ready. Would you please wake my father and ask the boys to wash?"

"Sure," Jason replied, going around the divider. "Wash up," he called, and the music stopped as the boys ran for the bathroom.

Jennifer drained the spaghetti and placed a pat of butter on the steaming pasta. She pulled French bread from the oven and placed the foil-wrapped loaf on the counter.

"Mr. MacFee!" Jason called more loudly the second time. A dog snarled. Jennifer dropped the hot pads and rushed into the living area.

"General!" she snapped as the dog bared its fangs at Jason. "They're very protective of Dad," she explained.

Osgood blinked and sat up.

"Dad, we're about ready to eat," she said. "Come on."

Jason shrugged and left to wash while General gave one more low growl.

Jennifer and Jason were the last to fill their plates. The small table in the kitchen was the only place left vacant, and they sat down together. It was dark outside now, with occasional flashes of lightning, a steady rain and intermittent rumbles of thunder.

Jason glanced at Goldie and Terrell sitting close together. Goldie was laughing at something Terrell had said. "You and your sister seem very different."

"We are. Goldie is more outgoing and carefree. She's younger than I am, and sometimes I feel more like her mother than her sister."

"Did your mother die when you were young?" he asked. Jennifer was obviously the center of the Ruark family, the pole of gravity that kept them together and functioning.

"When I was twelve, but she was always frail. I took care of things when Dad traveled."

"What did he do?"

She pulled apart the golden bread, which carried a faint odor of garlic. "He was a sales rep for a business-machine company and he traveled a lot through New Mexico and Colorado."

"I've noticed that sometimes he seems to hear better than others," Jason observed.

She laughed. "Dad turns off his hearing aid when he doesn't want to listen. The boys get on his nerves sometimes, so he tunes them out. Unfortunately, he's learned he can also tune out everything else when he wants to."

"I can understand that," Jason answered, and her eyes twinkled.

"You're wishing you could have turned your hearing off today when the boys practiced."

He gave her a grin. "I suppose."

"Have your folks ever been here or are they still upset that you didn't join the family business?"

"They were here once but they don't like roughing it."

"Roughing it!" she exclaimed, glancing around. "You have a dishwasher and a washer and dryer plus a fantastic view."

Jason leaned back in his chair and thought about that visit. "Mom detests this tiny patrol cabin even though it's deluxe by park standards. Some of the others are badly in need of repair or replacement. Even so, this cabin doesn't have suites with king-size beds, room service, daily cleaning, fresh flowers and candy on the pillow at night. To my folks, this is pretty primitive."

Jennifer studied Jason, surprised by his answer. She thought the cabin was marvelous. And she was beginning to like Jason Hollenbeck. He was an appealing man in spite of his fussiness. Not that it mattered, she reminded herself.

"This dinner is great," he said, waving his fork over the spaghetti. "I get tired of my own cooking."

"Don't you get terribly lonesome sometimes?" she asked, unable to imagine living such a solitary life. "I can't remember when I was last alone for a whole day and night."

"I like to be alone. I fish, I read. I keep busy."

"I can picture you being happier alone than Terrell. He seems very friendly."

"And I don't?" Jason asked, arching a brow.

"Sorry, but not always, you'll have to admit." In spite of that, he was considerate, he was brave and he was very attractive. She glanced at the window. "When it isn't flooding, I think this is one of the prettiest places in the whole world." She flashed another smile. "Of course, I haven't been many places in the world. I've never been out of the United States. Have you?"

Jason looked at the window and back at her. "Yes, but I like it here, too. I love the river and the mountains. It's my favorite spot on earth."

"Have you ever been to Paris?"

"Yes," he told her, remembering the last time he had gone during spring vacation to meet his parents there.

"That's my dream. I want to see the Louvre and Notre Dame."

Jason couldn't imagine flying to Paris with the three Ruark brats and Osgood. It would be like traveling with a circus. But Jennifer's eyes sparkled with dreams of the French city and he smiled at her, reaching across the table to touch her hand lightly. "I hope you get to see them."

She looked startled, her cheeks turning pink. "Right now, I'd settle for just seeing home and getting out of your way. I hate to bring this up, because I know we're a burden, but we're already running short on food."

His eyes widened as he looked past her. "We can't be! I bought bags of groceries."

"Well, now you're feeding eight people and five— four dogs. Growing boys eat a lot."

"They couldn't have eaten everything."

"No, we haven't yet, but I know the food isn't going to last a whole lot longer."

He looked as if she had ruined his dinner. He lowered his fork. "I have loaves of bread."

"Not any more. One loaf. It'll go tomorrow."

"There's a freezer with a chicken, frozen dinners—"

"No. They ate the frozen dinners."

"They couldn't possibly have eaten eight frozen dinners," he repeated, sounding dazed.

"You don't know much about growing boys."

"I was one once, and I didn't eat my parents out of their home!"

"You probably have no idea how much you actually consumed."

"Well, I know there's a brisket. The pantry has rice, potatoes and noodles."

"You don't even have peanut butter or cereal."

"I didn't plan on this."

"I know, and I'm sorry. We'll cut back as much as we can." She gazed at the darkened window. "Of course, the rain has to stop."

"I'll go fishing tomorrow morning and that will give us something for dinner. We'll have the brisket for lunch and we'll have the fish for dinner."

She seemed doubtful. "You're sure you'll catch something?"

"When I go after something, I usually get it," he said, studying her more intently.

"You seem so controlled that it's difficult to imagine you fighting for anything."

"Controlled? Me? You make me sound as cold as the river."

She glanced up at him and was ensnared in a direct gaze that was about as cold as a blowtorch. "Maybe cold isn't the right word."

He leaned closer over the table. "What is the right word? Now I'm curious."

"Complex. You're a complex man."

He arched a brow. "How's that, Jennifer?" he said in a low tone that made the conversation seem intimate.

"You're so aloof and so particular, and then you can change as fast as a coin tossed in the air and you're—" She blinked and bit her lip.

He crooked his finger, motioning her to lean closer. His voice was softer. "You can't stop now. I change and I'm *what?*"

"You know what you are, and you're doing it right now." She knew she sounded breathless, too aware of him as a man.

"I'm not doing what I'd like to be doing if we didn't have six others with us. If we were alone, I'd—"

"Jason—" As she stood up, he caught her wrist in a high-voltage touch. His eyes were filled with speculation. She heard footsteps; Jason released her and the moment was gone.

"Want to go fishing in the morning?" he asked her.

"I've never fished before."

He arched his brows. "Never? You live so close to the river! Why did you buy that house?"

"Mark wanted it. He liked white water rafting, but he didn't fish. Mark was too impatient, too flamboyant to fish. Besides—" she flashed Jason a broad smile "—I'd think you'd prefer to fish alone, because I've heard you need quiet to fish."

He did look relieved. As she finished speaking, Will passed on his way for a refill. "Fish? We're going fishing?"

"Mr. Hollenbeck is going fishing in the morning."

"Can I go?"

"It's time they learned," Jason said after only the slightest hesitation. "You may go, Will, and your brothers, as well, *if* you'll do what I tell you to do."

"Awesome!"

"We'll get up at five-thirty."

"Night fishing! Hey, Kyle, Brett, Ranger Hollenbeck is taking us fishing in the night."

"Wow!"

"You're in for it now," Jennifer said, wondering how they would get along.

"You can come, too," he said, standing beside her as Will left. "You ought to give it a try at least."

"Five-thirty isn't my best time."

"You did all right today, and it was earlier than that. You look great in the morning—about sixteen years old. I thought you were the boys' sister that day in the flowers."

"*Sister?*" she asked incredulously.

"Well, you had your hair up in a ponytail and it made you look younger...."

She laughed. "You don't need to explain to a woman why she looks young! I can't imagine that I could possibly have looked *that* young to you."

"Well, I have to admit that on closer inspection you do have more...womanly qualities," he said, his gaze holding hers.

Jennifer drew a deep breath. His warm moments came without warning and could be as devastating as a brush fire.

Terrell walked into the kitchen with dishes in hand, and again the mood was broken.

"We're going fishing in the morning, Terrell. Want to come along?"

"Sure. I'll ask Goldie."

"I'm not sure how much we'll catch when there are seven of us and five haven't fished before," Jason said, "but we'll give it a try. I'll get out the fishing gear." He placed his dishes in the sink and looked at the disaster in the kitchen. Picking up his schedule, he went to the living area.

"Boys," he said, "tonight you have to clean the kitchen."

There were groans. "Mom, do we have to?"

"Yes, you do. Into the kitchen."

"C'mon, guys," Will said suddenly, standing and motioning to the other two to follow. Jason felt a ripple of surprise at Will's response, and he suspected it had something to do with the rescue earlier. He watched the two youngest glare at him as they passed, and he tried to avoid thinking about the Ruarks handling his dishes.

"I'll get the rods and poles and gear and we'll get ready tonight. Would you like to come along, Mr. MacFee?"

"We're going home?"

"We're going fishing," Jennifer said loudly.

"In this rain? And in the dark?"

"No, sir, in the morning," Jason said, raising his voice when he noticed that Osgood had removed his hearing aid.

"Thank you, anyway. I'll sleep in."

Jason gathered his rods, and he and Terrell checked them over. When the boys had finished the dishes, they sat around the tackle box looking at lures and lead weights and hooks while Jason and Terrell answered their questions. As Jason changed the lure on a line, Kyle leaned against his knee, studying the feathers and hook.

"Doesn't the fish know that's a bunch of feathers?"

"No. The trout will think it's a bug or something delicious to eat."

"What's a trout?" Kyle asked, his arm draped over Jason's leg. Jason studied the child, so close to him. Had Jason ever been that casual with his own father? Somehow he doubted it. His father had been curt and demanding and physically undemonstrative.

"A trout is a fish, and you'll catch one tomorrow and we'll eat it tomorrow night."

"Am I going to use this fishing pole?"

"No. You'll use a different one and I'll use this one."

"I want to see mine."

"All right. Let me get this one fixed, and then we'll get yours all ready. You'll have to be quiet to fish. Can you do that?"

Kyle nodded up at him. "Sure. Why do I have to be quiet?"

"A lot of noise will scare the fish away."

"You don't have any little boys, do you?"

"No, I don't," he said, untangling a knot in the line and then carefully reeling it in.

"I don't have a daddy anymore. My daddy died when his plane crashed."

"I know, Kyle. I'm sorry about that." Jason set aside the rod and picked up a cork from the tackle box. "Now, I'll put this on a pole for you," he said, picking up a long fishing pole and pulling the line into his lap to attach the cork. Kyle watched what he was doing, still leaning on Jason's thigh.

"Here, I'll show you how to tie a knot in this. You take the line, then fold that over." He watched Kyle's small fingers work with the fishing line. The little boy looked so intent, his tongue stuck out of the corner of his mouth. Jason glanced up to see the other boys working with Terrell. His gaze met Jennifer's where she sat with a paper on her knee, her legs folded under her. He winked at her, feeling an unusual sense of closeness.

Kyle wriggled around. "How's that?"

Jason pulled the knot tight. "That's great. Now we need to put a lead weight on this line."

"Why?"

"So it'll sink under the water. The cork floats until a fish takes the bait, but the hook with the bait has to be down where the fish can get it."

Kyle looked at him intently. "I like it here."

"Do you? That's good, because until the rain lets up, you're going to have to stay here."

"You don't want us to stay here, though, do you?"

Kyle watched him unwaveringly and Jason felt a twinge of guilt. "Yes, I want you to stay. I wouldn't be sitting here showing you how to get the fishing poles ready if I didn't."

Kyle nodded as if accepting Jason's answer.

"We'll get to bed early, because we're going fishing at five-thirty," Jason said, closing the tackle box and standing.

"Can't we go at ten-thirty?" Brett asked, looking up at Jason.

"Terrell and I will be busy with park duties then. We'll get up at five-thirty, and by six we'll be on the creek bank. Perfect time for fishing, and it's pretty out early in the morning."

"In the rain?" Brett asked, his brow furrowed in a frown.

"Yes. Sometimes the fish bite better in the rain."

Jason went to the kitchen to look for a lead weight in one of his drawers. The counter was covered in bits of food and the sink hadn't been rinsed clean. He should have known what kind of job they would do.

"Boys, come in here."

The three walked in, looking guilty.

"Finish the job. This isn't a clean kitchen."

"Mr. Spotless," Brett said under his breath as Jason left the room.

Osgood was given the sofa, and the dogs settled in with him. The boys had blankets on the floor, and Jason and Terrell had sleeping bags.

The boys and their grandfather were asleep by ten, while Goldie and Terrell talked softly together in the living area. Jennifer and Jason sat in the kitchen with steaming mugs of cocoa.

"Goldie and Terrell seem to be hitting it off," Jason said thoughtfully. "Don't you ever think you'd like to start dating again?"

"How can I date with this?" she asked, waving her hands toward the boys. "How many men want to go out with someone who comes with three boys, a grandfather and five dogs?"

"They're not all that intimidating," he said easily, leaning back in his chair and stretching out his long legs.

"Easy for you to say, Hollenbeck," she teased, and he grinned. "What about you?" she asked, then blushed. "Or is that too personal?"

"Ask anything you want. Sure I date sometimes, but not all that often."

Suddenly she remembered hearing that Barbie Watkins went out with Ranger Hollenbeck. Barbie was pretty; she worked in her dad's café when she was home from college and she was probably about twenty-two years old now.

"I'm not a hermit." He sounded amused.

Jennifer shook her head. "Not anymore, you aren't. Not with all of us living here. Do you have to rescue people often?"

"Not very often, fortunately, but occasionally things happen. People come out here who aren't experienced in a natural setting and they do things they shouldn't. Even when you know everything, you can still get into trouble, but that's much less likely with an experienced camper."

Jennifer felt her heart skip as she gazed into his eyes. She couldn't look away, but she didn't want to have that kind of reaction to Jason Hollenbeck.

"When did you get married?" Jason asked quietly.

"When I was a freshman at the University of New Mexico."

"And you were probably a young mother, so it was easy for me to mistake you for Will's sister."

"I was twenty when Will was born, and he's tall for his age so people often think he's older."

"I had the same problem when I was a boy. People tend to expect more from a child who looks older."

"And now? What are your plans?" she asked. "To stay here always?"

"Not always, but for a long time. I like it here and the life-style suits me."

"If you get married, you'll live here? Your wife would have to like all this."

"I haven't given much thought to marriage any time in the near future." He looked at her intently over his cup of cocoa.

"Usually I don't give the future much thought," Jennifer said slowly.

Jason set his cup down and leaned closer. "You should. Someday the boys will be grown and gone and you'll be alone."

"According to you, that's a grand way to live. I'll worry about being alone when it happens. It may come as a welcome relief."

"It seems a waste," he said softly, and Jennifer felt her cheeks warm with a blush. "Are you an elementary or secondary schoolteacher?" he asked suddenly, changing the subject.

"I teach seventh grade and I teach everything. I have almost one hundred and thirty pupils throughout the day."

One hundred and thirty seventh graders! He couldn't imagine it. No wonder she coped so well with the boys. "I figured you were an art teacher."

"No, for a long time I treated art as a hobby, but after Will was born, I quit teaching until the year before Mark was killed. During those years, I devoted any spare time I had to my art and became really serious about it."

"Jason?" Terrell stuck his head around the latticed divider. "It's midnight. I've been in the bathroom. Goldie said to tell you to go ahead."

Amazed at the hour, Jason stood up. "Sure." He glanced down at Jennifer. "How about one more cup of cocoa when I come back. That was good."

"Sure," she said, standing up and carrying the cups to the counter.

She was pouring milk into the pan as Goldie came into the room. "Want a cup of cocoa?"

"No, thanks. I'm just waiting for Jason to get out of the bathroom and then I'm going to bed. I'm so glad the house is still standing. Terrell said if it made it through the first rush of water, it ought to last through anything now."

"I hope so. The furniture may be ruined, but everything is insured. I'll call the agent in the morning."

Terrell walked into the kitchen just as Goldie said, "I feel so safe here. No one can find us. No one—"

Jennifer glanced sharply at her and then at Terrell, who had cocked his head to one side and was looking at Goldie curiously.

"I mean it's private here," Goldie added quickly, blushing, and Jennifer wondered what Terrell must think.

"Well, I'll tell you ladies good night," he said, and turned to go. Goldie hurried after him, and Jennifer heard her whispering to him as they went into the darkened living area. She made the cocoa and carried the two cups to the table. Glancing at the clock, she saw it was now twelve-thirty. She was enjoying talking to Jason; it was seldom she had a chance to converse with an interesting man and she hated to bring the night to a close.

"I laid out a shirt for you to sleep in," came Jason's deep, soft voice as he crossed the room to the table. Jennifer's pulse jumped as she looked up at him. He was bare chested and barefoot, and blatantly male. He sat down at her right, so close to her.

"Goldie and Terrell are still talking," he said. "Do you think she's interested in him?"

"I don't know. She has a . . . sort of . . . boyfriend."

"And you don't like him or approve of him."

Surprised, Jennifer studied Jason. "How could you guess that?"

He shrugged one broad shoulder and she noticed the bulge of muscle in his upper arm. "You just didn't sound very enthusiastic."

"You're perceptive."

He chuckled and lowered his cup of cocoa, giving her an amused glance. "Don't sound so shocked."

"Sorry," she said, blushing.

"I'm teasing you. Is your sister going to marry this man?"

"I hope not, and I doubt it. I don't think he's the marrying kind, but they've gone together five years now."

Jason looked down at his cup for a moment, lost in thought, before taking an appreciative sip. "Are you as talented at your artwork as you are at making cocoa?" he asked with a smile. "What kind of work do you do? Paintings, pottery?"

"Watercolors and charcoal drawings are my favorites. I do a lot of portraits."

"Did you have much of your artwork with you?"

"No, thank heavens. I have two acrylics that I'm working on and I keep them upstairs. My bedroom has a balcony, so I paint there and keep my artwork in the bedroom so I don't have to worry about the boys getting into it."

She thought about how she and the boys had disrupted his life and wondered what he would do if he knew of the money Goldie had hidden under his bed. She decided it was better not to think of that. "Did you grow up in Santa Fe?" she asked brightly instead.

"Yes."

"Does your mother work? Is she someone I would know, too?"

"It depends on the circles you move in, because she's a lawyer. If you spend much time at the courthouse—"

"Thank goodness, no! I don't spend any time at the courthouse. And did she want you to become a lawyer?"

"No. As far back as I can remember, I was told I would go into business with my dad."

"Do you spend time with them on holidays?" she asked, unable to imagine a life as solitary as his.

"Not often anymore. They travel a lot. Dad has a man who manages his business very well. It's grown a lot since Randall came to work there, so Dad can get away. My parents don't like what I do and it's an issue between us—and don't look at me as if I were Little Orphan Annie."

"Sorry, but I can't imagine being alone on holidays. I like having Dad and Goldie and the boys around. Often we have the boys' friends, too. You don't spend Christmas alone, do you?"

He leaned closer and his eyes twinkled. "If I say yes, are you going to invite me to spend Christmas with the Ruarks?" Laughing, he touched the tip of her nose. "I'm teasing. Yes, I've spent Christmas alone and it's not the end of the world. I'm on duty in the park, so I have things to do, and my folks enjoy taking a cruise to warmer climates during the holidays. Actually, I don't miss being home, because our visits are strained."

"You have some things in common with my husband. Mark was very self-sufficient. When he flew, I think he forgot he had a family."

Jason touched her hand lightly, running his fingers across her knuckles. "I don't think he forgot you or the boys, Jennifer,'' he said softly, his blue eyes focused intently on her.

She felt herself flush, aware of his scrutiny.

''I'll go see an ophthalmologist when the waters go down.''

''Are you having problems?'' she asked, wondering what had prompted such a comment.

Amusement glittered in the depths of his eyes. ''I'd say I must have definite problems to mistake you for one of the boys.''

''Oh!'' She blushed, leaning back and glancing at the clock. ''Good heavens, it's after one o'clock!''

''Why's that so bad?'' he drawled lazily.

''I don't stay up this late ever, and we're getting up in just a few hours to go fishing. I won't be able to stay awake to hold a pole.''

''The past few hours have been nice, making up a little for the flood.''

They stood at the same time, and he took her cup from her hand, his warm fingers brushing hers. ''I'll clean up.'' He was standing so close to her. ''Good night, Jennifer. May tomorrow be a better day.''

''And we'll pray for sunshine so you can get back to your peaceful, orderly life.''

''I'm doing all right.'' He winked and moved around her to the sink. She glanced at his muscled back, the jeans riding low on his hips, a tiny triangle of white briefs catching her attention.

''Thanks for everything today,'' she said, and he nodded. She started out of the room.

''Jennifer,'' he called softly, and she paused to look back at him.

''Good night,'' he said.

"Good night," she whispered, turning away. Jason Hollenbeck was an interesting, complicated man and she couldn't believe they had spent so long talking. Was she as starved for company as he seemed to be? As quickly as the question came, she dismissed it as foolishness.

Later, as she lay in bed and listened to the rain, she thought about Jason and his life. It seemed somehow empty to her. How could he not be with his family at Christmas? And what a sad childhood he must have had. She felt sorry for him, but she knew he would consider her sympathy misplaced. His patience with Kyle tonight had amazed her, revealing another side to Jason Hollenbeck. She glanced around his bedroom, wondering about the man. A spy thriller rested on the bedside table and the art on the walls was all Western. She recognized some of the artists. The cabin was comfortable but not really cozy, and she couldn't imagine coming back to an empty house every night. With a sigh, she turned over in bed, remembering Jason's closeness in the kitchen and how he had pulled her up on the bank in the flood, holding her steady in his strong arms.

It had been a day to change all their lives, but thank heavens it hadn't been any more tragic. She only prayed Oats turned up, because she couldn't bear to see her father grieve for his pet. Saying another silent prayer of thanks that they had all survived, she closed her eyes and went to sleep.

THE ALARM BUZZED. Jason shut it off, wriggled out of the sleeping bag and pulled on his jeans. He moved to the bedroom. The door was ajar as Jennifer had promised to leave it. He tiptoed through the room, his clothes in his arms, glancing at the bed. Goldie's blond hair spilled over the pillow on the far side of the bed. Next to her Jennifer slept, one arm outflung, a riot of red curls spilling over her shoulder and face.

Making his way into the bathroom, he shaved and dressed swiftly. Terrell rose on schedule and started breakfast, and Jason thought he heard the women moving around. Fifteen minutes later he glanced at the kitchen clock. "Where are those women? The oatmeal will be done in another minute and it's time the boys get up and into the bathroom."

Twenty minutes later as Jason closed an ice chest and placed it beside a stack of things to carry out, he looked at Terrell. "My schedule is blown to hell."

"I knew it would be. I'll get the boys up and that'll be it." Terrell paused as he headed toward the door. "Jason, instead of cream in your coffee, you might put in a shot of bourbon."

"Why would I do that? I'm not a drinking man and you know it."

"Yeah, but you might become one if the river doesn't go down soon." He left Jason staring at the darkened living area. Jason heard him call the boys and then let the dogs outside for their morning run. Obviously neither ranger cared to announce that the park had a leash law, and the Ruarks probably didn't even own a leash.

By seven-thirty they were all in the Jeeps and headed toward Owl Creek. Jason drove with the boys, and the two women rode with Terrell. Jason wasn't sure exactly how that had happened, but during the ride home he intended to see that the situation was reversed.

"Mom said you're mad," Kyle announced beside him.

"No, I'm not mad. Whatever made her think that?" He inhaled deeply. "We're off schedule, but what difference does an hour make?" He looked down into Kyle's solemn green eyes. It really didn't matter. He and Terrell would get to work on time and they could be contacted by the office if an emergency arose before then.

"Mom said I have to be quiet and sit still."

"You need to be quiet, but you don't have to sit all the time. We can prop your pole on a tree branch, and if you'll keep an eye on the cork to see if a fish bites the bait, you can wander around a little."

"If I catch a fish, I'm not sure I want to eat it," Kyle said with a frown.

"Well, then we don't have to. If you catch one, you can put it back in the creek. How's that?"

"I might like that better."

"That's dumb," Brett said, glancing at Kyle.

"No, it's okay, Brett," Jason said, "because the rest of you may catch the limit anyway."

"I hope I catch a big one," Will said. "Are there big fish in the river?"

"Plenty big," Jason told him. "You'll see." He hoped they each caught one so they wouldn't be terribly disappointed. Fish were abundant, but Jason didn't have much faith in the boys' patience.

When they arrived at the creek, Terrell took Brett aside and Jason showed Will how to cast. In seconds he realized the oldest Ruark boy was a natural outdoorsman.

"Use your wrist, Will," Jason instructed, watching the boy. "That's it, now pull back slowly. Keep your line taut and the fly will skim over the water."

Jason stood with his hands on his hips, watching Will. "Make sure you're not going to snag your line on a tree," he cautioned. He glanced around to see Jennifer seated on a rock, watching him. She smiled at him and he smiled in return. Brett was attempting to cast and caught his line in a pine branch. He yanked at it impatiently until it was hopelessly snarled. Terrell had Kyle's pole braced in the fork of a branch, the red cork bobbing on the swift current, while Kyle was studying rocks nearby. Terrell was beside Goldie, showing her one of the rods.

Jason walked over to Jennifer, who was watching her oldest son. Will had taken to fly-fishing like a seasoned pro, flicking his wrist and sending the line snapping across the surface of the creek.

"He's doing great," Jason told her.

"So are you," she said, gazing up at him. "You're a good teacher, and I'm glad they're learning to fish. It seems ridiculous to live on a river and never fish."

"I agree." He held out his hand. "C'mon. It's your turn next." He pulled her to her feet and placed his arm lightly across her shoulders. "Will—if you get a fish, give a jerk and then reel him in. Call me and I'll help."

"How will I— Hey!"

The line bowed and Will yanked it.

"You've got one, Will! That's it, keep the line taut and reel him in," Jason directed. "Keep it going slowly, and when he gets close, you can take the net and scoop him in. That's it, Will. That's it."

In seconds Will held up a flopping silvery pink trout. "Look what I caught!" he whooped.

His mother and aunt applauded and his brothers crowded around eagerly. Jason showed Will how to take the fish off the hook and put it into the creel, then the boy was excitedly casting again. Jason went to join Jennifer.

"Will is so pleased," she said warmly, "and so am I. You were great with him."

"You sound as if I just jumped up and grabbed a star."

"Well, I didn't think you'd have the patience to teach the boys," she admitted. "I was wrong."

"As much as I like the praise, I don't deserve it. All I did was tell Will what to do. You have a son who's a natural. Some people can't cast like that after years of trying."

"No kidding? Will? He's never been interested before."

Jason took her hand. "C'mon. You have to give him room to cast, and Terrell and Goldie are with the little guys."

He led her downstream and around a bend. "Now here's what you do." She stood facing him, her hands on her hips. She was dressed in her jeans and sweater and one of his windbreakers. Her hair was tied back with a ribbon and she looked as appealing as ever. He wanted to toss the line aside and reach for her, but he knew their privacy would last all of two minutes.

"I'm not sure that I can learn this. I have a feeling I should be sitting on the bank and tossing out a line and cork like Kyle."

"Give it a try." Jason gave a demonstration and then handed her the reel. Standing close behind her, he held her wrist. "Hold it like this, draw back, give it a flick and let the line play out. He let his hands drift to her waist as she practiced flicking the rod backward and forward. She was warm, smelled sweet like soap, and he moved even closer.

"Yeow!" He jerked backward as he felt the hook sink into his thigh. Grabbing the rod, he pulled back on it. "Be still! You've hooked me."

"Oh, no! I knew I should've sat on the bank with a line and pole."

The hook had gone through his heavy pants, the bright yellow feather still fluttering above it. Jason gritted his teeth and yanked it free with a grunt of pain. A bright spot of blood stained the faded jeans.

"I'm sorry," she said.

"It's out now. Anyway, I shouldn't have been standing behind you."

"You distracted me," she confessed, looking up at him.

"Did I?" he asked, momentarily forgetting the pain. "I didn't know whether you noticed me or not." He took the rod from her hand and reeled in the line, then placed it carefully on the ground.

"I can turn my back if you need to put something on that or wash it."

"I'll live," he assured her. "It was a tiny hook and I've had my tetanus shot."

"Mom!" came a high-pitched shout, and Jason turned to the river to see Kyle swirling along in an inner tube.

"How the blazes did he get into that?" he cried, turning cold with fear as he watched Kyle bobbing along. "Call to him, Jennifer."

"Kyle, come here this instant!" Jennifer yelled.

"Kyle!" Terrell came crashing through the bushes and ran alongside the river, waving at the boy. "Paddle that over here *now!*"

"Where'd he get that thing?" Jason demanded. "I thought you were watching him."

"I was! He was there on the bank one minute and out in the creek the next. Jennifer, I'm sorry—"

"Get him over here, Jennifer."

"How can he get here? He doesn't have a paddle." She was starting to sound panicked.

"He can use his hands."

"We've got to get him quick!" Terrell shouted, running along the bank.

As all three ran alongside the river, Jason's stomach knotted. "Kyle, paddle that tube to the bank now!" he ordered.

"Mom, this is fun!"

"We're half a mile from the San Saba. If he dumps in there—" Jason yanked off his jacket.

"Kyle, do what they're telling you!" Jennifer cried.

"We've got to catch him here," Jason said. Terrell turned to him.

"Are you going in?"

"One of us has to. You know what's ahead. Kyle," he yelled, "row that over here now! You're headed for the river!"

Kyle waved and paddled with his hands, but he continued bobbing on the swift current down the middle of the creek.

"I'll get him," Jason said. He raced ahead, Terrell plunging after him and Jennifer trailing behind. Yards ahead of Kyle, Jason waded in to intercept him.

As the icy water swirled around his calves, Jason swore under his breath. Carefully he made his way from rock to rock, watching Kyle spinning toward him. The boy looked worried now, his eyes big as he paddled frantically. Was the kid finally cooperating or just trying to get away from him? Jason wondered. The tube veered toward the bank and Jason moved farther out, bracing himself against the strong current. His legs were numb now and he gritted his teeth.

Suddenly the tube was there, swirling before him. As it slammed against him, he lost his balance, the icy water closing over him. Kyle spilled out, and the tube bobbed away.

CHAPTER SIX

JASON SURFACED, gasping, and grabbed Kyle. The tube slipped away, spinning along on the powerful current and disappearing from sight. As Jason carried the sobbing, shivering child up the bank, Jennifer ran toward them. Jason motioned to her. "Give me your jacket—we need to get something around him. There's a blanket in the Jeep."

"Mom!" Kyle cried.

Jason didn't break stride as he grasped her jacket and threw it around Kyle. Jennifer hurried along beside them, wrapping her arms around herself. She was cold and knew that Kyle as well as Jason must be freezing.

"Get the blanket, Terrell," Jason called as they rushed toward the Jeep. He set Kyle inside and wrapped the blanket around him. Kyle was shaking and his teeth chattered.

Jennifer sat beside her son and hugged him, while Jason wrapped another blanket around her.

"You need this more than I do," she protested.

"Keep it on," he said, his hands arranging it across her shoulders. "Let's get him home. Terrell and the others are staying."

Jason climbed in on his side while Jennifer pulled Kyle onto her lap. She glanced over at Jason, who sat gripping the wheel.

She tugged the blanket over his legs. "I know you're freezing."

"We'll be there before long," he said, turning on the heater. In minutes the interior of the Jeep warmed, and she could feel Kyle's shaking diminish. He sat quietly, crying and hiccuping, until they reached the patrol cabin.

When they walked in, Osgood was working with his dogs, who were perched on various chairs. "How was fishing?" he greeted Jason. "Great grief, you fell in?"

"No, sir. I waded in to get Kyle," Jason answered loudly, then hurried toward the kitchen. "You and Kyle change first," he instructed Jennifer. "I'll put on some hot chocolate. Would you like a cup, Mr. MacFee?"

"Sure would. Hope you don't have to pull any more Ruarks out of the river. Good lands, you'd think we jumped in every few hours. I can't recall the boys having to be pulled out for several years now. Kyle, what happened? Did you fall in?"

"Dad, we'll explain after we're dry," Jennifer said, pushing Kyle toward the bedroom. "I need to get him into a hot tub." Osgood turned around to look quizzically at Jason.

"I don't think I'll have to worry about it happening again," Jason said.

"Little fellow looked scared to death. Was he really in danger?"

Jason paused and glanced at Osgood, realizing he had his hearing aid turned on. "Yes, he was in danger. He got into an inner tube and was floating down the creek. It empties into the San Saba River, and I don't think we could have fished him out of that."

"Great grief! Poor little tyke. No wonder he looked terrified."

In the bedroom Jennifer knelt down and faced Kyle. "That was very dangerous. In just minutes you would have been in the big river and we couldn't have gotten to you!"

Tears spilled down Kyle's cheeks.

"You heard Terrell tell you to paddle for shore, and you heard me, too. You know we weren't yelling because we wanted to spoil your fun."

"I'm sorry!" he said, his shoulders shaking and his lower lip quivering.

She hugged him. "All right. Get your things off and get into a hot bath while I find some dry clothes for you. You need to tell Mr. Hollenbeck that you're sorry."

Looking bedraggled and frightened, Kyle nodded and hurried into the bathroom.

While Kyle bathed, Jennifer changed her clothes. Once both of them were warm and dry, Kyle seemed to want to linger in the bedroom. Jennifer suspected he dreaded facing Jason again. "Are you okay now?" she asked him.

"Yes."

"Then let's get some hot chocolate." She opened the door and she could see Jason moving around in the kitchen. Her father sat at the kitchen table with a cup of steaming cocoa.

"You can have the bathroom now," she said as they entered the kitchen. Jason had pulled off his wet shoes and socks and shirt, and as she glanced at his bare, broad chest, she felt that tingling awareness of him as a man. Kyle walked up to him.

"I'm sorry, Mr. Hollenbeck, that you had to go into the creek after me."

"I accept your apology, Kyle," he said, giving the boy's shoulder a squeeze. He knelt to look Kyle in the eye, his wet jeans molding to his long, muscular legs. "When you're outdoors, you have to stop and think before you do things that might be dangerous."

"Yes, sir," Kyle answered solemnly.

"Now that you're warm and dry, would you like to go back with me? After I shower we'll still have almost an hour to fish before Terrell and I have to report to work."

"Are you sure?" Jennifer asked, surprised he would offer to take Kyle again. She had expected him to explode—because he'd said he wasn't accustomed to children—but so far he was doing just fine. She suspected Kyle had expected an explosion, too. Either that or the experience had given him a real scare, because he was more subdued than usual when he was in trouble.

"I'm sure," Jason answered. He looked at Kyle. "Want to go?"

Kyle nodded. "Yes, sir. I'd like that."

"Good. Now drink your hot chocolate and I'll change." Jason stood up and moved toward Jennifer. He took her arm lightly, pausing to look at her. "Are you okay?"

"I'm fine and Kyle seems fine, too," she said, feeling an unsettling mixture of emotions and all too conscious of the light touch of his fingers.

"I won't be long." He headed toward the bedroom and she turned around to watch him, the muscles in his back rippling as he moved.

Jennifer and Kyle had almost finished their drink when Jason emerged from his shower. He wore a navy sweatshirt and jeans, and his damp hair curled against his neck.

"We'll get some jackets and we're off," he announced.

"You have enough dry things for us all to have jackets?" Jennifer asked.

"Sure. They won't win prizes for fashion, but they're warm. Want to come with us?" Jason invited Osgood.

"No, thanks. You folks looked like three icicles when you came in here."

"It isn't that cold, Dad, if you don't fall into the water."

"With this family, that's a possibility. I think I'll stay here where it's warm."

"Before we go, I want to call headquarters," Jason said. He made notes all the while he talked, then finally hung up the receiver. "Let's go."

When they reached the creek and found the others, Brett came racing up to the Jeep.

"Mom, you let him come back out here!" he said in amazement. "Gee, Kyle, are you ever goofy!"

Kyle jumped down. "Have you caught any fish?"

"Yeah, come look. Mom, I've caught three fish and Will's caught five. Come and see."

"That's great." Jennifer felt both surprised and pleased; Brett's enthusiasm was obvious. The boys ran ahead and she turned to Jason, who placed his arm casually across her shoulders. "If you get them to enjoy fishing, I'll be eternally grateful."

"I didn't do anything except show them how, but they must like it. Will hasn't even said hello. Let's go see the catch."

As they walked up, Goldie and Terrell watched them. Goldie's eyes sparkled when she looked at Jason. "My goodness, that was brave to go into the icy river and save Kyle!"

"That's part of my job," he told her, then glanced at Terrell. "I called Della. They expect the San Saba to crest this afternoon. And she wants us to look at the remaining bridges. They're still not allowing campers back into the park. I told her we'd come by the office in an hour.''

''We'll have our limit in another half hour.''

Jason and Jennifer walked toward the creek where the boys were fishing, Jason's arm still casually draped across Jennifer's shoulders. When Brett saw them, he grinned broadly and opened a creel.

''Look what I have!'' he called.

Jason picked up a rainbow trout. ''That's great, Brett. Good job.''

''Brett, that's wonderful!'' Jennifer exclaimed, delighted her sons had learned a new sport. She glanced up at Jason as they walked toward Will.

''This really is great,'' she said. ''They've given you such a hassle. . . .''

''Before the flood as well as after,'' Jason agreed dryly, and she blushed. His arm tightened and he squeezed her against him. ''Don't look so worried. They're not incorrigibles.''

''I know they're wild, but this will be good for them if it lasts.''

''I would bet my paycheck it'll last with Will. Probably Brett, too. Kyle hasn't caught anything yet and he had a bad morning, so his enthusiasm might be dampened now, but if his brothers take to fishing, he should, too.''

''I caught three more,'' Will said proudly when they reached him. ''How's Kyle?''

''He's okay,'' Jennifer told him.

''The little goof. Didn't he know the water would be icy cold?''

''I don't think he minded the cold at first.''

"I'll show you how to clean and cook the trout," Jason offered. "About four more and we should have ample for dinner."

"Mom, aren't you going to fish?"

"Sure she is," Jason said, and Jennifer shrugged good-naturedly. "We'll go in about forty minutes, Will." The two of them headed back toward Goldie and Terrell. Goldie sat on the ground beside Kyle and his fishing pole while Terrell cast from the bank.

"I want to talk to Terrell a minute," Jason told her, "and then we'll start your lesson again."

"I don't know. All I did before was hook you."

"I survived—and I'll watch out next time."

He dropped his arm from her shoulder and she sat down to talk to Goldie. Jason caught up with Terrell, who was moving south along the creek's edge.

"What's up?" Terrell asked. "Did Della say if any more bridges are passable yet?"

"You can't get to your cabin. After the river crests, if we don't get more rain, the water should go down swiftly." The two men looked each other in the eye, and Jason suspected Terrell was thinking the same thing that he was. The bridges under water meant another night with the Ruarks.

"I'm not real sorry," Terrell admitted, and grinned. "I want to get to know Goldie better."

Jason turned to watch Will downstream. One of Jason's battered sailor caps was on his head, brown hair sticking out beneath it at the back. He was totally concentrated on fishing.

"Will has a knack for this," Jason remarked.

"Probably can't pry him away from the creek bank. The little one was hopeless. Brett's improving, but he has the line caught in the trees half the time."

"How about Goldie?"

Terrell grinned again. "Never in a million years will Goldie take to this. What about Jennifer?"

"She hooked *me*. I never got a line in the water. And I'm going to go let her have another try."

"Watch out for flying hooks."

Jason went back to Jennifer, who was seated on the ground beside Kyle and Goldie. Kyle held a fishing pole and solemnly watched the cork bobble on the water.

"Want to try again?" he asked Jennifer.

"I'll stay with the boys," Goldie offered. "You go ahead and fish."

"Come on—you might as well learn how and see if you like it," Jason said, knowing they would probably catch more fish if he just let her watch the boys.

Sunshine slanted through the trees and glistened on the cascading water. Jason inhaled deeply, relishing the clear air tinged with the pungent smell of damp pine. He found a spot down the way from Will and handed Jennifer the rod, his fingers brushing hers. He moved behind her.

"I'm scared I'll hook you again," Jennifer joked.

"Don't worry about me," he said, inhaling the sweet scent from her hair. "I'll watch out for you this time."

She tried to cast, but the hook landed at the water's edge. "Jason, I can't do this."

"Sure you can. Try again and I'll help." He clasped her wrist. "Bring your arm up, that's it."

This time the hook landed in a tree.

"Maybe if you didn't stand so close," she said huskily, glancing over her shoulder at him. He gazed down at her and felt a longing to pull her into his arms and kiss her. The mother of the Ruark boys? He caught sight of Will and knew they wouldn't have any privacy, so he eased back and let Jennifer try to cast again. This time the hook sank beneath the water a good distance from the bank.

"That's it," he said quietly.

Within twenty minutes they had their catch and climbed into the Jeep to return to the cabin.

After lunch, Jason and Terrell had park duties and Goldie was taking a shower. Jennifer assessed the supplies. With the fish and the bag of rice, they would manage dinner. Tomorrow there was enough oatmeal for breakfast, and Will couldn't wait to catch more fish. She felt a swift surge of gratitude for Jason. Fishing was a good pastime for Will; she should have tried to teach the boys, but she didn't know anything about it. She glanced outside. The sun was shining now and she wondered how fast the river would go down. Without television or a newspaper, she felt cut off from the world, held captive in a timeless bubble.

She sat down with her sketch pad and picked up the small drawing of Jason. She began to sketch out a larger one, shading the plane beneath his cheekbones. What a complex man he was, so particular about his surroundings, yet showing patience and flexibility with the boys—along with a genuine warmth. She only hoped he didn't have to rescue any of them again.

Wrinkling her nose, she studied the sketch, and a jolt shuddered through her like the aftershock of a quake. She had never been able to draw Mark or her family, and she had always thought it was because she was too close to them. She stared at her sketch pad with dissatisfaction and surprise. Why couldn't she draw Jason? She wasn't close to him. She crumpled up the paper and tossed it into a trash basket.

Goldie appeared from the shower, toweling her golden curls. "I hope it rains and we never have to go home. Jenny, Terrell is the most interesting man, and he's the first man I've ever known who just wants to talk! He's asked me all about the pet shop and I've told him what I'd really like to do...."

"What's that?" Jennifer asked, knowing Goldie's career aspirations changed daily.

"I really want to have my own pet shop. I want to take in strays and get them adopted and have a boarding kennel."

"Goldie, that takes a fortune to maintain. Strays can't pay you."

"I know," she said, looking disappointed, "but I just feel so sorry for all those little animals."

"That's why we have five dogs now," Jennifer pointed out. "We've taken in every stray Dad and the boys have found."

"I think that's nice. Rat doesn't like animals."

"Goldie, Rat *is* an animal."

Goldie tilted her head to one side and moved closer to Jennifer. "You know what?" she said, whispering and looking over her shoulder even though they had the place to themselves for the moment. Osgood and Kyle were walking the dogs, and Terrell and Jason had taken Brett and Will with them so the boys could watch the rangers at work.

"What?"

"I think I'm having more fun with Terrell than I have with Rat."

Jennifer looked up, then shook her head. "Goldie, you always have fun with the man you're with."

"No, this is different. Terrell is just so—" she paused as if groping for the right description "—interested in me. No one else really has been. Rat can't bear to listen to me talk about the pet shop.''

"I imagine that pales in comparison to a drug heist," Jennifer said dryly.

Goldie sat down near Jennifer. "I've been thinking about what you said about Rat, and maybe I should stop seeing him."

Relief swamped Jennifer, yet at the same time she thought about Terrell. As much as she loved her sister and wanted only good for Goldie, she also hated to see someone as nice as Terrell get hurt.

"Goldie, Terrell has lived out here alone for years. Jason told me. He's bound to be vulnerable where women are concerned."

"Who's vulnerable? Jason?"

"No! Terrell! Will you listen? You don't want to hurt someone."

"I'm not going to hurt him. I happen to think he's very nice, too. He's more than nice, Jennifer, and I like him and..." She lowered her voice. "I wish the sun hadn't come out and we could stay here for days. This is the best time I've had in *so* long."

Jennifer studied Goldie and wondered if she would truly break away from Rat. There had been other men in her sister's life, but Goldie always went running right back to Rat Tabor. Yet Terrell, with his quiet manner and stability, would probably be like a rock for Goldie, something she had never had with Rat. And right now where *was* Rat? How many men were searching for the money? Jennifer felt safe at the patrol cabin—no one could find them there with the park closed to campers—but what would happen when they returned to Santa Fe?

She went to shower herself, wishing she had some clothes of her own to change into. She realized she was eager for Jason's return.

Restless, she walked outside, meandering down the trail until she heard an engine. She moved to one side and waited as a Jeep came around the bend. Jason slowed down and stopped beside her, and Will leaned out the side.

"Hi, Mom. We pulled part of a bridge out of the river. It fell in and smashed against the bank."

"Want a ride?" Jason asked.

"Sure." She climbed inside and Will slid into the back. "How's the park?"

"Flooded badly toward the southeast. Most of the bridges are still submerged or washed away completely, but the water should go down soon. I spotted two men across the river. I tried calling out to them that the park was closed, but they ran into the woods, so I guess they knew they weren't supposed to be here."

"They were down near our house," Will said. "Our house has water all over the first floor. Mr. Hollenbeck took me to see."

"I called the insurance agents today about the house and the Bronco. The agent for the house will come out and look at it as soon as the water goes down." Jennifer thought about all the money hidden at Jason's cabin and a vague fear returned. "Can anyone in the park get to this side of the river?"

"Not unless they travel miles upriver and come back down, and I'm not sure they could get through then, because I don't know if there are any roads." He shook his head. "No, we're still cut off from the world. If this weather holds, though, we can get through tomorrow."

She felt a mixture of emotions, primarily relief that no one could cross the river. It was foolish to connect the two men with the money, yet what were they doing in the park and why had they run from a ranger? She also felt reluctant to leave the patrol cabin, and she knew it was mostly because of Jason. She glanced over at him as he drove. He looked so strong and capable. And he was great with the boys. He and Terrell were a good influence on them. In spite of being cooped up for the second day in tiny quarters without a television, they had been less rowdy than at home, and she had to credit Jason for that. Quietly he had insisted they take more responsibility for cleaning the cabin. The fishing jaunt had subdued Kyle and made Brett and Will proud of their accomplishments and more interested in the park and the rangers.

"Mr. Hollenbeck found a rifle on the riverbank, and we had to move a log off a trail," Will said enthusiastically. "It was neat, Mom."

"Sounds like a good day."

Jason parked beside the steps to the cabin and Will bounded out, taking the stairs two at a time.

"Thanks for taking him along today. He really seems to have enjoyed himself. I hope he wasn't a burden."

"No. He was a help. He's tall and strong for his age, and I enjoyed having him along."

"All three of them act more mature when they're separated. When they get together, they seem to rev each other up until they're all in trouble."

Jason laughed as they stood together in the sunshine. A faint dark stubble of beard shaded his jaw, making him look rugged, and his hands rested easily on his hips. His eyes studied her with undisguised interest.

"You washed your hair," he said, his gaze roaming over her features. "It looks pretty."

"Thank you," she replied, aware of his intense scrutiny.

"I need a good soaking myself. We were in mud up to our knees. I wonder how long it'll take the park to dry out. I hope Terrell gets here soon. I'm famished."

"Trout dinner sounds wonderful."

"I'll take care of cooking the fish. I'll show Will how to do it. Does he know how to light a grill?"

"No."

"Time he learned, then. I'm cleaning up first and then we'll get dinner."

She walked upstairs with him and found Will finishing a box of cereal, eating it dry as he leaned over the sink. Jason called to him from the bedroom.

"You can shower when I get out, Will, and then we'll get the fish on for dinner."

"Yes, sir."

She bit back a smile, knowing how recalcitrant Will would have been at home if she had suggested he cook dinner. A short while later she looked outside and saw Jason showing Will how to work the grill. She glanced at the timer on the stove. The rice had another twenty minutes to steam.

Terrell had showered and was outside with Goldie and the other two boys; Osgood was napping. Kyle's exuberance had returned and he didn't seem any the worse for his dunking in the creek. Jennifer noted the trees and their lengthening shadows, and she wondered again about the men Jason had spotted. Could it have been someone after the money? Telling herself that that was ridiculous, she still felt a chill. Should she tell Jason about the hidden money? As she stared at the darkening trees, she debated the matter. In the end she decided to keep quiet. There was no way for anyone to find them until the water went down, and then they would take the money to Rimrock.

After dinner Will stood in front of the gun rack. "Mr. Hollenbeck, would you show me your guns?"

Jason looked at Jennifer. "I hunt. Kyle is too young, but if you want, I'll show Will and Brett my rifle and the .45 I carry."

Jennifer was silent while she thought it over.

"Go ahead," Osgood urged. "Might as well let someone who knows what he's doing show them."

She nodded, thinking there were a lot of similarities between Jason and Mark. Jason was as much a rugged outdoorsman as Mark had been, and in his own way, as willing to take risks. She watched him open the gun case and prop a rifle butt against his thigh as he showed the weapon to the boys. He was undeniably attractive, but she didn't ever want to be seriously involved again with another risk taker. Not that there was any danger of that. Jason would soon be rid of them and she would probably see him as seldom as she had before the flood. At the thought that he would go out of their lives tomorrow, she felt a pang, because he was winning the boys' friendship and hers, as well. And it was heaven to have an appealing, intelligent male to talk to and be with.

"Will," Jason said, pointing to the bedroom, "get my field kit off the dresser, please." When Will returned, he took the two boys into the kitchen, and Jennifer listened to him describing the parts of the rifle, telling them how to clean and care for it.

When he locked up the gun case again, Will appeared in front of her. "Jason said Brett and I can go with him tomorrow and he'll let us shoot at targets if you say it's okay."

She didn't approve of guns, yet when she thought about Will's enjoyment of the time he'd spent fishing with Jason, she decided to relent. "Yes, it's okay," she said, looking past him at Jason who winked at her.

Will moved to join his brothers on the floor, where they were playing cards with Osgood. Jason nodded toward the door. "Come on, let's take a walk."

"Sure," she said, wondering how often he took walks after hiking through the park all day. She stood up, and as they went to the door, he took down two jackets and handed her one.

The sky was clear, stars twinkling brightly as Jason looped her arm through his and they walked down the steps. The smell of burning pine from his fire was in the air, and a plume of gray smoke trailed upward from the chimney.

"Do you ever have to work at night?"

"Sure, if I'm on duty. We have to check on campers at night. People have noisy parties—even fights—and we get called in."

"You have to deal with fights?"

"I'm the law in the park," he said, and Jennifer thought again about the money. Yet what would it accomplish to turn it over to him? It would be better to stick to her plans.

"The Blathey family are regulars at fighting," Jason continued. "They camp one weekend a month from April to November. In college, along with all my other courses dealing with nature, I had to take sociology and psychology to help me deal with campers." He draped his arm across her shoulders. "When we get away from the cabin you can see even more stars," he said in his deep voice. Their footsteps crunched on the graveled path and she was aware of his arm around her as they walked together. ''Now look at the sky.''

Stars glittered like diamonds against black velvet. The moon was full, shedding white brilliance over the spruce and aspen, and she moved away from him, gazing upward.

''I think the river will go down and you can go home in the morning,'' he said. ''You might as well stay here again tomorrow night, because you won't be able to sleep at your house.''

''We can't inconvenience you any longer. We can stay in Rimrock.'' She faced him as they walked, moonlight spilling over his face with a dusky clarity.

''At the Shady Acres Motel?'' he asked, laughing. ''I wouldn't wish that on my worst enemy. No, you stay at the patrol cabin tomorrow night.''

''When we first moved in, I didn't think your nerves would last, but you've done a good job of putting up with us. And you've been more than tolerant of the boys. They like you.''

''Maybe it'll make up for past differences. I like them. They're good kids.'' He studied her, his blue gaze electrifying in the moonlight. ''I like their mother, too,'' he added softly. ''Life is full of surprises, isn't it?''

Her heartbeat speeded up as he watched her, and she felt a warmth inside, a longing. ''Yes, it is,'' she answered in little more than a whisper.

''Jennifer...'' He reached for her, sliding his arm around her waist and drawing her closer. She caught her breath, her heart pounding now as she felt his strength and his lean body pressing against hers. She sighed. It had been a long time since she had been in a man's arms. ''You're remembering, aren't you?''

"Yes," she replied, surprised at his perception. She started to move away, but his arms tightened slightly and he kissed her temple and trailed light kisses on her cheek.

"There's no hurry, and remembering is natural," he whispered.

His lips brushed hers lightly and memory spun away. Mark would never come back to her, and what they had had was locked away in her heart. Right now she wanted Jason's kisses, wanted his strong arms holding her.

"This is the last night, the last time we'll be together," she whispered. She placed her hands on his upper arms, feeling the texture of his quilted down jacket. He bent his head to kiss her.

Her arms slid around his neck. His muscular body felt marvelous and she clung to him, returning his kisses, relishing the moment, because she knew it wouldn't last. She refused to think about tomorrow, about telling him goodbye.

His hand slid over her hip and down along her thigh, a warm, heavy pressure. When his fingers roamed back up to her rib cage and the full underside of her breast, she felt faint with longing and moaned softly with pleasure. His hand slid to her taut nipple, and all the while he kept kissing her. How long since a man had made her burn with desire? She was vulnerable and his kisses and caresses were volatile. It had been so long.... Was that why she was trembling in response, or was it simply because it was Jason Hollenbeck who was kissing her?

His hand slipped beneath her T-shirt to caress her. He cupped her full breast, his thumb making circles over her nipple while he trailed kisses along her throat. She ached with longing for more, knowing she was running risks with her heart, but it was nice, so nice to be held and kissed like this. Caution whispered like wind through pine boughs that Jason was filling gaps in their lives, in hers and the boys', that the kisses could be dangerous . . . that he was becoming too much a part of their family.

Startled, she looked up at him. "Maybe we're playing with fire here."

He gazed at her solemnly, his arm still tight around her waist. With his fingers he smoothed a lock of hair away from her cheek. "How's that?"

"I don't want my life disrupted. And you don't want yours disturbed, either."

"I'm not going to disrupt your life," he said gently. "How could I?"

"I suppose you won't, because after we go home, I probably won't see you again."

"You know you'll see me again," he said, lightly touching the corner of her mouth with his finger.

"Then it's risky, because I don't want to become involved again with another man who likes to flirt with danger."

"I don't run big risks," he said, his fingers traveling around to caress the nape of her neck.

"You've run several in the time I've known you."

"What would you have had me do—stand on the bank and wring my hands?"

"Of course not, but you're like Mark. You love the outdoors, its hazards and its wonders, and you're not afraid to wade right into trouble. I can't risk my heart again with a man like that." She shook her head. "Listen to me. All we've done is kiss a little and I'm talking about forevers. We'd better go back."

"Jennifer," he said, and his voice was full of amusement. He tilted her chin up and his smile faded. "You're still wrapped up in grief. You have to take risks in life. I did what I had to do to save your sons. That's not the same as daredevil stunts in an air show."

"It seems the same to me."

"I'm afraid of things just like everybody else. And some things that you do so easily scare me."

"Like what?" she asked, aware that they were still standing pressed together, that his hand continued to caress her, moving lightly from her nape to her cheek.

"You open yourself to people. It's an effort for me to get close to people—really close. Maybe it goes back to my childhood, because my family is so cold and self-sufficient."

"You're not that way, Jason!"

"Yes, I am. Somehow, with you and your boys, you're all outgoing and you make it easy. Terrell and I have become friends over the years I've been here, but I don't have any other close friends. My relationships with women never get to the serious stage, so you're pretty safe from any heartbreak."

At his last words, she gazed up at him. Again she wondered if beneath his self-possession was an incredibly lonely man.

He framed her face in his hands. "Take a little risk," he whispered, and leaned down to place his mouth over hers, his tongue touching hers.

She trembled in response, feeling a warmth spread through her veins. His arms wrapped tightly around her, and she could feel their hearts pounding as his kiss deepened. He shifted slightly, his hand again drifting down to cup her breast, his thumb caressing the hard peak. Moaning softly with pleasure, she turned her head as he trailed kisses down her throat.

"Jennifer," he whispered, his voice a rasp, his need clear.

She turned her face up, his mouth moving over hers to kiss her again as she pressed against him and felt his arousal. Since the flood he had become a friend; now he was becoming more—a man in her life, kindling desire that had lain dormant for so long. She pushed back, feeling shaky, both of them studying each other.

She shook her hair away from her face and he pressed her back against his chest. She listened to his heart, staring at the darkened trees on the mountainside, wondering how much their relationship had changed in the past few minutes. Suddenly a bobbing light in the darkness caught her eye, and she drew in a breath.

"Jason! There's someone in the woods!"

CHAPTER SEVEN

JENNIFER STARED AT the bouncing light, her heart beating wildly.

"You're right," Jason said. "The park's closed so they shouldn't be here. Look, head back to the cabin and tell Terrell I need him."

"I don't want to leave you and I don't want to walk back alone."

"You're safe between here and the cabin, because I can hear if you yell. I'm going to call out to them," he warned her before he raised his voice. "Hey! The park is closed!"

Instantly the light vanished.

"Dammit." Jason sounded annoyed. "Trespassers, probably wanting to see how high the river is or wanting to fish while the water is up and running. Let's go back and I'll report it."

Jennifer stared at the dense woods, shadows blotting out the moonlight, and she shivered, thinking about the money. "You said no one could get across the river."

"I don't know how they did. They must have gone far enough upriver or waded through one of the creeks like I did this morning. Someone would have to want to get across mighty badly."

He walked with his arm around her, his presence reassuring. At the foot of the stairs to the cabin he turned her to face him. "I'm glad you and your family are here," he said.

"So am I," she answered.

"I better make my report." Inside he called headquarters and left a message with the night dispatcher, then he talked quietly to Terrell. In minutes both men pulled on jackets and Jason disappeared into the bedroom. When he returned, Jennifer noticed he was wearing the revolver.

"We'll be back soon," he said, before going out and closing the door quickly. She stared at the door, worrying about the safety of the two men, worrying about the rest of them if someone was wandering around outside. Jason denied taking risks, but here he was charging into something that could be dangerous. Was she making it worse by not telling him about the money?

She went to the bedroom and closed the door, her thoughts on Jason. Switching off the lights, she moved to the window and gazed out. Moonlight splashed over the boughs of trees, but the shadows were too many and too thick for her to see anything; she couldn't spot the Jeep or any lights. She felt the cold glass against her fingertips as she remembered Jason's kisses and his statement that his relationships with women never got too serious. What would happen when she went home? Would they see each other again only in the most casual way?

The door opened and she turned around.

"Jennifer, are you all right?" Goldie asked, switching on a light. "What are you doing?"

"I was looking out the window."

"Jennifer, I have a date next Saturday night with Terrell," Goldie said, her eyes sparkling. "He said we're going to have to stay here while the house dries out even after the river goes down, but whether we're here or we're there, he's asked me to go to a movie in Rimrock."

"That's nice," Jennifer said cautiously, "but I hope you don't lead him on and hurt him."

"I won't hurt Terrell, so you can just stop worrying about him. He treats me nicer than any other man I've known."

Jennifer was afraid it was premature to feel relieved; she had had similar conversations with Goldie before. But she couldn't help thinking Terrell was just the sort of man Goldie needed.

"Goldie, when you go to Rimrock, keep your eyes open and watch out for strangers. We still have the money to worry about."

"I will," she answered airily, and Jennifer knew she wasn't giving a thought to the money. Goldie left the room and closed the door, and Jennifer crossed over to the mirror to stare at her reflection. She looked the same as she had last week, but she didn't feel the same, thanks to Jason Hollenbeck.

By the time Jason and Terrell returned, the boys were asleep and Osgood and the dogs were snoring noisily. Jennifer, Goldie, Jason and Terrell went to the kitchen to sit at the table over coffee. Jason found crackers and cheese and brought them over.

"Did you find any trespassers?" Jennifer asked him.

Jason shook his head. "No. We've looked, and no one seems to be camping along the river."

"Somebody's in the park who isn't supposed to be?" Goldie asked, frowning as she gazed up at Terrell.

"Jason spotted someone, but we couldn't find anybody. It reminds me of that time they closed the park because of a fire. Jason and I saw some smoke and we went to check. It was four couples who thought they would bring food for the animals who wouldn't have any because of the fire. They slipped into the park and dumped all the stuff they brought along the riverbank, then built a campfire for their dinner. That brought a couple of bears on the run. The people had to lock themselves in their cars, but their keys were in a tent, so they just had to sit there. They couldn't get out because of the bears."

"What did you do?" Goldie asked.

Terrell grinned. "Our vehicle scared away the bears. We told those people to get their keys and get out and come back later for their tent. They didn't come back until summer's end."

"Once we had a lion that escaped from a small traveling circus and got into the park," Jason added. "That kept everyone hopping until it was caught."

"The boys should hear your stories," Jennifer said.

"Did your family go camping when you were kids?" Terrell asked.

"No," Goldie answered, smoothing thick yellow cheese on a cracker and taking a bite.

"Dad was traveling so much of the time," Jennifer explained. "Goldie and I used to sleep in the backyard when we were little."

"I'd be frightened to sleep out here because of bears," Goldie said.

"They're not that big a hazard," Jason told her, setting down his coffee cup. "We have hundreds of campers, and if they're careful and follow the rules, they don't get hurt. You keep everything that will attract them up high or locked away—sweet-smelling things, food, even toothpaste."

"Did you camp out when you were a kid?" Jennifer asked, and Jason shook his head.

"Not with my family, but I was sent to a camp every summer starting about the time I was ten years old, and I loved it. I went to Wisconsin most summers, sometimes Missouri, sometimes Colorado."

They finished the cheese and crackers and Terrell stood up. "I'll take my turn in the bathroom first. Before I do, Goldie, show me those pictures you told me about."

"They're in my purse," she said, rising. Terrell took their plates and cups and saucers to the sink and the two left the room.

"I think we can get to your house tomorrow," Jason said quietly, leaning back in the chair and rubbing his neck.

"I dread seeing what the water has done, but I'm thankful we still have a house. Where's Terrell from? I haven't heard him say."

"His family is from Albuquerque. He played football at Tech when he was younger."

"He looks like he played football sometime in the past. Were you in sports, too?"

"A little."

She laughed, and he arched his brows. "I think you're being modest. Did you play football?"

"No. I played golf and tennis and I was on a track team."

"In high school or college?" she asked, easily imagining him doing any of the three. He had the long legs of a runner.

"Tennis and track in high school and college. Golf was in college."

"Did you get your letter?" she asked, amused at his reluctance to talk about his participation in sports.

"Yes, I did."

"You don't like to talk about it, do you?" she said, suddenly realizing it wasn't modesty but reluctance that made him so closemouthed. "Sorry if I pried."

"You didn't," he answered quickly. "It was just never important to me. It was important to my folks, though."

Jennifer decided not to pursue the subject. Any reference to his parents always acted like a dead weight on their conversation. Her thoughts shifted to the trespassers. "Do you lock the door to the cabin?"

"Yes, I do, but no one would break in here, and if they did and saw all these people and dogs, they'd leave fast," he joked.

Not if they knew how much money was in the cabin. Again, she was tempted to tell Jason about it, but she suspected the blossoming relationship between Terrell and Goldie might suffer a fatal setback if Terrell realized how deeply she was involved with Rat.

Jennifer glanced at the clock and was surprised to see it was after one in the morning. She stood up. "We'd better turn in. I'll get the dishes."

"I'll help."

He carried dishes to the sink, and as she turned to look for more dishes, she saw Jason studying a piece of paper. When he tore it in two and dropped it into the trash, she looked at him questioningly. "A grocery list?"

"No, my schedule for tomorrow. I know I won't need it."

"We caused you to toss it away, didn't we?" she said, thinking how much they had disrupted his orderly life.

He touched her cheek lightly. "Could be you did. I don't think the Ruarks run on schedules. Except you must do something different when you teach and the kids are in school."

"It's very different, but it's summer now and I don't want to go by a schedule, although while we're at your place, we'll do what you say."

"Sure enough?" he asked, teasing her.

She laughed and turned back to the dishes, rinsing them and placing them in the dishwasher. As she finished, Jason reached around her to switch off the light, leaving only the glow from the light above the stove.

He placed his hands on the counter on either side of her, leaning close. "We're alone," he said softly.

"Only after midnight," she whispered, tilting her head as he leaned forward the last few inches to kiss her. His lips were warm, brushing against hers.

"Mom."

She looked around, and Kyle stood in the kitchen in Jason's oversize T-shirt and his own shorts. "I want a drink of water."

"All right, and then you have to get back into bed. I thought you were asleep."

"I was, but I got thirsty."

She reached for a glass and Kyle moved closer, looking up at Jason. "You're kissing Mom."

"I was."

"You love Mom?"

"Kyle, here's your water, drink it," Jennifer said briskly, her cheeks pink.

He accepted the glass, staring at Jason and drinking without taking his eyes from him.

"Now you get back to bed," Jennifer said, and Kyle turned and ran out of the kitchen. "Well, you'll probably get asked about this again, and I'm sure I will, so you might as well get ready for the questions."

"I'll manage," he said, and she realized he probably would. He seemed to be getting along fine with the boys, but his status with them might have just changed.

Jason reached out to pull her back to him, but she resisted.

"If I know my sons, Brett will be in here in minutes, and then Will." She tilted her head to look up at him. "This is something unique in their lives and Kyle won't wait until morning to discuss it with his brothers."

Jason glanced toward the darkened living room. "I don't hear anything or see anyone moving around in there."

"Take my word for it." She placed her hand on his arm. "Jason, thanks for all you've done for the boys, especially Will, but I'm still not sure that it's right to teach Will and Brett to hunt."

"I don't hunt in the park, because it isn't allowed, but it won't hurt them to learn how to handle a rifle and to appreciate nature. They were curious about my .45."

"Guns and nature don't seem compatible."

"If handled right, they can be. I hunt game birds and that's all—mainly pheasant." He leaned forward to kiss her throat and she closed her eyes, letting him for a moment.

"I don't see Brett," he whispered.

"You will." She moved away. "Good night, Jason."

"Can I get a drink?" Brett asked, emerging from the darkened living area and staring at Jason as if he had turned purple.

"Yes, you may," Jennifer answered.

"Good night to both of you," Jason said, heading for the bathroom.

"Why did you kiss him?" Brett whispered loudly enough for Jason to hear. "He isn't going to be our new dad, is he?"

Jason wondered what her answers would be. How serious did he feel about Jennifer? He knew she wasn't someone to be taken lightly. He looked at the mounds of blankets and bodies strewn on the sofa and floor. With the exception of Terrell, all of them belonged to Jennifer and would go along with her if she married. The mere thought of exchanging his solitary existence for three children, a wife, a live-in father-in-law and five dogs was staggering. Yet there was something very special about Jennifer. He felt more relaxed with her than he had with any other woman. There was a comradeship between them that made it easy to talk to her. And he liked the boys. Brett was the most standoffish, but maybe that was because Jason had rescued the other two. Pray he didn't have to rescue Brett from some disaster to win him over.

When everyone was settled for the night, Jennifer lay in Jason's bed and looked through the window at the twinkling stars. Her thoughts centered on Jason and the boys' questions. Jason was becoming very special to her. She knew he had won Will's trust, but she wasn't sure about Kyle, and now Brett seemed to see him as a threat.

She sighed, thinking it was ridiculous to worry about their relationship, because when she went home there wouldn't be a relationship. Jason would never become seriously interested in a woman with such a sizable, unusual family as hers.

TERRELL AND JASON had left to check the bridges before anyone else was up the next morning. When they returned, they were met by the smell of hot coffee.

"How are the bridges?" Jennifer asked, stepping into the living area. Jason's sleeves were rolled up and he was pulling off his muddy boots. His hands were also covered in mud and he headed toward the bathroom.

"There's a bridge above water now," he said, pausing in front of her, and she felt a swift rush of longing. He was so handsome, so full of vitality. He held out his dirty hands. "I have to get washed. We'll grab a bite to eat and then take you home. It's six-thirty, and Terrell and I don't officially report until nine. Today we'll be busy with repairs and campers coming back into the park."

"It'll be open to the public again?" she asked, thinking about the money.

"Yes, but if we move along, we'll have time to help you with some of the cleanup."

"You don't have to do that."

"Sure we do. It's in the ranger handbook—clean flooded houses after any dam collapse."

She smiled and returned to the kitchen while he went to wash up.

"Are we going home today?" Brett asked, coming into the room and reaching for a piece of buttered toast.

"Yes, as soon as we get ready and the rangers have breakfast."

"Then we won't see them anymore, will we?"

She glanced down at Brett, who stood frowning at her, and her worst fears were confirmed. He'd definitely seemed relieved when she had told him Jason wouldn't become their new daddy.

"We'll see them a lot more. And we're staying here tonight, because our house won't be dried out."

"Aw, gee, Mom. I want to stay home."

"We will as soon as we can, Brett. I think when you see the house, you'll want to stay here tonight."

"No, I won't," he said stubbornly, and left the kitchen.

After breakfast, they piled into the Jeeps, Jason leading the way with Jennifer, Will, Kyle and two of the dogs. There was still no sign of Oats, and Jennifer held a slim hope that he might have gotten home and was waiting for them. Jason had to drive farther north to the passable bridge, taking a circuitous route to the valley. As Jennifer gazed at the river flowing swiftly past, she had a strange feeling that life had changed in more ways than a house being flooded. Twisting to look over her shoulder, she saw Goldie laughing at something Terrell was saying.

The river hid the road in places, and water splashed high as the Jeeps hit puddles. When they reached the house, the high-water mark, a dirty brown stain, was two feet above the ground floor, and weeds and branches were caught on the front steps where they had been swept by the rushing river. Vehicle tracks were deep in the yard and Jason frowned at them; they looked fresh.

He stopped and they climbed out. The ground squished beneath their feet, and the stench of mud and wet wood was overpowering. Jennifer was thankful for the bright sunshine. They were going to need a lot of it.

"You're fortunate the house is standing," Jason said. The river ran only yards away now and the road was still underwater.

Jennifer reached the door first; it stood slightly ajar. "I had to kick it open when I came to warn you," Jason said. "I couldn't wake you." When they stepped inside, a dank, musty odor assailed them.

"Dad, I don't think you'll want to come inside until we air the place out," she called as the dogs ran around the yard and barked.

Jason stared at the house. The flooding had been high, leaving mud and silt and a thick covering of water over the floor. The smell of the wet rug was repugnant, but he was looking at the room in shock. He had expected the floor damage. What he hadn't expected were the ripped cushions, the holes gouged in the walls, the drawers pulled out.

"Jennifer, what the hell—" he asked, and then he looked at her. Her eyes were wide and all color had drained from her face.

CHAPTER EIGHT

"OH, NO!" THE BOYS brushed past her and stopped.

"Jeez, what a smell!" Will said.

"Phew," Brett exclaimed, holding his nose.

"Mom, what happened to our house?" Kyle asked.

Jennifer glanced up the stairs as ripples of fear shot through her. She knew why the house was in shambles. "I want to look upstairs," she said. She needed to get Goldie alone. Someone had been in the house searching for the money, and one look at the chaos around her brought the danger home. Yet how could she get the money to Rimrock without Jason knowing?

"We've had looters," she said as Jason took her arm and they crossed the living room.

"This isn't the work of looters. You've had someone in here searching for something. Looters grab and run, they don't rip and tear."

The upstairs, too, reeked of the flood, and the damage was just as extensive. Mattresses were slashed, drawers and their contents flung around the rooms. She drew a deep breath and glanced at him. "I don't know what happened."

"Jennifer, is there any reason someone would do this? Are you in some sort of trouble?"

She was tempted to tell him about the money, but she wanted to talk to Goldie first. "Nothing like this has ever happened before," she said evasively, turning away.

"Mom, someone's wrecked the house," Brett said, thrusting his head into the room. "They've yanked out all my drawers and cut up the mattress."

"I know. We'll just have to start putting everything back and trying to dry it out."

"I'm reporting this, Jennifer," Jason said. "I'll call the sheriff in Rimrock. You shouldn't touch anything until then."

"Will he come out here?" she asked, worried about Goldie's part in the theft.

"Yes, he will. Is that a problem?"

"Before you call him, let me talk to Goldie and see if she has any ideas about this."

Jason studied her closely, and she felt a flush rise to her cheeks. His blue eyes were intent as he stared at her. "All right," he answered carefully. "Tell me when you've finished talking to her." He left the room and she followed him into the hall. Goldie stood at the foot of the stairs.

"Goldie, will you please come up here." Jennifer hoped her voice sounded casual, and she watched Goldie rush up the stairs. They went into the bedroom, and Jennifer closed the door.

"This was someone after the money, wasn't it?" Goldie asked, her face pale.

"Yes. It had to be."

"I'm sorry," Goldie said, looking at the jumble around her. "I didn't think anyone would find me here. You know it wasn't Rat."

"No, it was someone after the money, maybe even after *you*. Jason wants to notify the sheriff. We need to give the money to the sheriff right now."

"We can't." Goldie wrung her hands and bit her lower lip. "I don't have the money."

"What do you mean you don't have the money?" Jennifer suddenly felt cold. "Where is it?"

"It's hidden at Jason's place."

"Goldie, how could you!" Jennifer closed her eyes and thought about the thousands of dollars in Jason's empty patrol cabin. "You left the money behind?"

"Yes, because we're going back tonight. I thought it would be safer at his place."

Jennifer rubbed her forehead. "I have to tell him, and we have to get the money."

"Please, please, not yet," Goldie begged, reaching out to grip Jennifer's hand. "Please, Jenny. Terrell won't want to see me again if he finds out I've hidden that much money for Rat. And I don't want to tell him where it came from."

"Goldie, if you're going to have a good relationship with him, you have to be truthful with him. He's going to find out sometime, anyway." She glanced at her watch. "Lordy, Goldie, they have to go to work in an hour."

"That's all the more reason not to tell them now. A day or two really isn't going to matter. We're staying at the patrol cabin tonight."

"We just can't wait," Jennifer said finally, staring at a slashed mattress and thinking about her boys. "We're getting that money to the police this morning. Where's it hidden?" She crossed the room and put her arms around her sister. "Can't you see? The sooner we get rid of it, the safer we'll be. And the less chance of you being prosecuted."

"How can I be prosecuted when I didn't take it?"

"Because you've hidden it—that makes you an accessory," she explained patiently. "Goldie, this is the worst thing Rat has ever done. He's put you in danger and jeopardized your future."

Goldie started to cry and Jennifer patted her back. "Now tell me where you hid it."

"In Jason's bookshelf in his bedroom...behind some books," she said, trying to control her sobs, and Jennifer felt sorry for her.

"Goldie, just don't forget how many tears Rat has caused you to shed. I'm going now, because I have to tell Jason." She went downstairs and found him outside, assessing the damage with Will.

"Jason, may I see you for a moment?" she asked, her heart beating rapidly. She had no idea what his reaction would be. He was the law in the park, the same as a policeman. She knew he would never understand about Goldie and Rat. Would he arrest Goldie right away? She rubbed her arms as if a cold wind had blown across her, even though she was standing in warm sunshine.

With curiosity evident in his eyes, Jason walked over to her.

"I have to tell John Wainworth, our insurance agent, because he wanted to come see the damage, but he'll have to wait a few more minutes, because I need to talk to you." She took Jason's arm and steered him toward the Jeep. "I know you need to get to work before long." They walked around the vehicle and stopped out of earshot of anyone in the house. "I have to tell you something."

"Go ahead," he said easily, folding his arms across his chest and leaning back against the Jeep.

Wind caught locks of his black hair, curling them back from his face. Jennifer wondered if the next few minutes would change their growing friendship forever. She took a deep breath. "My sister dated a man who got involved in a theft of drug money. He told her to hold on to the money because some men were after him." When nothing changed in Jason's expression, she felt a little better.

"He gave the money to Goldie and told her to keep it for him, and then he disappeared. Last month some men tried to kidnap her, but she escaped. Her place has been broken into and searched. She was frightened so she brought the money here."

"Where you and your boys are?" he asked, his brows arching and anger flashing in his eyes.

"Yes, because she didn't know where else to go. She said she was careful—"

He made a dismissive motion. "You have three boys and you don't know how to use a gun. You don't have any protection. Didn't she stop to think about that?"

"Probably very little. I'm like a mother to her. She didn't have anywhere else to turn." She could understand Jason's anger, yet at the same time she felt love and pity for Goldie.

"Go ahead and finish telling me about it," he said in a grim voice.

"When she arrived the night of the flood, she had the cash hidden in money belts. I was going to take the money to the sheriff in Rimrock, but the dam broke and we had to flee. She took the money to your place." She paused, dreading to tell him the next part, because it would directly involve him.

"And?" he asked, the word coming out clipped.

"The money is still at your place," she said swiftly, bracing for a storm.

He inhaled and stood up. "We'll go get it."

She stared at him, momentarily taken aback by the way he was reacting. She had expected an explosion, remembering his fury over the hole the boys had dug in the park and the way he had lost his temper the first time the boys practiced and the dogs started howling. She shifted her thoughts back to the money. "I want to turn the money over to the sheriff, but when I do, I want Goldie to tell him her story. Jason, if she cooperates and turns in the money voluntarily, can she get off without being charged as an accessory?"

"She might. Garcia's lenient that way." He looked at his watch. "It would be better to turn the money in rather than have him come out here. I'll report in and tell the office where I'm going and why. I can make arrangements to take you and the money to Rimrock."

She closed her eyes in relief. "Thank heavens. I'm so afraid for the boys. We've been at your place almost since Goldie arrived, and at least I felt safe there."

He glanced at the house then back at her. "Even after you turn in the money, someone may come looking for it."

"I know, but I don't want Goldie charged with this crime if we can prevent it."

"She should have thought of that when she took the money," he said, his voice suddenly sounding rough. "She must like this guy a lot."

"I think it's over between them," Jennifer said, guessing that Jason was angry because he felt Terrell was going to be hurt.

"Let's get the money and come back for Goldie. Is she going to tell Terrell about this?"

"I don't know. I suppose she'll have to now. Let me tell her we're going." She hurried toward the house, where she found her father mopping up water.

"Dad," she said, "I'm going to the cabin with Jason. Where's Goldie?"

"Off somewhere with Terrell."

"Tell her we'll be back to pick her up in a little while. We need to get into Rimrock to talk to the sheriff about the break-in."

Osgood nodded. "What about the insurance fellow?"

"I'll call him as soon as I get back, but I have to take care of this other matter first."

"Jenny, I'll call him if you'd like and tell him we're here so he can come out and look at the damage."

"Thanks, Dad." She smiled at him. "Here's the number." Fishing a slip of paper out of her pocket, she handed it to him. "We'll get this back in order."

"I know. I was just hoping Oats would be here waiting."

"He may show up yet. You know how he always got lost if he was by himself."

Osgood nodded and she hurried across the yard. Jason waited with one arm braced against the Jeep. Beneath all her worries was relief that he had taken the news as well as he had—and that she had at last been honest with him. He opened the door for her and she climbed inside.

"Where's the money hidden?" he asked when they were on the trail, water splashing high against the sides of the Jeep.

"Goldie said it's in your bookshelf behind your books."

"Terrell asked her to go out with him next Saturday night," Jason said quietly, yet she could detect anger in his tone.

"I know. She's excited about it. She's talking to him now."

"Who is this guy, Jennifer?"

She had dreaded that question. "His name is Rat Tabor—Rudolph Allen Tabor—and she's known him a long time. He's never been involved in anything big like this before, just petty things that he can always wiggle out of without any real consequences."

"This is a stupid question, but what does she see in the guy?"

"He's as handsome as a movie star, he's charming, he's good to her in his own way. I've tried to talk her out of going with him for a long time now. Who knows why people fall in love?" Jason looked over at her and she wondered what he was thinking. "Rat owns part of a nightclub in San Francisco," she continued, "and Goldie worked there until recently."

"What did she do?"

"She sang and then she was a hostess. And at one time she was an exotic dancer."

"Lord, Terrell and an exotic dancer," he muttered under his breath, frowning.

"She's my sister!"

"And Terrell's my friend. The guy hasn't gone out with anyone in the past couple of years. Do you know how vulnerable he is?"

"I haven't gone out with anyone in the past couple of years either, so I understand all about that," she answered stiffly, thinking that she had been as easily drawn to Jason as Terrell had been to Goldie.

Jason glanced at her as he drove up the mountain to his cabin. "Jennifer, sooner or later Rat will show up to claim the money. Would he hurt Goldie?"

"I don't think so. At least he never has in the past. Sweet-talking is more his style."

"Even when you turn in the money, that won't stop someone from coming to search for it again. I've said this before but you've got to expect it."

"I know, and that's what scares me. And when we get home, I'm going to call my neighbor in Santa Fe. Sally has a key to our house. Someone may have ripped it to shreds, too."

Jason stopped the Jeep and they climbed out. "Has Rat ever served time?"

"Yes, for theft and for writing bad checks. I know he sounds terrible, and he is, but I think Goldie finally sees him for what he is."

"She's been with him a long time, you said?"

"Yes. I know you like Terrell and don't want to see him hurt, and neither do I, but my sister is a nice person and wouldn't knowingly hurt anyone. And she likes Terrell. Jason, he's all the things she's never known in a man, and she appreciates that."

"I hope she isn't just entertaining herself while she's stuck out here in the woods."

"She's not, but in many ways she's still like a child, and—"

"But she's not a child," Jason said harshly, unlocking the door to his cabin. "She's a grown woman now. Jennifer, she had to know what danger she was placing herself in and that she would become an accessory by hiding the money."

Jennifer followed him into the cabin. "Jason, I don't think you've ever been so infatuated with someone that you would do anything for them. Goldie is softhearted and not the most logical person in the world. I think she's finally seeing there are men who are better than Rat. She's scared what Terrell will think."

"She should be."

"Goldie didn't know she had become an accessory when she accepted the money. She still doesn't quite understand what serious trouble she's in."

He strode to the bedroom and Jennifer followed. "She said it was on the bottom shelf behind some books."

Jason knelt to remove the books and pulled out the money belts. "If I'd even glanced over here, I would have noticed these," he said, his voice changing as he stared at the bulging money belts. He looked up at Jennifer. "How much money is here?" he asked, opening one of the pouches and pulling out hundred-dollar bills. When he shot her another glance, his blue eyes were fiery.

"Dammit, Jennifer!" he exclaimed, his tone furious. "Men would kill without a qualm for this. I thought you were talking about a couple of thousand dollars. Who's after her, anyway?"

"I think it's an organized group," she admitted reluctantly.

"Lord, she should have run straight to the police." He looked at her solemnly. "I think your sister's in trouble up to her pretty blue eyes. Someone tried to kidnap her, you said. Can she give a description of them?"

"I didn't ask her."

"She may be as hot as this money. If she can identify the men who tried to kidnap her and they can tie this money to drugs through Rat, she'll be a good witness for the prosecution that someone will want to silence.''

Jennifer drew a deep breath and a chill shook her. ''You think they'll be after her whether we have the money or not?''

''Of course they will! Hell, Jennifer, Garcia will have to call in the Feds. This isn't petty theft. Call your neighbor from here and get her to check on your house as soon as she can. You can put it on my bill.''

As she went into the living room and picked up the phone, Jason crossed the room to the gun case. He removed his holster and revolver and buckled the belt around his hips. Next he took out an automatic pistol and a rifle, then closed the door.

''Sally?'' she asked when she heard her neighbor's familiar voice. ''This is Jennifer. Would you do something for me, please? We've had a break-in and I'm worried about our house. Take Jack with you and have a look, please. You can probably peer in through the kitchen window. You have my phone number here.''

''Give her mine,'' Jason added quietly.

''Let me give you another number, but I'm leaving here soon. It's 555-3172. Everything okay with your family?'' She listened to Sally's affirmative answer and then said goodbye, replaced the receiver and turned to face Jason.

''I need to call headquarters and Garcia,'' he told her, picking up the phone. ''Remember when you call from your place that someone could have tapped your line.''

She stared at him. ''Jason, I'm scared for the boys. I thought when we got rid of the money, that would be the end of it.''

''Not if these guys don't know Goldie got rid of the money, and not if she can identify them. Even if she doesn't remember, they may think she can. Have you talked to her about this?''

Before she could answer, he turned away. "Della? Jason. Something's come up."

Jennifer worriedly stroked her forehead, staring at his broad shoulders and gaining some reassurance from his presence and his calmness. She hadn't thought about Goldie being able to identify anyone and she rubbed her arms, truly frightened now.

She went to the kitchen to get a drink of water while Jason talked in a low voice to his office. When he had finished, he picked up the phone again, and she heard him ask for Sheriff Dan Garcia.

When he hung up, Jason turned to her. "Do you have a lawyer?"

"No, I don't," she said, trying to think whom to call.

"I have a friend who has a mountain home in the area. If he's available, I think he can get to Rimrock about the same time we do. I think Goldie should have someone there."

"Fine. Jason, Goldie may go to pieces. She's never been involved in anything like this and she's accustomed to someone taking charge of everything for her."

"She looks reasonably strong, Jennifer. She may surprise you. And she has to do this. She doesn't have a choice and neither do you. Tonight, and until your house dries out, you and your family will be safe here. When you move back home, I want to stay at your place until this is settled and the men are under arrest."

"They may never be under arrest!" she exclaimed. "You can't stay at our place just to protect us."

"You don't want me there?" he asked, his voice charged with a different emotion. She had a sudden feeling that more was involved here than mere protection for her and her family.

"Yes, I'd like you there, but it'll interfere with your life."

"I wouldn't offer if I didn't want to stay, and you need protection."

"They might not ever come back," she argued, but that protest died as she looked into Jason's implacable gaze.

He lifted a money belt. "I can promise you, they'll be back." His voice was grim. "When there are hundreds of thousands of dollars at stake, they'll be back if for no other reason than to teach Rat a lesson."

"Oh Lord!" she exclaimed, closing her eyes. "I wish to God Goldie had never met that man!"

The phone rang and Jason picked it up. "Hollenbeck." He paused and glanced at Jennifer. "Here she is." He held out the receiver.

"Jennifer," came Sally's voice, and Jennifer felt goose bumps prickle her arms; she could detect fear in Sally's tone of voice.

"Someone's been in the house," Jennifer stated flatly, picturing in her mind how their mountain home had been torn apart.

"Yes. I didn't wait for Jack. I went in the back door, and the kitchen is a shambles. I just left."

"Will you notify the police for me, please. Let them in and give them my number here. Sally, please tell them we've had a break-in here and we're going to Rimrock to talk to Sheriff Garcia."

"Let me write it down," she said, and Jennifer heard the phone clatter. She thought about her artwork and the boys' rooms and the family photo albums.

"I'll call the police," Sally said. "I'm so sorry, Jennifer."

"Thanks a lot. I'll phone you tonight, Sally." She turned to Jason. "The house was ransacked. You heard what I said to Sally."

"I'll call my lawyer friend and we'll go." She watched him pick up the phone and her gaze drifted down to the revolver on his hip. The pistol and rifle were nearby on the sofa and made the menace more real and threatening. Jason talked in a low voice then hung up, turning to look at her.

"Are you all right?" he asked, studying her.

"Yes, but the danger seems much closer now, and looking at all the guns... are they necessary?"

"I hope not, but I want them along. I'm surprised your husband didn't keep guns."

"He did, but he kept them at our home in Santa Fe. I've never fired one."

"Let's get Goldie. Garcia's expecting us now." Jason tucked the pistol into his belt and picked up the rifle.

"Aren't you a little heavily armed?" she asked, wondering what he expected.

"I'm taking the pistol to Terrell and I want the rifle at your house. Do you have a place we can keep it where the boys won't get it?"

"Yes, in my room. They leave my things alone and you can place it on a closet shelf."

"It isn't loaded right now. The other guns are. I'll bring it back when we all come to the cabin tonight, but Terrell and I will be stopping by your house during the day and I want it available. Does your father know how to shoot?"

"He fought in Korea so he should, but I don't think he's owned or touched a gun since then."

"Okay, let's go." He held open the door and locked it behind them.

"I suppose I need to tell the boys to watch out for strangers," she said when they were heading down the mountain.

"Yes, you do, and tell Osgood, as well. None of those mutts are watchdogs. They wouldn't bite a prowler—they'd welcome him."

"They do bark at people, so they let you know when someone is around. General is protective of Dad, but you're right, they wouldn't deter anybody."

"Your bunch will be sitting ducks for anyone who wants you. Three boys, an elderly man, two women who don't know how to use a pistol and five—four—overly friendly mutts."

What he said was true, but now she was endangering him, too. "Jason, the bookie they stole the money from was fished out of the bay with bullet holes in him."

Jason glanced over at her, his expression grim. She rubbed her fingers across her forehead, dreading the task of trying to calm Goldie and praying they could keep her from getting arrested. "I'll be glad when this morning is over. Thanks, Jason, for what you're doing. Always to the rescue," she added wryly.

"This isn't your fault, so you shouldn't have to suffer for it. I know you're worried about Goldie and your family. I'd keep the boys where you can see them."

"Santa Fe won't really be any safer than here. Maybe not *as* safe, because I can keep them closer here." She was silent a moment, worrying about the boys. "I'll tell the boys as soon as we get back from Rimrock. They'll be busy at the house, so they won't wander away from Dad."

Jason slowed as they reached the driveway. Goldie and Terrell emerged from the house and crossed the patio as Jennifer climbed out, and when she looked at Goldie's face, she felt trouble brewing.

"Terrell is going with us to Rimrock," Goldie said, sounding worried.

"I need to speak to Dad before we leave," Jennifer told her, and headed for the house.

Jason came around the Jeep and handed Terrell the pistol.

"Why don't you wait in the car, Goldie?" Terrell said, and she hurried away from them. Jason watched her go.

"She told me about Rat Tabor and the money," Terrell said, his voice harsh. "She's an accessory now. Until today, I thought she had broken off with the guy, that he was history."

"I think it *is* over as far as Goldie's concerned. That's what Jennifer says."

"Yeah, well, I feel stupid. She had to be madly in love with him to do what she did."

"She didn't know you then," Jason said in a half-hearted attempt to cheer his friend.

He might as well not have spoken. "How could she like a guy who would do that to her, place her in such terrible danger?"

"Apparently he's never done anything like this before," Jason said, trying to keep his anger from showing. He hadn't ever known Terrell to needlessly hurt anything or anyone. He was capable and kind and intelligent, and it was easy to see he hurt badly now over Goldie. "I want to talk to Garcia and see if we can keep him from pressing charges, but she'll probably have to agree to testify against the guy.''

"I don't know if she'll do that. She doesn't understand why she might go to jail. There's something very trusting about Goldie.''

"You two are different, but they say opposites attract.''

"What do you mean by that?'' Terrell asked, his voice gruff.

"I mean you're not very much alike and I'm surprised you're attracted to each other.''

"You're not very much like Jennifer, either, but there's something going on between the two of you,'' Terrell countered, glancing beyond Jason to Goldie, who was waiting in the Jeep. "I know we're different. She's flighty and irresponsible—she's even been an exotic dancer.''

"She told you?''

"Yeah, she did. But she's bighearted and kind and optimistic and a lot of things I'm not.''

Jason's thoughts drifted to Jennifer and he understood what Terrell meant. Jennifer *was* unlike him, and he found her carefree warmth more than a little appealing. Hell, even the boys were growing on him. "When they move home, I told Jennifer I'd stay with them at night. I think they're in far more danger than they realize.''

Terrell tucked the pistol into his waistband. "You're right. I've been so damned angry I haven't stopped to think about the danger, but whoever is after the money will be back for it—and Goldie.''

"Jennifer went to tell Osgood to keep an eye on the boys. She'll explain everything to them when we get back. Meanwhile, Garcia's sending out some men to check out the cabin." He heard the back door slam and turned to watch Jennifer stride toward them. She had changed into a navy dress and high-heeled blue pumps. Her legs were long and shapely, and he felt a tug inside. Suddenly he wished he could take her away from all this—somewhere where, for once, it was just the two of them.

They climbed into the Jeep and Terrell sat in the back, talking in a low voice to Goldie. The air was fresh, and the deep blue sky was dotted by white clouds. In the distance Jennifer could see Mount Rainy, while down the mountainside through the trees was the silvery expanse of the tumbling river. She wondered where the Bronco was and what had happened to Oats, though that seemed less important than the immediate problem. Neither Jason nor Terrell could be with them day and night. What if the intruders returned?

She glanced at Jason in his crisp uniform, his hair blowing in the wind, the revolver big and powerful looking on his hip. She hated having guns around the boys, but now there wasn't a choice. When they were finished in Rimrock, she would have to go home and explain everything to her father and the boys.

They wound out of the mountains and followed the highway where it descended into the valley that housed Rimrock. Jason pulled to a stop in front of the one-story stone police station.

With all the money belts in one hand, Jason held open the door with the other, and they entered the lobby of the Rimrock police department. Sheriff Dan Garcia strode out to meet them, his dark eyes resting on Goldie a moment.

"Hi, Dan," Jason said, shaking hands with the dark-haired, powerful-looking man.

"Jason, Terrell," he said, shaking Terrell's hand. He turned to Jennifer, his eyes filled with curiosity. "Hi, Jennifer."

"This is my sister, Goldie MacFee. Goldie, this is Sheriff Dan Garcia."

"How do you do," Goldie said, sounding fearful.

In the hallway behind them a door opened, and Jason turned around. "Here comes Rick." He shook hands with a tall man in rimless spectacles and a dark green suit. He introduced him to everyone except the sheriff, who knew him. When he turned to Jennifer, he said, "Rick, this is Jennifer Ruark, Goldie's sister. Jennifer, meet Rick Waverly."

"Thanks for coming," she said, shaking his hand and feeling hers grasped firmly.

"I'd like to talk to Goldie a minute," Rick said, and Garcia nodded.

"Sure, you can have the first room on your right. I want to talk to Jason. Let's go to my office. If you folks will excuse us, we won't be gone long."

Jennifer glanced at the money belts now in Dan Garcia's thick fingers. He had barely given them a glance. She nodded to Jason then took a seat on a long mahogany bench against one wall.

Terrell moved to the front window, and she noticed he was no longer wearing the pistol. He turned around to look at her. "We're going to be here for hours, Jennifer. I'm going to walk around town, see what's going on."

"Sure," she answered, thinking that very little went on in Rimrock, but she didn't care if he left. She wondered how long they would have to wait; she was growing increasingly nervous about Goldie. And what was Sheriff Garcia discussing with Jason?

Her eyes scanned the empty lobby. The building was only ten years old and still looked new compared to some of the older stone buildings in the town. A receptionist sat behind a desk, and glass doors closed on the hallway leading to the offices. Rick Waverly and Goldie emerged after twenty minutes, and Goldie's eyes were red. She rushed over to sit down beside Jennifer while Rick looked around.

"Where are the others?" he asked.

"Jason and Sheriff Garcia are in the sheriff's office and Terrell said he was going to walk around town."

Rick nodded and walked down the hall toward the sheriff's office.

"Jennifer, Mr. Waverly thinks I have to agree to testify against those men who tried to kidnap me, and I may have to testify that I got the money from Rat."

"Rat should have thought of that before he gave you the money. You'll have to tell the truth in a courtroom."

Goldie started crying. "You were right about Rat. I almost wish he would move away and I'd never see him again, and that's terrible."

"No it's not, Goldie. It just means you're not infatuated with him any longer."

"You're right. Terrell wouldn't do anything so awful to me. He wouldn't get all mixed up in things like this." She spoke in a subdued voice. "I won't go out with Rat again, ever."

Jennifer studied her and hoped with all her heart that Goldie meant exactly what she said.

"Jennifer?" Goldie's eyes brimmed with tears and her voice quavered. "I'm afraid Terrell won't want to go out with me now. He's being nice, but he's angry."

"He'll think it over, Goldie. This all came as a shock. Give him time. And tell him you're through with Rat forever."

"I don't know if he'll believe me. And I've put you and the boys in danger. Terrell said those men will be back, that they won't stop until they get Rat or me or the money."

Jennifer stared out the window at the lazy activities in the broad main street of Rimrock. The sun was shining and columbines bloomed in tubs in front of the police station. An American flag waved in the breeze. Everything looked safe, ordinary, but somewhere out there were men who were tracking Goldie.

She glanced at the glass doors to the sheriff's office and wished Jason would come out. She felt an urgency to get back home to the boys, and her eyes lighted on the pay telephone near the door.

"Goldie, I'm going to call home and make sure everything is all right."

"You think there might be trouble while we're gone?"

"No, but I just want to make sure."

"Jennifer, I'm sorry I caused all this trouble for you."

"Sh. Don't worry. It'll all get straightened out." She hoped she sounded more confident than she felt. She crossed to the phone and made a credit-card call to the house.

"Hello," came her father's voice, and she relaxed a little.

"Dad? We've been delayed here in town and I just wanted to let you know. Is everything okay?"

"Everything's fine. The boys are working outside like mules, and I talked to that insurance man. He'll be here this afternoon. The police have already come and gone.''

''I'm guessing we'll be home in about three hours,'' she said, hoping they wouldn't be that long.

''Don't worry. We're getting things cleaned up in the yard here. Thanks for calling me.''

''Bye, Dad.'' She replaced the receiver as Jason appeared.

''Goldie, can you join us now?'' he asked, and crossed the hall to Jennifer, taking her upper arm lightly and running his finger back and forth. ''Dan wants to talk to Goldie now. Are you all right?''

''Yes. Should I come along? Goldie is so nervous. Jason, she's never been through anything like this before. She doesn't even get traffic tickets. I know she seems flighty to you, but—''

''Honey, your sister's fine,'' Jason interrupted. ''But I don't think you should go with her. Let her fight some of her own battles. It's time. Where's Terrell?''

''He said he wanted to walk around town. I just called Dad and everything is all right there. Jason, I don't think the intruders could have gotten into the house until last night or this morning. It would have been underwater and the road was too deep to ford.''

''They may have come part of the way on foot, but you're right about the time. It was probably early this morning, a couple of hours before we got there. We'll get back as soon as we can, but I have to go now. Dan wants me to sit in while they talk to Goldie. You're okay?''

''I'm fine. I'm just worried about Goldie.''

''*Don't* worry. I think Garcia and the Feds will be very lenient if she'll cooperate.''

"She'll cooperate. She's told me she's through with Rat, and I think this time she means it. She's truly worried about Terrell and what he'll think of her."

"It'll work out," Jason said, and winked. She caught his arm as he started to go.

"You said the Feds. Is that necessary?"

"This involves drug money, and maybe organized crime, and Goldie has crossed state lines. It's a federal case. There's an FBI man with us, Hube Turnbull."

"Oh, Jason, no!" she exclaimed, aghast at what Goldie was involved in. Jason clasped her arm firmly.

"They're being very lenient, Jennifer, and I think Goldie will come through this just fine."

Jennifer looked up into his serious blue eyes. He smoothed her collar and brushed his hand lightly over her shoulder.

"The question is," he said in his deep, solemn voice, "how loyal will she be to Rat?"

Jennifer stared at him, unable to answer. She knew what Goldie had told her, and she wanted to believe it. She *did* believe it! Yet Goldie was so unpredictable....

Jason smiled at her, and her spirits rose again, but as she watched him stride away, the revolver on his hip was a grim reminder of the seriousness of the situation. He vanished through the glass doors and she went back to the bench to wait. After a few moments she crossed over to the phone again to call the insurance agent for the car.

Twenty minutes later Terrell returned and sat down beside her. "They still in there?"

"Goldie and the lawyer are talking to Sheriff Garcia and an FBI agent. Jason's still with them, but he seemed hopeful about it all."

Terrell folded his arms and leaned back, patiently waiting, and Jennifer thought again how different he was from Rat. Terrell was quiet, yet she suspected he would be a tower of strength for her sister.

Finally the glass doors opened and Goldie emerged.

CHAPTER NINE

GOLDIE'S EYES AND NOSE were red and Jennifer's heart went out to her. Terrell moved forward awkwardly, reaching out to Goldie, who rushed to him and stood crying against his chest. Jason spoke briefly to the sheriff and then to Rick Waverly. Another man waited a few feet behind them, and Jennifer guessed it was the FBI agent. As Jason came toward her, she couldn't tell from his expression what had happened.

He took her arm. "We can talk outside, but Garcia wants a word with you first."

Curious, she crossed the hall with Jason. "Jennifer," the sheriff said, "I talked to the Santa Fe P.D. I told them about your break-in at the cabin and the money. Jason said you'll be in the city on Saturday, so would you go by the station and make a report about your house there?"

"Yes, I expected I'd have to see them."

"They've been to your house and checked it over. They'll keep an eye on your place to make sure no one comes back."

"I'll talk to them Saturday," she said, "and thanks for everything."

"Sure." The sheriff turned to Jason. "Keep in touch, Jason."

Jason nodded and took Jennifer's arm. She glanced up at him. "Goldie can leave?"

"Yes, she can," he said, stretching out his arm to hold open a glass door.

Relief made Jennifer weak as she stepped outside into the sunshine.

"I told Terrell we're walking down to the coffee shop. He needs to be alone with Goldie, so we'll meet them back here in an hour. Garcia will come out to look at your house this afternoon."

"Thank heavens this part of it is over," she said, grateful for Jason's quiet strength. "I'm so relieved to be rid of that money."

Jason was ominously silent, and she shivered. Placing his arm lightly across her shoulders, he gave her a reassuring squeeze, but she didn't feel much comforted.

As he walked beside her, the wind caught locks of his black hair. He appeared unperturbed, but she knew he was concerned about the danger to her family. They headed along a wide sidewalk past small shops—a bakery, a shoe store, an ice-cream store. Cars moved slowly up and down the street and kids rode past on bicycles. They crossed a small wooden porch to reach the café, and Jason held open the door. Inside, ceiling fans slowly revolved, cooling the booths lining one wall.

Jennifer slid into a booth and faced Jason. They waited in silence while a waitress brought glasses of water.

"Hi, Jason, Jennifer."

"Hi, Terri," Jennifer said to the tall blonde who had worked at the café for the past three years.

"Sorry your house was broken into. I hope they catch whoever did it."

"How on earth did you hear about it?" Jennifer asked in surprise.

"Terrell was in here this morning to get a cup of coffee and he said you folks were at the sheriff's office. I guess someone was taking advantage of the flood. Terrell said your house will be okay, though."

"Yes, once we get everything dried out and cleaned up. Right now it's ankle deep in mud."

"Too bad. The Wilsons' cabin and the Lomaxes' little house washed away."

"I didn't know," Jennifer said, feeling sorry for her neighbors down the river. "We were fortunate to get out."

"What can I get you?"

"I don't know. I'm really not hungry." She was surprised to see that it was a quarter after eleven.

"Better eat lunch," Jason urged. "What would you like?"

"A grilled cheese sandwich," she replied after a moment. He ordered a hamburger, and then they were alone.

"What happened this morning?" she asked, almost dreading to hear about it.

"Charges won't be pressed against her if she'll be a witness. She gave them descriptions of the men who tried to kidnap her."

"She won't mind doing that, but what about Rat? That's what will be difficult for her."

"If they catch him, she may have to testify against him, but she told Rick she's willing to do that if she has to in order to avoid charges." Jason took Jennifer's hand, his thumb rubbing back and forth across her wrist. "She's going to be all right as long as she cooperates."

"Do you think Terrell will forgive her? He's so quiet, I couldn't tell if he was angry or just solemn."

"He's angry, but he's standing by her, and when he sorts things out, if she truly is through with this guy, then he'll calm down. Jennifer, she has to return to Rimrock two days from now. Terrell said he would bring her to town, and if he can't, I will. She's to meet with an artist who'll come out from Santa Fe and do a composite of the men who tried to grab her. You get her to give you a detailed description of them today, so if you see anyone who fits the description, you'll know. Garcia will talk to the San Francisco department and see what he can learn."

She nodded. "Thank you for talking to the sheriff on our behalf and getting the lawyer," she said, wondering what she would have done without his quiet support.

"Sure. Now comes the bad part. I think those men will be back and they'll want Goldie to tell them where Rat is and where the money is. And when she tells them she turned it in, they aren't going to be happy with her."

Jennifer gazed into his worried blue eyes and felt apprehension growing. "How long do you think it'll be before they'll come back?" she asked, aware of his thumb moving lightly over her knuckles. "The boys are eager to be back in their own place."

"I doubt if it'll be very long. Those guys will be anxious to get their money. Once you move back to the cabin for good, Terrell and I will trade off staying at night. Both of us work in the daytime tomorrow, so you'll have to be especially vigilant when you're there."

"We'll be careful."

"I'd like to teach you to use a gun."

She shook her head and thought again how much like Mark he was. "Mark always wanted me to learn. I can't do that, Jason. I couldn't shoot anyone."

"You could if they threatened any of the boys."

She thought about that, her gaze going past him to the window. "How did we get mixed up in this? It's all so unreal."

"You can thank your sister's boyfriend."

"I hope Goldie means what she says about Rat. She's so softhearted." She prayed her sister wasn't tied to the man by some misplaced loyalty. She forced herself not to think about that. "This morning while I was waiting, I called the insurance agent about the Bronco. The insurance covers a rental until I get a new one, but I have to go to Santa Fe to pick it up."

"I'll take you. I can go Saturday. Let's stay in town and I'll take you to dinner. Terrell can stay at your cabin with the boys."

"That sounds great," she said eagerly. "But Terrell and Goldie were going to go out in Rimrock."

"I think they have a lot of talking to do first," Jason said. "But I'll make sure it's all right."

"I'll have to look at the Santa Fe house and see what the damage is there. Our insurance premiums will probably go up after all the break-ins," she said, but her thoughts were only half concentrated on such practical matters. On Saturday night she was going out to dinner with Jason—their first real date even though they'd been together constantly since the flood—and the prospect was exciting. She saw Terri crossing the room toward them with a large tray, and Jennifer pulled her hand away from him.

Terri placed the hamburger and fries in front of Jason and a grilled cheese and potato chips in front of Jennifer.

"Hi, Jason," came a cheery greeting, and Jennifer turned to see Barbie Watkins. "Hi, Jennifer. Sorry about your break-in. Terri told me. Was much stolen?''

''We haven't sorted it out yet,'' she replied as Barbie came around the counter to their booth. Jason stood and motioned her to sit down with them, but she shook her head. Her smile was for Jason, and then she turned to Jennifer. ''Terrell told us you got washed out and had to stay at the ranger cabin with all your family.''

''That's right.''

''Must have been crowded.'' She looked back at Jason. ''Daddy got that new car he promised me. It's out back and you'll have to see it sometime soon.''

''Sure, Barbie,'' he answered easily. ''What did he get?''

''I'll surprise you—'course in Rimrock, nothing much is a surprise except the dam breaking. I guess you folks had an exciting time of it, didn't you?'' Her last words were directed at Jennifer.

''It was a busy few hours. We still haven't found one of the dogs.''

''Too bad.'' Barbie paused and glanced at Jason. ''I'm glad the water's gone down enough for everyone to get around again. I know you couldn't get out of the park. See you soon, Jason.''

She left and Jennifer bit into her sandwich, feeling the silence stretch between them. Would Jason rather be coming into Rimrock Saturday night and going out with Barbie?

''Jason,'' she said, remembering an appointment she had made, ''next Friday I'm doing a portrait of a rancher who lives north of here, Harvey Roth. He's coming to the house so we can discuss it, and he's bringing pictures. I work from pictures rather than sittings. Even so, he'll be at the house for a short time. If it's going to be dangerous for him, do you think I should cancel?''

Jason thought it over a moment. ''It might be better to avoid any risk.''

''I can call him and ask him to mail the pictures and we'll make the appointment for later.''

''That would be the safest way. And I want you to reconsider learning to use a gun.''

When they had finished, Jason paid the check and they walked back to the station. Terrell and Goldie were waiting, seated on a bench outside. Goldie dabbed at her eyes with a tissue and stood up, climbing into the back of the Jeep. Terrell sat down beside her.

They were quiet on the ride back and Jennifer could feel the tension; Jason and Terrell talked about the park and Terrell said he had called Della while he was waiting. At Jennifer's house Jason stopped in the driveway and Goldie climbed out, hurrying inside while Terrell remained in the back of the Jeep.

''Now comes the hard part,'' Jennifer said. ''Telling Dad and the boys.''

''Look, Terrell and I both wear beepers. If there is the slightest sign of trouble, call for help.''

''I will. And thanks,'' she replied. Both men were reliable and courageous and she was grateful for their presence.

''Why don't you send Will out, Jennifer, and let me talk to him,'' Jason said.

''All right.'' She hesitated. ''Jason, you're not going to give him a gun, are you?''

He shook his head. ''No, I'm not, but don't underestimate your son. He did some fast thinking when he rescued Priss.''

She nodded and climbed out, trying to avoid mud puddles. "Will!"

He came out of the house, smudges of mud from head to toe and his hair a tangle. "Yeah, Mom?"

"Jason wants to talk to you," she said, wondering what Jason would tell him and what he expected Will to do. She walked on to the house, but turned at the door to see Will standing on the driver's side, listening while Jason talked to him. Will nodded his head, a frown creasing his brow, and she realized that in many ways Jason treated Will like another adult. And Will seemed to act more responsibly around Jason. How much would the events of the past few days affect him?

She went inside to find Osgood in the kitchen, washing the refrigerator.

"Everything was ruined, because all the power was gone. I think I got the odor out."

"Dad, I need to talk to you and the boys. I'll round them up. Do you know where Goldie is?"

"She went running upstairs," he said, looking at her with curiosity in his eyes. Jennifer nodded and left to find Brett and Kyle. Will came through the front door.

"Would you get your brothers? I need to talk to all of you and Granddad."

"About Aunt Goldie?" Will asked, standing with his hands on his slender hips.

"Yes. Did Jason tell you about the money?"

"Yeah. He thinks we're in danger and he told me to watch the place. He gave me a radio to wear so I can contact him."

She looked at Will, who sounded confident and so grown-up, and again thought how good Jason was for him. "He didn't tell me he was going to do that. Will, keep Kyle and Brett where you can see them all the time.

Jason said those men will come, and they're very dangerous.''

"I will. Mom, what about our home in Santa Fe? Is it all right?''

"I called Sally from Rimrock, and it's been broken into, too.''

"Shoot!'' he said, kicking the air. "They broke my bank here and took the money, so they probably did that at home, too.''

"Sorry, honey. If that's all we lose, though, it isn't the end of the world.''

"Yeah. I hope they get caught. Man, I'd like to see them hanging around here,'' he said, suddenly sounding like a kid again.

Kyle and Brett appeared, and she motioned to them to follow her to the kitchen, where she told them about Goldie and the money.

Brett tilted his head. "Is Mr. Hollenbeck still going to be around here?'' he asked.

"Yes,'' she answered, aware of how unhappy he sounded. "You don't want that?''

"He's okay, but he's not part of our family, Mom. I thought we wouldn't see him anymore when we came home. Do we have to go back to his place tonight?''

Jennifer nodded.

"He's only trying to protect us,'' Will said. "Can I go now?''

"Yes, you may.''

"C'mon, Kyle. You can help me outside,'' Will said, leaving the kitchen with Kyle trailing behind him.

"We'll stay at Ranger Hollenbeck's cabin tonight, Brett, and when we move back here for good, he and Terrell will take turns staying at night with us.''

"We don't need a ranger here. We'll be safe.''

"We'll be safer with one of them here. Don't you like Mr. Hollenbeck?"

"He's okay, but I don't want him here all the time," he said. Big blue eyes leveled on her. "He isn't going to be, is he?"

She motioned to Brett to come with her and they walked out of the kitchen, leaving Osgood cleaning the stove. "No, he isn't going to be. He thinks those men will come back sometime soon, so you have to stay with Kyle and Will and especially keep an eye on Kyle."

"Okay."

"I'm going to Santa Fe with Jason on Saturday to see about the Bronco."

"When you're in town are you going out with him on a date?"

"Yes, I am."

Brett's jaw thrust out belligerently. "Mom, he isn't going to be our new dad, is he?"

"No, he's not," she answered quietly. "He likes his life the way it is and he's accustomed to living alone. We're friends, Brett, but I enjoy him and I like going out with him."

"I don't want a new dad. I just want our dad."

She hurt for him and hugged him tightly. "Honey, your dad isn't coming back to us. I know you love Dad and you always will. He's your real father, and that will never change." She held Brett away, feeling him stand stiff in her embrace and seeing the anger and hurt in his eyes. "Brett, I like going out with Jason. That isn't going to change anything."

He stared at her and his lower lip jutted out. "I'd rather you didn't go out with him. You kissed him."

"Yes, I did, but that doesn't mean he'll become part of our family. Brett, give him a chance. He doesn't have to take your father's place in your heart.'' She longed to make Brett happy, yet she didn't want to tell Jason to get out of their lives. She wanted his protection and help—and she realized how much she had enjoyed his companionship during the past few days.

Brett started to walk away, then turned back to shout, ''I don't want Mr. Hollenbeck here!'' before running outside.

She drew a deep breath. Brett was having such a hard time accepting Mark's death. His father was gone, and no matter how much it hurt or how much they loved him, he wasn't coming back. She brushed her hand across her eyes and then remembered Goldie and the trouble she was in. Jennifer sighed. Nothing was easy these days.

She found Goldie upstairs in her bedroom, her eyes puffy. ''Jennifer,'' she cried, running across the room to hug her sister.

Jennifer patted her shoulder to calm her down. ''Sit down now, and tell me what happened.''

''They won't press charges if I'll be a witness.'' She looked up and frowned. ''And I'll have to testify against Rat, but I will, Jennifer, because he shouldn't have involved me in this. He shouldn't have given me the money and run out on me.'' Tears welled up again. ''I didn't know I might go to jail!'' She wiped her eyes and sat up straighter. ''I'm in love with Terrell and he's so angry with me!''

''Goldie, you haven't known Terrell very long. You might not really be in love.''

''Oh, yes, I am. He's special, Jennifer. I haven't ever known a man like him and I think he's wonderful, but I don't think he's interested in me anymore. He's furious with me.''

"Did he tell you he's going to stay here at night sometimes?"

"Yes." She took her sister's hand and looked at her intently. "I'm sorry I brought all this trouble to you and the boys and Dad. You know I didn't mean to put you in danger."

"I know. Well, at least we have some protection, and let's hope the men will be caught. Goldie, just be yourself and Terrell will calm down."

"I don't know. He seems like a man slow to get angry and then slow to get over it."

"Maybe not," Jennifer said, patting Goldie's hand, then going to her own room. She closed the door and moved to the window, looking out at the mountainside that now seemed deceptively peaceful. So much had happened in the past few days, and the future was so unsettled for all of them. She thought of how unhappy Goldie and Brett were and of the danger that surrounded her family. That stormy night had swept into her life and turned it upside down. Somehow she felt better knowing that Jason was there for them. She went to her closet and changed into jeans and sneakers so she could help clean.

That night they all piled into the Jeeps and returned to Jason's cabin. As soon as they reached the patrol cabin, Terrell said goodbye and left to go to his own place. Goldie watched him drive away with a forlorn expression, and Jennifer hoped they could work things out between them.

Jason showed Will how to grill the burgers, and after dinner Jennifer glanced from the kitchen to the living area to see Jason seated with Kyle, helping him untangle a fishing line and replace a cork. Will sat close by working on a lure, but Brett was across the room with her father and the dogs.

As the evening wore on she became aware how much Kyle and Will followed Jason around, and how much Brett avoided him. Had Jason noticed? Would it matter to him?

But finally the boys were ready to call it a day as one by one they drifted off to bed. Jennifer waited until they were asleep before voicing her fear. "I wonder if our house is safe," she said.

"There's no reason for anyone to come back and ransack it again," Jason replied. "They must think you have the money with you." He leaned back in his chair at the kitchen table with his shirt unbuttoned to his waist and his boots off. His faded jeans were frayed at the knees, and her gaze kept drifting down the long length of him, playing over the expanse of dark hair showing on his bare chest.

"I need to get back to my artwork, because summer is when I get my paintings done. And I have some lesson plans I want to change and get ready for fall. I hope my things aren't ruined at home in Santa Fe. They smashed the easel I keep here."

"I have one. Some camper left it behind and never claimed it. If you want to go down to the storage shed, I can get it for you."

"That would be great." He slipped his feet into moccasins and she followed him downstairs and outside to a small shed, where he switched on a light. Everywhere boxes were piled high. Tools lined one wall and fishing equipment another, along with a golf bag and clubs and a tennis racket. As he rummaged through things, she noticed a shelf laden with dozens of trophies. She picked one up and saw it was for a swimming championship.

"Jason?"

He turned around and glanced at her and the trophy.

"Are all these yours?"

"Yes, from college and high school."

"Why are they down here?"

He shrugged. "I don't give a damn about them. Mom sent these to me but I should have packed them up and sent them back to Dad. He's the one who really cared about them. I should pitch them, but I haven't yet. That's a lot of my life tied up in those trophies."

Jennifer wondered once again about his relationship with his parents. He might not have had a happy childhood, but he had no trouble relating to her boys. "I really appreciate the time you're spending with my sons," she told him.

"They're easy kids to work with," he said, straightening to look at her, "though Brett isn't happy about my being around. He's changed since Kyle saw me kiss you."

"He misses Mark so badly, Jason. I've tried to tell him we're just friends and that you're helping me and I enjoy being with you and there's nothing more to it than that...." Her words trailed off as she faced him across the crowded, jumbled shed. He was watching her closely, the search for the easel abandoned. She felt caught in his gaze, wondering what was running through his mind. He put down the box he was holding and stepped over another one to approach her.

"There might be more than just friendship, Jennifer," he said in a husky voice, and her pulse skipped. Placing his hands on her shoulders, he leaned down to kiss her.

She felt a rush of warmth inside as she went willingly into his arms, her body pliant against his solid frame. His hands drifted down over her, and she felt a deep longing for him. It seemed so right to be in his arms. She wound her slender arms around his neck, molding her body to his as she kissed him in return.

"Jennifer," he whispered, "I want more than just friendship between us. A lot more." He trailed kisses up her throat to her lips, brushing her mouth and then covering it with his, his tongue thrusting deep as his arms tightened.

Her heart pounded and she returned his kiss, wanting to be held and loved, yet at the same time feeling a reluctance; it was complicated for them to become more than friends. And then logic drifted away and she trembled with need.

His hand lightly stroked her nape while he bent over her, his tongue deep in her mouth, his erection pressing against her.

"Mom!" Dimly she heard the cry. "Mom!"

She pushed against him. "Jason, someone is calling me."

"Mom! Jason!"

She heard the dogs barking as Jason looked into her eyes. He was breathing heavily, but at the next cry of his name, he turned and vaulted a box, racing out of the shed.

CHAPTER TEN

THE BOYS STOOD on the stairs with flashlights in their hands while the dogs raced around, barking madly. The door to the cabin was open, light spilling out across the top steps.

"Mom?" Will asked, looking from her to Jason. "Brett woke up and couldn't find you and got us up. We were scared something happened." Suddenly he sounded embarrassed.

"Jason was getting an easel for me," she said, heading toward the steps. "Sorry you were worried."

"Go with them and I'll find the easel and bring it up," Jason told her.

"We can get it tomorrow," she said, watching Kyle go back inside with the dogs while Brett and Will waited on the steps for her.

"I saw it at the back of the shed. I might as well get it out now." Jason turned toward the shed.

She nodded, then joined Will and Brett.

"Sorry, Mom," Will said.

"That's all right. It was better to check than regret later that you didn't. I didn't think about your waking up and getting worried or I would have stayed in the cabin."

"I was scared something happened to you," Brett said, and she glanced at him. He didn't look the least bit worried, and she wondered if he had really been more concerned about her being alone with Jason. It wasn't like any of the boys to seek her out at night when they got up.

They climbed back into their sleeping bags and she put away cups and saucers in the kitchen and sat down at the table to wait for Jason.

He brought the easel and propped it against the kitchen wall. "There you are, one new easel. Glad I found a use for it. I didn't realize what a clutter I have in the shed. I'll clean it up the first chance I get."

"Which may be a while if you keep giving so much attention to us. It's almost two in the morning, Jason. I'm going to bed."

He nodded, and when she stood up, he drew her to him.

"See you in the morning," he said softly.

She nodded and walked past him, wondering if the boys had heard them.

When she was in bed, she stared into the darkness, remembering what it had felt like being in Jason's arms, wanting his kisses, wanting his touch—wanting him to love her and then loving him in return. Yet that would only complicate their lives all the more.

Before dawn, Will and Jason went fishing, and by seven Terrell appeared to help drive the Ruarks home. As soon as Goldie and Osgood climbed out of his Jeep, he told everyone goodbye and drove away, leaving Goldie looking sad and drawn as she went inside the house. The boys and dogs spilled out of Jason's vehicle, and Jennifer was left alone with him.

"Call me if you see anything the slightest bit suspicious," Jason told her, taking her hand in his. "I wish I could keep all of you with me while I work."

She smiled. "Fat lot you'd get done! We'll be all right." She glanced around. "When the sun is shining and the boys are racing through the house, it's hard to believe there can be any danger."

He placed his hands on her shoulders. "Don't forget for one second that you *are* in danger. All of you. Even if Goldie left now, they might think you have the money or at least know where it is. Honey, you're in it now until someone gets caught."

She felt cold as she listened to his grim words. "We'll be careful."

"I wish I didn't have to go to work. Sometimes Terrell and I have different schedules and then we can be here more often, but today we're both needed at the same time. I'll come by at lunch if I get a chance."

"Don't worry. We'll call if we need help."

He brushed her cheek with a kiss, climbed into the Jeep and drove away. She watched him awhile then turned to find Brett standing a few yards away, a scowl on his face.

"He'll be back tonight, won't he?"

"Yes, he will, and if we can get the house aired out and in any kind of order, we'll all stay here tonight."

"Mom, I don't want Jason here."

He looked so worried she wanted to hug him. "Honey, we need his help and protection. Give Jason a chance, Brett. Kyle and Will like him."

"That's just 'cause he's tried to get on their good side."

"No, it isn't. And he wants you to like him, too. Be fair."

He scowled and turned to run off. Jennifer wondered if he would be the same no matter whom she dated.

She felt a prickle across her shoulders and turned to glance at the swift-flowing river and the dense woods beyond. There were so many shadows on the mountainside, places in the thick of the forest where men could watch without being seen. Should she learn to use a gun? She couldn't imagine holding a gun on anyone, much less shooting them, yet if the boys were in danger, she knew she could. She stared at the dark spruce. Tonight she would ask Jason to show her how to use a pistol.

John Wainworth, the insurance agent, arrived and went over the damage with her, snapping pictures and taking inventory. The place still reeked of muddy water and mildew, but the upstairs at least was livable and they decided they could stay at home.

It was the first time since childhood that Jennifer had seen Goldie so subdued. She hoped that Terrell would stop by or at least phone. Jason had called to say he would drop by, and at one she went upstairs to shower and get ready.

As she pulled on her loafers, Goldie stopped in the doorway. "Jennifer, have you seen Dad anywhere?"

"He was here just a while ago. I thought he was taking the dogs for a walk."

"That was at ten o'clock. It's one now and he hasn't come back."

Jennifer stood up. She didn't need anything else to worry about. "He didn't eat lunch with you and the boys?"

"No. The dogs aren't back and we haven't seen him."

"Maybe he's fishing."

"All his fishing poles are on the back porch."

"That's not like him at all." Jennifer glanced out the window at the mountainside and imagined her father having a heart attack or falling. If he was out there alone, the dogs would stay with him. "You're sure he's not around here?"

"No, he's not in the house."

"Jason should be here any minute. I'll round up the boys and we'll look for him."

Jennifer went downstairs and out to the porch. Goldie was right. Osgood's poles were lined up, the tackle box beside them, so he wasn't fishing. Then where was he? She went to the front of the house and gazed up and down the river. When she glanced at her watch she felt a chill. Osgood had never been gone this long before.

An engine hummed in the distance, then drew nearer. As Jason turned into the yard, she hurried over to him.

He climbed out, striding toward her. "What's wrong?"

"Dad left to walk the dogs hours ago. He's not back and neither are the dogs."

"You're sure he wasn't going fishing?"

"He said he was going for a walk, and all his fishing gear is here."

"I'll call Terrell and see if any rangers can be spared to look for him." He broke off as Goldie ran toward them, a piece of paper fluttering in her hand.

"Jennifer!" Her eyes were brimming with tears.

Knowing something disastrous had happened, Jennifer took the paper and Jason moved close enough to read with her.

To my girls:

I feel I should pack and move on. You both have met nice men who might become serious if you aren't encumbered with an aged parent and four dogs. I feel like a burden and don't want to stand in your way. Don't worry about me. I'll write when I settle and I'll be fine. My love to you and the boys. I know this is best. Dad.

P.S. I couldn't carry the dog food, so it's in the pantry. Give it to the Matthews down the road, because they have two retrievers.

"Oh, no!" Jennifer looked at the road, thinking about Osgood trudging through the mountains.

"I don't think he took much with him," Goldie said. "All his dog things are here."

"He's probably climbed up the mountain to the highway and then he'll try to hitch a ride." Jennifer's father had been raised in an era when hitchhiking was considered safe, and she knew he wouldn't think about the danger. "Nobody's going to let four dogs into their car, and he's too old to be walking that far—and he's probably turned his hearing aid off!"

"Just keep calm," Jason said. "I'll go look for him. I told you, I'll alert the other rangers, then I'll call the highway patrol." He turned to Goldie. "Goldie, if Terrell can't come, he'll get someone to help. How long has he been gone?"

"I'd guess over three hours," Jennifer replied.

"I'll get on the phone now. Call the ranger office if he comes back to the house. That will get word to all of us quickly."

Jennifer nodded, but she was finding it hard to quell the panic rising in her.

Jason placed his hands on her shoulders. "Don't worry. We'll find him. A man with four dogs isn't exactly inconspicuous."

"If he's hitchhiking and someone did pick him up, there's no telling where he might be."

"We'll find him." Jason picked up the radio in his car to make his calls, then climbed behind the wheel.

He raced up the mountain road, descending on the other side to get on the highway and head toward Santa Fe. His gaze continually swept the land ahead and in minutes he was out of the trees and on level land where he could see clearly. Then he slowed for curves as the highway slashed through the narrow canyon, its steep sides streaked by falling water.

Cottonwoods and willows grew along the San Saba River, and Jason continued to drive slowly, because there were innumerable places Osgood could have stopped to rest. "Oh, Osgood," Jason muttered, but he couldn't hold back a wry smile at the old man's eccentricities. He sobered again as he thought of the danger those quirks might have placed him in. Then, as he rounded a curve, he saw Jennifer's father seated on a suitcase beside the road. The dogs were sitting behind him.

Osgood held up his thumb for a ride, and Jason braked, slowed and pulled off the road. He radioed the news to the search parties before he stepped out of the Jeep.

Osgood's eyes narrowed, and he shook his head. General growled.

"It's time to go home," Jason spoke loudly. "Jennifer and Goldie are very upset."

"I don't have your phone, Jason."

"I said, it's time to go home!" Jason repeated more loudly. "Your girls are worried. Please get the dogs and get into the truck, Mr. MacFee."

"Good luck to you, too. Now don't go telling Jennifer and Goldie that you saw me. I'll get a ride in a minute and be on my way."

"Sir, would you please turn on your hearing aid!" Jason shouted in exasperation.

"I know I'll freeze if I wade. I wasn't getting in the river, Jason."

Jason leaned down and bellowed, "You need to come home!"

General bared his teeth.

"I'm tying that dog up and putting him in the back of the Jeep if he doesn't stop that."

"He's not for sale."

Jason wondered if Osgood did this to Jennifer and Goldie. "Turn on your hearing aid!" he yelled.

"I know, that's why we picked it."

"Picked what?"

"Eh? What say, Jason?"

"You picked what?"

"This clearing. It's got shade."

"Sir, I'm putting General in the Jeep."

"You want to keep General? I don't think he likes you."

Jason reached to unfasten his belt. "That dog goes into the Jeep so I won't have to deal with his interference."

"We won't be here long for you to deal with him."

He heard that perfectly. Jason felt his temper fraying.

Osgood stood up. "General. Quiet!" The dog sat down and stopped growling immediately. "You just have to be firm."

Take a lesson, Hollenbeck. "Sir, will you and the dogs get in?"

"Nope. I'm not going back. I'm a hindrance to Jennifer, and maybe to Goldie, too. You might want to marry my daughter someday and you don't need all of us as well as the boys."

"Thank you, Osgood, but Jennifer and I are only good friends."

Osgood stared at him intently, and Jason suddenly had a peculiar feeling in the pit of his stomach.

"Are you going to hurt my little girl?"

"No, sir!"

Osgood continued to look at him. "You're young. If you take on three boys and a wife, you're a bigger man than many. I'm not adding to that burden. And maybe I'm worrying Terrell, too. I don't want to be part of the reason he's stopped seeing Goldie." He sat down on the suitcase and waved his hand at Jason. "Go back, son. Tell the girls I'm fine." He touched his hearing aid. Jason wanted to swear because he suspected Osgood had just turned it off again.

"Sir, will you please get in the car."

Osgood gave him an assessing look. "It's a little early in the day to be looking for a bar. Don't know where there is one, anyway."

"I want you in my Jeep."

"You want to jog in the creek? It's going to be cold."

Exasperated, Jason bent over and took Osgood's arm and motioned to him with his finger to come along. Osgood shook his head and looked at Jason's hand on his arm. Three of the dogs growled.

"Oh, for God's sake!" Jason snapped, glaring at the growling dogs. "Sir, will you please get in!" he shouted in Osgood's ear. The dogs began to bark and snarl.

Osgood reached up to touch his hearing aid. "Eh?"

"Will you get into the Jeep? Jennifer wants you to come home."

"Can't do that, Jason."

"Sir," he said, grasping Osgood's hand, "everyone's very worried about you!"

"Mister, do you need any help?" a driver called out, slowing down beside them.

"I could use a ride to Santa Fe, me and my dogs," Osgood said, standing up.

"Sir." Jason hurried to the van to talk to the couple, who were staring at him with frowns. The woman rolled the window up slightly. "I'm Jason Hollenbeck," he said, "a ranger at the San Saba Park, and this is the father of a friend of mine and he wants to run away from home because he thinks he and his dogs are a burden. I'm just trying to get him to go back."

The couple looked at each other, and the man assessed Jason's ranger uniform. Jason produced his wallet and flipped it open to show them identification.

"We just wanted to help."

"That's nice," he said, returning the wallet to his pocket. "But it's a family matter and it'll get straightened out. Thanks for your concern." As they drove away, Osgood frowned.

"Now why did you do that, Jason?"

Jason walked back to the Jeep and reached inside to get his radio. "Della, call the Ruark house and tell them where I am. I can't do anything with Mr. MacFee and people are stopping because they think I'm trying to harm him. And he isn't helping matters."

He thought he heard a laugh. "Right, Jason."

He walked back to Osgood, who was scowling at him. "Jason, you run along. I'm not going back with you and that's that. And I can't hear you, so don't try to argue with me.''

Had Osgood's daughter inherited his streak of stubbornness? Jason stared at the man, who lifted his chin in a familiar manner.

He squatted down, knowing he was in for a long wait. He pushed his hat to the back of his head and thought about getting his fishing rod from the Jeep, but Osgood might flag down a ride while he was at the river.

A car approached and Osgood raised his thumb. Jason stood up so he would block the driver's view and waved the car past. Another couple drove by, glancing at Osgood.

"Jason, you're a little ornery.''

He smiled and held up his hands, then squatted down again. Osgood looked at him. "You can't stay all day, because you have to go back to work.''

Jason smiled and pointed to his watch.

Osgood turned on his hearing aid. "What did you say?''

"I said your family is on the way to get you.''

"Now why did you do that? Confound it! Do you know how much trouble it was for me to get this far with all these dogs?''

"I can imagine.''

Osgood stood up. "I love my girls and I don't want to cause them grief.''

"Then you should go back home with them.''

"Will you marry a woman who has three boys, an old father and four dogs under her roof?''

"I might,'' Jason said evenly, surprised at his answer. "I just might.''

"Son, I don't think you have the stomach for it. You're mighty nice, but that takes nerves of steel. You can't turn off your hearing."

"No, sir, but I'm adaptable." Why was he arguing this way?

Half an hour later Osgood announced, "Well, here they come." Jason turned as Terrell's Jeep skidded to a stop and the Ruarks piled out. The boys ran to hug Osgood, their eyes bright with tears. Jason went back to his vehicle.

Terrell walked over to him. "Old guy all right?"

"As ornery as ever. And stubborn. It might run in the family. Look, let's get everybody home so we can get back to work."

Jennifer turned and walked over to them. "Thank goodness you found him!"

"He's fine. Look, we'll get you home and then we've got to get back to the park."

"That's fine with me," she said, "but I might need some help with Dad."

In the end it was the boys who convinced their grandfather to come peaceably.

JASON HAD TO WORK a bit later that night to make up for his lost time searching for Osgood, but at last he found himself free to be with Jennifer again.

The boys had gone to bed and Osgood and the dogs had retired for the night. Jennifer sat on the patio beside him, their chairs close together and all the lights off. The front of the house was securely locked and protected by a new alarm system.

Jennifer felt reassured by Jason's presence, and she also felt vulnerable sitting outside. All the dogs were in the house except Priss, who lay at her feet. Priss would bark if any stranger came within several hundred yards of the house, but even then she couldn't relax.

"Osgood seems perfectly content being back," Jason said.

"We had a long talk, and he promised me he wouldn't do that again," Jennifer told him, but her mind wasn't on her father. "I've thought it over," she said quietly. "I suppose I should learn to shoot."

"Good. I have to start work at nine in the morning. If you'll get up a little earlier, we can get in half an hour or so."

"It may take a year before I can be competent with a gun."

He laughed. "If you can hold it and aim in the right direction, you'll stop someone. Most people don't want to take a chance when they're looking down the muzzle of a gun."

"Jason, I feel so tense. This is getting on my nerves, and I worry about going into town this weekend."

"Terrell will be here—and he has Saturday and Sunday off—so don't worry. He'll keep them safe."

"My client, Mr. Roth, is mailing his pictures to me. I'll have to pick them up at the box in Rimrock. I'm getting so far behind on my work. I have three portraits due by next month."

"Maybe you can get back to it now," Jason said. "It looks to me as if you've done as much with the house as you can. It's ready for the professionals to move in now."

"The workmen are coming to repair the walls tomorrow. This weekend if I get time, I'll pick out some new furniture. We're going to repaint once the walls are fixed. I figure Will and Brett and I can manage the painting."

"If you do the painting yourself, can you still get your portraits done on time?" he asked, taking her hand in his and stroking her fingers, then lifting them to his lips to kiss her knuckles lightly.

"Yes, I think so. If it interferes, I'll hire someone, but I think we can do it." He tugged her hand lightly.

"Come sit on my lap," he urged softly.

She moved over and he drew her close to kiss her. She stopped worrying about all her problems and yielded to his kisses, aware of how special he was becoming to her.

Finally she pushed away. "I should go in."

He nodded and they both stood. "I'll see you about five-thirty in the morning," he said, stroking her cheek lightly. "You go inside. I'm going to look around. I'll take Priss with me."

"Please be careful. How will I know when you're back?"

"If you're going to worry, you can wait downstairs. I want to circle the house and yard."

"I'll wait in the front room."

She left him, closing the door quietly behind her. When she looked out the window, the patio was empty. Feeling cold, hating the thought of Jason prowling around alone in the dark outside, she went into the front room. For long, nervous minutes she sat on the sofa and waited, finally hearing the door click in the kitchen as Priss came bounding into the room.

"Everything looks fine," Jason said, joining her.

"Thank heavens. I'm really grateful you're staying here tonight. There are sheets and a blanket on the couch and I put a towel and washcloth out in the bathroom. If you need anything, just help yourself or come and get me."

"I'll be fine," he said, pulling her to him for one more lengthy kiss.

"Good night, Jason," she whispered, her heart drumming. The last thing she wanted to do was leave him, but she turned and hurried upstairs, and it was Priss who stayed behind.

At noon the next day she was sitting in the shade of a tree in the front yard, working at the easel Jason had found her. With a piece of charcoal she shaded in an area on the picture she was finishing, glancing back and forth between the small snapshot she was working from and the drawing in progress. She picked up a pencil with a soft lead and shaded the face.

At the sound of an approaching vehicle, she looked up from her work. It was Jason. Her pulse accelerated at the sight of him and she smiled as he climbed out of the Jeep and strode across the yard.

"Wow, that's good!" he said, studying the drawing, and she felt a rush of pleasure.

"Thank you. I wanted to get it finished so I can deliver it when we go into Santa Fe on Saturday."

"That's really good," he repeated. He turned to look at her. "My folks called this morning when I stopped by the cabin. They're leaving for a two-month cruise. I told them a little about you and your family."

"You did?" she asked, surprised.

He shrugged. "Your family is so warm and close. I've been thinking about it, and I figured that I might be partly to blame for some of my alienation from my parents. Maybe I should start including them in my—" He broke off and shrugged again. "It wasn't a big deal."

"Are you saying my family and I are not a big deal?" she asked, teasing him, and he grinned, leaning forward to kiss her.

"You're a very big deal," he said.

The door burst open and Brett ran toward them. Suddenly he stopped and walked away.

"I'll be back in a minute," Jason said quickly, jogging across the yard and catching up with the boy. He placed his hand on Brett's shoulder, and Jennifer watched as her son jerked away. She pressed her lips together. If only Brett would let go of his resentment and try to get to know Jason.

As Brett ran off, Jason stood watching him, his hands on his hips. He crossed the yard back to her.

"I'm striking out with your middle son."

"Sorry. It's just that he sees you as a threat."

"We were getting along great until he discovered I'd kissed you, so maybe time will help. Is everything okay here?"

"Yes. Maybe those men won't come back. Maybe they've decided Goldie doesn't have the money."

"Then why did she flee San Francisco? They'll figure she's either got the money or knows something about it."

"Well, at least they aren't bothering us now," she said. "So come inside and we'll have a sandwich." She covered the drawing with a sheet of tracing paper and weighted it down. "Peanut butter or ham and cheese? And thanks for bringing the groceries with you last night."

"Ham and cheese sounds good. And you're welcome."

As soon as Will and Kyle spotted Jason, they raced over, and then Osgood joined them. Finally Brett came in, but he kept as far away from Jason as possible. Things were no better between them that night when Jason came to stay. Brett remained aloof, but the sparks between Jason and Jennifer were hotter than ever.

JENNIFER FELT A FLUTTER of excitement Saturday morning as she showered and dressed and gathered her things together to go into Santa Fe with Jason. At last they would have some time alone. While she placed the drawings in her leather portfolio, Brett came into the room and stood watching her.

"Don't go," he said.

"I have to get some new furniture and pick out a new truck and rent a car so we'll have transportation." She turned around to face him. "Look, while I'm gone, you and Will are to take care of everyone. Granddad doesn't hear very well, so it's up to you two to stay on the look-out for trouble and to keep Kyle with you all the time. And for this weekend, you can't go out of Terrell's sight."

"Terrell said we could all go fishing, and he'll have a raft we can ride in tomorrow."

"Great!" she said, although it hurt to hear Brett talk with such enthusiasm about Terrell when she knew how he felt about Jason.

She held Brett's shoulders. "Please, Brett, keep an eye on Kyle."

"Sure, Mom. Don't worry."

She hugged him and he ran out of the room, and she went in search of Will to give him the same message.

Terrell arrived first, looking solemn until the boys began asking him questions about the day's activities, and then Jason drove up. Twenty minutes later Jason and Jennifer were heading up the mountainside toward the highway to Santa Fe.

As they left the muddy park road and turned onto the paved highway, Jennifer put all responsibilities and cares behind her. For one weekend she wasn't going to worry about yesterdays or tomorrows. The last remnants of the winter's snows glistened in crevasses. As they drove out of the mountains, mist was rising off Snow Wind Lake. They passed a basalt-capped mesa that dropped down to slopes covered in piñon and juniper and buffalo grass, then the road cut through a canyon, winding out at last onto a stretch of flat land, the San Saba alluvial fan north of Santa Fe.

"I love this country," Jason said, "and my job is ideal, but living in a patrol cabin isn't all that appealing to most women."

"Have you ever asked one to?"

"No." He grinned and changed the subject. "Where do you exhibit your art?"

"At the Saenz Gallery. I have some things with a gallery in Taos, too, and some in Phoenix. Mostly in Santa Fe, though."

"I'd like to stop at the gallery today and see your work."

"That's fine, because I have to take some other drawings there, anyway." She leaned closer to the open window, enjoying the morning breeze.

The road cut across the caliche and sandstone of the barrancas as Jason took Highway 84 through Pojoaque. Shifting in the seat, Jennifer glanced at him. His dark head turned and he gave her an inscrutable look, then squeezed her hand. "Stop worrying about your boys. I can promise you they're safe with Terrell. He won't let them out of his sight. And you can count on Will to take some responsibility."

"That isn't what you would have said two months ago," she teased, and he grinned.

"I have to admit you're right." His expression became almost wistful. "When I was growing up, I wanted a brother in the worst way. Your boys are lucky to have each other."

"Do you want a family?" The moment she asked, she wondered if she was prying.

"Yes, but I haven't given it much thought." Jason glanced at her and realized that was no longer true. Jennifer and her family were becoming very special to him. "I've always known that someday I would want to marry and someday I would want to have kids. And when I do, I want to be close to them, not too busy to give them my attention. And I hope to God I never push them into things they have no interest in doing. Looking back, I suppose all the athletics Dad pushed me into when I was too small to make my own decisions—Little League and that sort of thing—I suppose in the long run they were good for me. What wasn't good was being made to feel a complete failure if I wasn't the star of the team and didn't make the highest score."

"Maybe that drive—that competitiveness—has helped you do your job so well. When you rescued Kyle, you acted as if you wouldn't let anything or anyone stand in your way. And I don't know what I would have done if you hadn't pulled me out of the San Saba during the flood."

"You can be pretty determined yourself," he said lightly. "I think you would have made it."

"I would have tried my best for the boys."

"I know. Your kids are really lucky. I had a child-hood most kids would envy. I didn't lack for anything I wanted. I had a nice home and got to travel and do all kinds of interesting things. It just wasn't the warm family you have. I've really enjoyed being around the Ruarks."

She laughed. "My goodness, what a change! That first hour at your cabin, you looked as if you'd just as soon step outside and slit your throat."

"Maybe so," he admitted with a grin. "Your boys were a big change in my life, but maybe I needed that change." He looked into her green eyes and pulled her hand up to brush her knuckles with a kiss. "I know I'm glad you were there."

"We've got this whole weekend to look forward to without kids interrupting and dogs howling," she said, and her pulse raced with anticipation every time she looked at him. He was so handsome in the short-sleeved blue shirt he wore and jeans that molded to his long, lean legs.

"What's the agenda?" he asked. "I'm at your dis-posal all day."

"That's nice. First I think I should go home and see the damage and then go to the police station. Then I have a list of errands—and the first is to see about re-placing the Bronco. I want to make arrangements for an alarm system to be installed at the Santa Fe house and I have to see the insurance agency. Then I'm going to shop for furniture." She paused and bit her lip, glanc-ing out the window at the shimmering heat waves ris-ing above the level ground. The blue mountains were in the distance now and she could see the trees and roof-tops of the town. "Maybe everything at home is ru-ined, too."

He squeezed her shoulder. "Just remember—furniture is replaceable."

"I know you're right. I have to go to the art gallery, too, but that can wait till this afternoon. Then I need to go to the bank. Sure you're still at my disposal?"

"I'm here to chauffeur—at least until the sun goes down. Then all the errands go out the window and we have a real date."

At his words she felt her pulse leap. "That's a deal, Ranger Hollenbeck."

They drove into Santa Fe and turned onto Guadalupe. "Where's your favorite place to eat?" he asked.

"La Fonda has great blue-corn tortillas and La Hacienda has good enchiladas. You decide."

He drove past the Plaza, the end of the old Santa Fe Trail, and then the long Palace of the Governors and the La Fonda Hotel. "I'll surprise you tonight."

"Don't you ever want to live in town again?" she asked, looking at the city she loved so much.

"Not in the near future. I like being a ranger and I like the mountains. You must, too, or you wouldn't keep your mountain place."

"I love it up there, but I love Santa Fe, too—the adobe buildings, the art, the people. This town is unique, keeping the old flavor of both the Hispanic and Indian cultures. Oh—turn right at the next corner." She gave directions to the canyon where she lived, and in minutes they were on a winding road with brush and trees on either side, hiding the houses scattered over the canyon walls.

"Take the next turn to the right," she instructed, and Jason whipped off the asphalt onto a narrow dirt road. They rounded a final curve and Jennifer pointed out her house—a sprawling adobe on the side of the canyon.

"You can afford this on a teacher's salary?" he asked as they climbed out of the Jeep. He had been expecting something cluttered and rustic like the mountain house and was surprised at the size and elegance of her home.

"No. My husband bought this on his pilot's salary. Now, with my art and my teaching and his insurance, I maintain it. It's home to the boys."

"You really rough it at the river. This house is a far cry from what I'd pictured." Jason grinned.

"I can imagine," Jennifer said dryly, and then she stood staring at the house. Jason moved closer, sliding his arm around her waist, knowing what she must be feeling.

"Even if it's trashed, you can fix it up again," he reassured her. "You said it's insured, and the insurance people have been very cooperative."

"There are pictures and things that I'm sentimental about. I hope they didn't destroy those."

He took the key from her hand. "Let's stop standing out here worrying about it and go see." He turned the lock, bracing for the worst. The damage inflicted mirrored that at the cabin. Drawers had been pulled out, their contents scattered over the floor. A mirror had been torn off the wall. Jennifer stepped through the entryway grimly and put her purse on a kitchen counter cluttered with jars and spices and broken dishes. Canvases were propped against the walls, and he studied them. "This is your work?"

"They didn't destroy it? Thank goodness," she said, brushing back her hair and looking at the open cabinets.

"Jennifer, you may be the most wonderful teacher in the world, but you're a damned fine artist. Why don't you do this full time?" he said, looking through the pictures.

"Every year I toy with the idea of quitting, but it seems a big step to give up the regular paycheck and the pension and insurance for the precarious security of an artist," she answered distractedly, her thoughts on the chaos at her feet. "I'm going to look at the rest of the house."

Jason followed her out of the kitchen. Jennifer Ruark was a complex woman, he thought. She gave herself almost totally to the practical side of life, and yet tucked away inside her was an incredible talent, one she should have the time and resources to develop.

She led him through an open hallway with thick wooden posts dividing the rooms, a dining room to the left and a sprawling living room to the right. The destruction was throughout. Chairs had been slashed, pictures yanked off walls, furniture overturned. Even the plants had been ripped out of their pots and soil scattered over the floor. Yet beneath the present chaos, Jason could tell that this would be a comfortable, cheerful house. The walls were white plaster and the earth tones of the furnishings were brightened by colorful cushions and throws. The ceilings were timbered, and wide-arched doorways led from room to room.

He stepped over a cushion and bent down to pick up a picture from the floor. It showed a younger Jennifer with a baby in her arms, probably Will, and a handsome, curly-haired man standing beside her. Mark Ruark was smiling at the camera, and Jason set the picture down carefully on a table.

"If I hadn't already started learning to fire a gun, I would now," Jennifer said grimly. "I guess I could shoot someone if I had to, because this makes me so angry.''

He nodded. "Let's check the rest of the house and make the police report. You can stay at the hotel tonight. I'll call and make a reservation.''

"I can stay here.''

"If you stay here, I stay here, so while we run your errands, how about my getting a cleaning crew out here and getting this place in order?''

"Oh, Jason, that would be great!''

He went to the phone to make the arrangements, and a short while later he joined her in the dining room.

"Thank heaven, they didn't break things in here. My good linens will have to be washed, but the damage could have been much worse.''

"The cleaning crew will be here in twenty minutes.''

They walked down the hall to a large bathroom and then to a bedroom with bunk beds and football posters. Toys and the contents of emptied drawers were strewn everywhere, but Jason found himself concentrating more on the tempting fragrance of Jennifer's perfume and her soft, lightly freckled shoulders, bare except for the skimpy straps of her sundress. It was all he could do not to bend over and brush her bare flesh with a kiss, and the realization that no bra covered her full breasts beneath the blue cotton dress tantalized him still further.

"This is Kyle and Brett's room," she said, then moved down the hall to another bedroom. "And this is Dad's room.''

It was a large bedroom with a fireplace. Books had been pulled off the shelves and clothes dragged out of the closet. The various hoops and props used in the dog act were scattered around the room. They went farther along the hall to check Will's bedroom, where a tank of fish remained intact.

"Who feeds the fish?"

"Chase. Will's friend next door."

They turned a corner in the hall and entered a bedroom isolated from the others. In spite of its present upheaval, the room looked inviting. It was large, with sliding glass doors, a fireplace and a king-size bed. Paintings were lined against the walls—Western scenes in watercolors and acrylics. Several easels lay toppled on the floor. Jason walked over to the glass doors and looked out at a hot tub in an enclosed deck surrounded by a ten-foot-high fence.

"You enjoy the hot tub?"

"Sure. It's a great way to relax."

"You and the boys and your dad and the dogs?"

She laughed, adorable dimples appearing. "We don't all get in at once. Actually, it's pretty much mine so far. To the boys, it's too much like taking a bath, and they're at the stage where they balk about a nightly washing. Dad doesn't like it and the dogs aren't allowed."

She disappeared into a walk-in closet and in a minute he heard an exclamation.

"Are you all right?" he called.

"Yes," she replied, reappearing with a large photo album. "They didn't destroy my pictures."

He crossed the room and took the book from her, then pulled her into his arms and hugged her. "Let's go down to the police station and you can make your report. When we get back, the cleaning crew will have this place in much better shape." He gave her a squeeze and then held her away, looking at her with concern. "Are you okay?'' She smiled and nodded and left to call the insurance company.

The doorbell rang, and Jason answered it to find the cleaning crew. ''Come in,'' he said. ''I'm Jason Hollenbeck.''

''Mae Whitcomb,'' a matronly woman introduced herself as three other women in yellow slacks and yellow shirts entered the house.

''I made arrangements for a double crew because the house has been broken into,'' Jason said, glancing at the peaceful street and closing the door behind them.

''Yes, sir. We were told about it.''

''Look, try to get this in as good a shape as possible by six o'clock.''

''You understand it's time and a half,'' Mae Whitcomb said.

''That's right. I've also called a florist, and some flowers should arrive this afternoon. Could you put them in the living room, please.''

''Yes, sir.''

''The family is away and we're the only ones coming and going. If anything suspicious bothers you, call the police.''

''Is anything likely to happen?'' she asked, giving him a keen look. He shook his head.

''No. But the house was ransacked, so I thought it might be wise to be extra careful.''

''We will be,'' she replied while the other women disappeared down the hall.

''The agency said they would send a bill.''

''Yes, sir.''

He pulled out his wallet and peeled off several bills, handing them to her. ''This is extra. I know you'll do a good job.''

"Thank you, Mr. Hollenbeck," she said, flashing him a broad smile as the money disappeared into her pocket.

He found Jennifer placing spices on a rack in the kitchen. Taking her arm, he headed toward the door. "The cleaning crew will do that. Let's get started—you've got a long list of things to do."

Jason drove her to the police station and then took her to pick up the rental car. At that point they parted, agreeing to meet again for lunch.

By one o'clock they were seated on a shaded patio with a splashing fountain, and Jennifer ran over her list of things to do. "Now all I have left is to shop for furniture, go to the bank and stop by the gallery."

"What did the insurance people say?"

"I have to turn in a list of damages and then we'll settle. This morning it didn't look as if the furniture was as badly damaged as up at the cabin."

"It may not have been. Was Goldie in your home here with the money?"

"No. She came the night the dam burst, and whoever is following her probably knew that." She smiled, changing the subject. "You're welcome to come furniture shopping with me."

"Sure."

She laughed. "I didn't think you'd want to. That seems like the last way you'd want to spend your Saturday afternoon in Santa Fe."

"I think I can find shopping for furniture fascinating if it means I get to spend the afternoon with you." He gazed at her, his eyes as blue as a mountain stream.

She smiled back at him, feeling some of the burdens of the day lift. Lunch was enjoyable, and she was glad he would be with her all afternoon. She reached across the table to take his hand.

"You've been great, Jason. Thanks for all you've done."

Something flickered in the depths of his eyes and he wrapped his hand around hers, giving it a squeeze. "Shall we get started?"

"I suppose."

Thirty minutes later they stood in an aisle looking at rows of sofas. She purchased new ones for both homes and two armchairs for the mountain place. With Jason wandering around behind her, she bought new mattresses and made arrangements to have them delivered the following week. Sally would let the deliverymen into the garage and the boys would carry them to the beds later. Next she bought pillows and a new wall clock to replace one that had been smashed.

Finally, as they placed the pillows in the rental car, she turned to Jason. "I'm exhausted. I'd like to call the gallery and go there tomorrow."

"Fine. Then we'll call it a day. Now, do we both check into the hotel or do I take an extra bedroom at your place? You can't stay alone."

"Do you mind sleeping on a slashed mattress? The new ones won't be delivered until Monday."

"No. It can't be any worse than a sleeping bag on the floor."

"I'm sorry. You haven't been in your own bed since you met us. If you can stand the ripped mattress, I'd rather be at home tonight."

"Sure, home it is."

"My neighbors are going to ask questions about you."

"Does that bother you?"

"No," she said, smiling at him. "I can explain that you're there to protect me."

"Okay. I'll get my Jeep and meet you at your place." He caught her arm as she started to get into her car. "If you get there before I do, wait for me before you get out."

"When you say things like that you scare me."

"Let's not take any chances, okay? Will you wait for me?"

She nodded, wondering how long she was going to have to be so careful, worry about the boys, look over her shoulder, watch every shadow.

She climbed into her red rental car and pulled away from the curb, passing him as he strode down the street toward his parked vehicle. She glanced at him again in the rearview mirror, watching his long stride, feeling excitement grow as their evening together drew near.

As she drove up the winding canyon road, she kept glancing in her mirror. The road behind her was deserted. As she looked at the trees and brush lining the canyon, she realized how isolated her house was, even though she was in a residential area.

Jennifer arrived before Jason, and the cleaning crew's van was gone. Feeling ridiculous, she sat and waited, and in minutes the Jeep came up the driveway and stopped beside her. She got out and started to hand Jason an armload of pillows, but when she turned, she stopped in her tracks as she stared at the pistol in his hand.

"Jason?"

"That's a big house. I don't want to take chances. Give me the key and let me go in first."

"I can't do this every time I come home."

"No, but you can this weekend while I'm here. Let me have the key."

She handed it to him and watched while he went to the back door and quietly opened it, flinging it wide and rushing inside.

Finally he reappeared and came out to help her with the pillows. "It's fine."

She walked into the kitchen, stopping in amazement to look at the orderly room. "Oh, Jason! I didn't think they could get this much done," she exclaimed. "This is wonderful!"

"That's what they were hired to do. Where do all these pillows go?"

"Just put them on the table."

"I'll put them in the bedrooms," he said dryly, locking the kitchen door. "When will the alarm system be installed?"

"Not until I'm back in town and can make arrangements for them to come while I'm here."

Jennifer walked down the hall and into the living room. Except for pictures hanging in different spots and slashed cushions, the room looked normal.

"Jason!" she cried, noticing the huge bouquet of cut flowers—red roses, yellow, white and blue daisies, white baby's breath. "Jason, this is wonderful and the flowers are beautiful!" She flung her arms around his neck, smashing pillows between them while she kissed him. "Thank you for the beautiful flowers! And thank you for calling the cleaning people. I never even thought about hiring a service to put everything in place. I can't tell you how wonderful it is to come home and see everything almost back to normal."

"Anything to help, hon," he said softly, his gaze roving over her features. "See, time will pass and all this will get straightened out and your life will return to normal."

She wondered if it would ever be like the way it had been before she met him. She moved away, picking up the pillows she had dropped.

"Which bedroom do you want me to take?"

"Mine is the big one, so you can have any of the others. You can choose between football posters or dog hoops."

He grinned and picked Will's room, which was the closest to hers. He glanced at his watch. "I'll make dinner reservations for seven, okay?"

"Fine. How about a drink and a soak in the hot tub?"

"That's the best offer I've had today," he said, handing her the pillows. As she started past Will's room, Jason thrust his head back into the hall. "I didn't bring a swimsuit."

"Wear your jeans—they'll dry."

"Sure you don't want to go in the buff?"

She laughed and didn't bother to answer as he disappeared back inside the bedroom and closed the door.

Twenty minutes later she sat in the steamy water and sipped a margarita made by Jason while a cool breeze blew across her shoulders.

"I can understand why you like Santa Fe so much when we're sitting out here," he said. He had been under the water and his hair was in tight, damp ringlets, reminding her of the first morning when he had jumped into the river to rescue her. "This is peaceful, shut off from the world, but I guess it's not like this when your family's here."

She smiled. "When the boys aren't in school, they spend most of their time watching television. You've changed that, you know."

"What? Watching television?"

"Yes. Now they want to go fishing every chance they get, and with Terrell taking them down the river in a raft, I have a feeling there will be one more thing they'll like to do outdoors. I just hope they'll find more new interests when they're back in Santa Fe. Mark was a doer, not an observer, and he didn't have time to sit back and watch the boys learn."

"Sometimes they just learn by watching someone."

"He didn't take them with him very often, because they were younger then."

Jason sank down into the water and leaned back, closing his eyes. His arms were stretched out, one hand lazily stroking her bare arm, the other resting along the back of the tub, his hand holding the cold margarita. Her gaze drifted over his thick lashes—dark against his prominent cheekbones—his mouth, the slight stubble on his jaw. Then her attention shifted lower to his muscular chest, the mat of damp dark curls, his narrow hips enclosed in the faded jeans. She drew a deep breath, feeling a stir of longing for him, wanting him to turn and kiss her.

She turned to watch the mulberry leaves flicker in the breeze over the patio, wondering if they were safe staying at her house tonight. She felt warm, relaxed and contented, more than she had in a long time, and she knew it was because of the man beside her.

She thought about what he had said earlier about her artwork. The time was coming when she would have to let the school know if she didn't intend to return. New teachers were hired in August. She glanced at Jason, remembering what he had said about doing the work you like. If she concentrated on her art, she would have more time for the boys.

"Okay," Jason said softly, "a penny for your thoughts."

"I was debating about whether to teach another year or to quit."

"And..."

"I haven't come to a conclusion. When I think of all the security I have, I can't bear to give it up."

"I thought you said you have insurance money from Mark."

"I do, but the other makes everything very secure and comfortable. Art can be sold one day and not the next."

"Not the way you draw. The real question is, can you support yourself with it—and I'm sure you can—and which do you enjoy the most?"

"You're right. I can make a living from my art. Combined with teaching it gives us a very comfortable life-style. And, yes, I enjoy art the most."

"How much of that comfortable life-style would you have to give up if you retired from teaching?"

She thought about it. "If I could draw all year as much as I do in the summer, I might make more than I do teaching. Maybe it's just losing the security that frightens me." She sipped the margarita. "I almost forgot to tell you. While I was putting on my swimsuit—"

"Which is gorgeous," he said in a deep voice.

She smiled. "Thank you. I got a call from the insurance agent. Someone found the Bronco. It's been submerged in the river. It was almost at Rimrock."

"I'm glad they finally found out what happened to it. Are you ready to go to dinner?"

"That sounds good," she said, turning to look at him and gazing into his blue eyes. His hand slid behind her head, and he drew her closer to kiss her long and passionately, finally releasing her.

"Off to dinner," he said in a husky voice, studying her. "I can't believe I have you all to myself for hours this evening. No drums, no trumpets, no howling dogs."

"I'm looking forward to it too, Jason. I haven't had a date with a handsome man in oh, so very long."

"Oh, really?" he asked, his voice teasing. "A handsome man? That's a bulletin. Maybe we'll skip dinner and stay here," he said, drawing her closer.

She laughed and wriggled away. "I know you don't go without three meals a day, and it's been a long time since lunch."

"My stomach agrees with you, but the rest of me wants to stay right here." He stood up with a splash, his wet jeans molding his body, his arousal obvious. Her gaze flicked over him before she turned away, easing herself out of the tub and grabbing her towel. "Meet you in the living room."

"Aw, shucks. I was hoping you were going to say, 'Meet you in the shower.'"

"No such luck, Hollenbeck. Out," she said, pointing toward the hall.

With a grin, his gaze drifting down over her turquoise swimsuit and long legs, he closed the door behind him. Jennifer stared after him and began to smile.

CHAPTER ELEVEN

As THEY SAT ON THE PATIO of La Hacienda, three guitar players strummed music in the background and the smell of sizzling fajitas filled the air. Jennifer sipped ice water and gazed across the table at Jason, wondering if he had enjoyed the past few hours as much as she had. "This is heaven, Jason. I haven't sat down to a quiet dinner in a long time. During the school year we have such hectic schedules with band practice and Will playing basketball in the spring and my teachers' meetings."

"I don't know how you juggle it all around," Jason said, quietly studying her while he drank a cold beer. Realizing how much he enjoyed being with her, he wondered if his life would seem lonely when he settled back into his old routine. Somehow he couldn't imagine life without Jennifer and the boys. He'd promised Will he would take him along on his park duties again one day soon, because Will seemed interested in Jason's work. And he couldn't imagine long days on end without seeing Jennifer or talking to her. Since he had started back to work after the flood, he had missed seeing her during the day.

"I've been thinking about what you said."

"What's that?" he asked with amusement. "I think I've said a lot of things."

"About doing the work you like. I'm going to make the change this year. I'm going to turn in my resignation to my principal."

"You feel you can manage all right?" he asked, pleased by her decision.

"I think I can. I've gone over and over the figures. I almost made this decision last summer. Actually, I figured my income pretty much on what I'm making now, plus the income that I receive from Mark's insurance. I should do better than that, though, because I'll be drawing all year instead of only three months. If I don't succeed, I'll go back to teaching."

"Can you go back?" he asked, watching the play of light in her large green eyes. She was a beautiful, exciting woman and he admired the way she had juggled two careers while taking care of a large family. It was time she had a life of her own.

"Yes, I'm sure I can," she said, shaking her hair away from her face. It curled softly over her shoulders and the turquoise cotton sundress brought out the green in her eyes. His gaze drifted over her bare shoulders, and he longed to reach out and touch her. "I can substitute-teach, too, if I want to."

"That's great," he said, suspecting she was being very conservative in her estimates about her income from her art.

"I'm happy about it. Scared, too, because I feel so alone. I'm not accustomed to stepping out of my groove."

"You'll do great. You already are."

"I think I'll talk to an agent about handling some of my work, because an agent can make contacts I can't."

"So this is a celebration dinner to mark your new career. We should have champagne," Jason said, lifting the bottle of beer, and she smiled at him, her eyes lighting up with pleasure. He motioned to the waiter.

"Jason, you don't really have to order champagne. It's not that big a deal."

"Yes it is. A night to remember—the start of a whole new career." He looked up as the waiter approached. "We'd like a bottle of champagne, because we're celebrating."

She listened while Jason discussed various brands with the waiter and finally selected one. She felt reassured by his confidence in her, knowing she was taking a big step and a risk for the boys as well as herself, but it seemed like a good thing to do. She studied Jason as he talked, his navy-striped sport shirt open at the throat, his dark skin exotic looking in the evening light. Her gaze drifted down to his strong hands, so competent whether handling fishing rods or his Smith & Wesson, yet so gentle when he touched her.

"You didn't need to do that," she said when the waiter left.

"I wanted to, because tonight is very special," he said softly, and she gazed back at him as he watched her steadily.

He caught her hand and held it, and she felt another deep rush of longing, aware of how important he was becoming to her.

"I've had a good time today," he said.

She laughed. "Sure, shopping for pillows is a wonderful way for a park ranger to spend his Saturday."

He smiled and shook his head. "It was more fun to be shopping for pillows with you than to be sitting out on the creek alone," he said quietly, and she felt a catch in her heart.

"That's quite an admission from a man who loves his solitude." Her tone was solemn. "I'm glad, Jason, because I've enjoyed the day, too."

The waiter appeared and popped the champagne, and Jennifer watched it bubble in the glasses. When they were alone, Jason raised his glass.

"Here's to a great future for you, Jennifer."

"Thank you," she said, touching his glass lightly and taking a sip, wondering how much he would be a part of that future. Bubbles tickled her nose and the champagne tasted perfect, not too sweet. She felt carefree just being with Jason. Her gaze drifted across the patio. Strings of colored lights and bright piñatas hung from the ceiling, and ropes of red chili peppers wound around the wooden posts that ran up to the latticed roof. Most tables had couples, while in the center of the room was a large party of twelve. Across from them a dark-haired man sat alone at a corner table. Her gaze returned to him, sweeping over his plaid shirt, his thick hands and neck. When her eyes lighted on his fingers, wrapped around a glass of beer, a chill raced up her spine.

"It may be my imagination or just coincidence," she said, looking back at Jason, "but there's a man eating alone at a corner table who fits the description Goldie gave me of one of the men who tried to grab her off the street."

"Describe him if you can without looking at him again," Jason said quietly.

"Dark hair, dark eyes. The description would fit half the men in the room, except Goldie remembered his index finger was cut off at the knuckle. I noticed this man holding his beer and the tip of his finger is missing."

"Goldie did a good job if she got that much when she was being wrestled into a car."

"Goldie notices men," Jennifer said dryly. "She's very aware of them physically."

"Make a damned good witness. I knew Garcia was pleased with the composite and pleased with her cooperation. I'm going to the men's room and I'll stop at a phone. There's a man I'm to call if I see anything suspicious."

"Suppose I'm completely wrong?"

"He'll never know. The police will just watch him."

"He's following us and someone will follow him?"

"That's about it. They can't accost him in the restaurant. He's not doing anything and he can deny following us. I'll be right back."

He left, and she watched him stride away. Her gaze roamed back to the man again, who was looking at Jason now. The bubbly excitement of the evening was dulled by the threat of danger. Certain now, she wondered how long someone had been following them.

She was glad when she spotted Jason's broad shoulders and watched him weave through the tables and sit down across from her again. "It's done."

"He noticed you as you left the room. Do you think he followed us from San Saba?"

"No. I think he picked us up here. I was careful to watch whether anyone was behind us when we left the park. I've kept an eye out most of today, but I slacked off when we came here tonight." He looked at her warmly. "My attention was elsewhere. I'll have to be more careful."

They drank one more glass of champagne and then left without glancing at the dark-haired man. As Jason moved through the traffic, she twisted in the seat to look at him.

"Are we being followed?"

"Yes, we are," he said, leaning across her to get his revolver from the glove compartment and place it beneath the seat.

"That isn't very reassuring, you know. Should we go home?"

"Sure. We'll be safe enough. Don't worry about it."

"You aren't worrying about him trying to get us or break into the house?"

"Let him try," he said tersely. "I can get help instantly, and the police will be watching him, anyway."

She relaxed slightly. "I feel better about that. When we get home I want to call Goldie and see if everyone is all right."

"Sure, but I can promise you, they're just fine."

As they drove up the driveway to the darkened house, she shivered again and Jason reached over to give her shoulder a squeeze. "I wish I had left lights on at the house," she said.

"We're all right...relax," he urged as he came to a stop and climbed out to open the door for her. In the kitchen he locked the door and Jennifer went straight to the telephone to call her family.

While she talked to Goldie and then Will, Jason disappeared. As she replaced the receiver, she turned around to see Jason leaning against the doorjamb, his long legs crossed, two chilled margaritas on the counter. He picked them up and waited. "How about some quiet time in the hot tub?"

She nodded. "Sounds fine to me. Jason—the patio has a fence. If someone stood on the other side of it, could they hear our conversation?"

"We'll put on some music and talk softly so no one will hear us. If the man following us comes that close, the police will pick him up and charge him."

"With what?"

"Trespassing, Peeping Tom—there should be several interesting possibilities. Let's go, love."

In minutes they were in the warm, swirling water sipping the salty drinks while music from a CD played softly in the background.

Gradually she relaxed as Jason did his best to divert her. He was pale in the moonlight, the mat of hair across his chest a dark shadow. They talked for more than an hour while he gently stroked her arm and shoulder, his hand drifting over her nape. Gradually she forgot the danger and became intensely aware of Jason beside her.

"I want you to meet my folks sometime."

"They don't sound as if they would like my family. My boys don't win trophies or excel in sports. And look at Dad and his dog act. That's a bit much for a lot of people."

Jason laughed softly, his hand drawing circles over the back of her neck. "Your boys are great kids and probably a thousand times more well rounded than I was at that age. They'll excel somewhere down the line. And if they don't, the world won't end. Lord, I'd never push a kid to win the way I was pushed. And as for your dad, Osgood is unique. My parents are the difficult ones. At least your family is adaptable."

"I suppose we've had to be," she murmured, barely aware of her words. All evening, desire had been building in her, and as their hips touched, she felt a quivering longing for his arms to be around her.

"Jennifer," he said softly, and she turned to look at him, knowing this man was so special, so important to her. He drew her to him, and when his gaze lowered to her mouth, she couldn't get her breath. His lips covered hers, and she returned his kiss with a passion held too long in check. With a soft splash she wound her arms around his neck, and he pulled her close, sliding her warm, wet, pliant body over his, her breasts pressed against his solid chest.

She trembled with need, feeling his hot arousal press against her, the warmth of his body excited her. His hand slid along her ribs, his thumb caressed the side of her breast, and then slipped down over her hip.

His kisses were hot, demanding, and intensified her desire. He shifted her, sitting her on his lap and peeling her suit away. Closing her eyes and tilting her head back, she gasped with pleasure as he cupped her breasts in his large hands, his thumbs rubbing lightly over her taut nipples.

Jason ached with need, trying to curb his passion and love her with care. Her enticing breasts were full, beautiful in the pale moonlight, filling his hands with such softness that he felt consumed by a longing for all of her. She was warmth and laughter, and he needed her badly. He lowered his head to take her nipple in his mouth, feeling her fingers wind in his hair and listening to her soft moan as he kissed the hard bud.

"Jennifer, I want you," he whispered with an urgency that had been building for days. Moving aside with a splash, he stood up and peeled away his tight, wet jeans, his hands yanking at the buttons. Moonlight played over his virile body, splashing a silvery sheen on his broad shoulders, showing the ridges of bone, the curve of firm muscles.

Jennifer looked up at him in awe. His shaft was dark against his flat, pale belly and she reached up to caress his throbbing, heated flesh, hearing his deep intake of breath. Her gaze traveled the length of his body to rest again on the dark hair between his thighs, his strong legs, the silvery drops of water on his skin. His body was taut and ready, and she drew a deep breath. She caressed him, then leaned forward to trail her tongue over him.

Reaching down with his hands under her arms, he picked her up and pulled her wet body against his. His erection pressed against her feminine mound.

"Jason, I want you," she whispered, knowing she did, her heart pounding with joy. He held her hips, bending his head to kiss her, sinking back down and pulling her onto him while he caressed her everywhere. They wound together in the water, their heated, slippery bodies moving sensually. His hand slid lower between her legs while she gasped with pleasure.

"Go on, baby, let go. Oh, Jen!" he groaned, his fingers exploring her softness, caressing her until she tensed and clung to him tightly. Her body arched in a spasm as she climaxed, clinging to him tighter. "I want to love you all night, to find what pleases you."

"Jason—" Her words were bitten off as he kissed her again, his hands driving her to a greater need. She wanted him desperately. She was ready, eager.

Jason felt he would burst. Hard and hot, he wanted her softness to surround him, to ease his raging desire. This woman was so many things to him now. He tried to hold his own need back, kissing and stroking her, discovering what gave her pleasure, learning the secrets of her body. She gasped with pleasure, writhing beneath his touch, tugging at him.

"Jason," she whispered, "please—"

Jennifer's heart pounded wildly. His body was a marvel of maleness, hard planes and muscle. He stood up, took her hand and pulled her over to lie on the chaise to feel her beneath him. He trailed kisses down her stomach, between her thighs. His tongue flicked over her as her body arched to meet him.

Suddenly she sat up between his spread legs, caressing him, leaning forward, her tongue touching him. He gasped with pleasure as she kissed and stroked him until he knew he was in danger of losing all control. He shifted her until she was lying back, his legs between hers, and he spread her smooth thighs apart. His shaft touched her, easing in slowly, filling her. He felt he would lose himself in her softness as he gave in to his driving hunger, thrusting deeply, hearing her quiet moans of pleasure.

"Jason," she gasped, her head thrashing back and forth as she clung to him, her long, slender legs wrapped tightly around him. Jennifer's heart pounded violently as she slid her hands over his powerful body. "Jason, please," she whispered, raising her hips to meet him, knowing he was holding back to please her while she was nearing the edge of the abyss. She wanted to give to him, to be one with him, because he made her feel complete.

He turned to kiss her passionately as he thrust deep, deeper. She clung to him, her cries muffled by his kisses as his rigid shaft took her to a peak. She cried out and they rocked together. Ecstasy burst inside, and she buried her face against his neck as Jason plunged into her, his arms tightening around her.

"Jennifer," he said, his voice a rasp, "I love you." He shuddered with release at last, his body tensing and shaking.

She slowly came back to reality, to her world, her house. To the marvelous, special man who held her tightly while their hearts pounded in unison. He rolled

over, keeping her with him, his leg wrapping around
hers and his arm pulling her close. They both struggled
for breath as he showered kisses over her cheek and ear
and temple.

Jason shifted to look into her eyes. "Jennifer, I love
you," he repeated, gazing into her eyes with a direct-
ness that took her breath away.

Her senses reeled from the past few minutes of rap-
ture. "Jason, this seems so right," she said tenderly,
kissing the corner of his mouth.

"It is," he answered solemnly. He raised himself
slightly and looked down at her. "I haven't felt this way
before and I need you, Jen," he said in a husky voice
that made her heart pound with joy. She stroked his
cheek, feeling the slight stubble of new beard.

She felt dazed, satiated with physical pleasure, but
her emotions ran much deeper, a satisfaction of heart
and soul, because it *was* right to be with Jason. He filled
the empty spaces in her life. She turned her head against
his neck and clung to him tightly, fighting tears.

"Hey!" he said softly, tilting her chin up. For a moment she tried to resist, pulling against him.

"Jason—"

"Honey," he said, the tenderness in his voice making her hot salty tears flow freely. He kissed the corner
of her eye, his thumb wiping away the dampness on her
cheek. "Jen, what is it?"

"I love you. This seems so good. I've been alone for
such a long time. Ever since you came into our lives that
wild night, it's been better for the boys as well as me."

He held her tightly against him, folding his arms
around her and stroking her hair away from her face.
"This *is* good and I want you with me all the time. It's
perfect. I feel as if I've waited for you forever, Jenni-

fer. It isn't better yet for Brett, but maybe with time—''

"The other two are crazy about you and follow you like shadows," she said, wiping her cheeks.

"I'm glad. And I'm glad for you, for tonight." His voice was husky. She held him tighter, feeling his heart beat, relishing the long hard length of his body, which had given her such pleasure. He stroked her bare back, his hand drifting over the soft curve of her buttocks and touching her legs, then moving up again. "You're a beautiful woman, so giving," he said, thinking how she had come into his lonely life like a ray of golden sunlight into a dark cave. And not just Jennifer, but her boys as well, giving him the sort of family he had never known. His lips grazed her temple and he trailed kisses down her cheek, knowing he didn't want to lose that. He would win Brett over, somehow, and work to turn Will and Kyle's trust into love.

"I need you—you and your family. All of you are so much a part of my life already."

At his words her heart beat swiftly with joy. She wanted it to be that way, she wanted him to need her as she needed him. She looked up into his eyes, darkened by passion, and remembered that moment on the bridge when the wall of water had borne down on them. She felt as devastated now, because in the past few minutes she had given herself to him completely, body and soul. She knew she should be physically satiated, but she wanted to touch him, to relish the maleness of him, to hold him, and he must feel the same, because he was aroused again. She slid her hand along his thigh, feeling the soft hair, his long muscles, his solid legs.

With a sigh, she shifted slightly and saw that he was watching her. He leaned forward to kiss her, their tongues playing together as they stroked each other. His hand moved down over her hip while he caressed her back.

"Jason..." she whispered, looking up at him. Shrouded with desire, his eyes gave her a look that touched her physically. Her nipples were taut, sensitive to the slightest friction, and low in her body was a longing that was again becoming unbearable. His head lowered and his mouth covered hers with another hot kiss that drove away all thought. He trailed kisses down across her narrow waist and flat stomach, down to the soft warmth between her legs, and heard her gasp of pleasure. She arched beneath his touch, winding her fingers in his hair and moaning softly until finally she shuddered with release. He stretched beside her, pulling her to his warm body.

With a groan he picked her up, lifting her over him and entering her as she held him. She gasped with pleasure, moving with him, feeling his hands stroke her breasts and then move down to her feminine core to heighten her pleasure. She cried out in ecstasy as she shook with an orgasm, feeling him thrust deeply.

"Jen, oh, no!" he gasped, his body overtaken by his own climax. She wrapped her arms around him and twisted her head to kiss him. As he held her close, he showered her with kisses and feather strokes, murmuring so softly she wasn't sure what he was saying.

"Jennifer, love. You're beautiful. I will never get enough, never...." She clung to him, holding his strong body, feeling weak and boneless, as if she couldn't stand alone. He settled her against him, holding her close, knowing she was the only woman for him. "Jen, I've never been happy like this," he said in a deep voice.

They lay in satisfied silence for a while, then Jason chuckled softly and she raised herself up.

"What's so funny?"

"I was remembering my early conversations with Osgood and how he would turn off his hearing aid."

"I still say you would have turned one off, too, if you could have. Whatever are your parents going to think of us?"

Jason would never tell her about his conversation with his mother.

"A dog act!" she had shrieked, for once in her life losing her composure.

"Yes, Mom. Osgood has terriers, and they perform on television and at malls."

"Good Lord, Jason! Three boys and a father with a dog act?"

"They're all adorable, Mom," he said, avoiding any mention of Goldie's possible indictment.

"They can't possibly be!"

"I want you and Dad to meet them, because no one could dislike the Ruarks." He thought back guiltily to his own first impression.

"Jason, you've lost your mind. This is what comes from living all alone out in the woods."

"You'll love them, Mom. I promise you."

Jason tightened his arm around Jennifer. He felt closer to her crazy family than he did to his own parents. And he really couldn't imagine anyone not liking the Ruarks—once they got to know them.

When the light of dawn filtered over the patio, he gazed lovingly down at her. Perspiration curled tiny locks of her hair damply against her temple, and he brushed them back, leaning forward to kiss her. "That was a perfect night and this is a perfect dawn."

"I'm exhausted," she said, moving sensually against him, warm body rubbing warm body. He took her hand in his and they climbed down into the hot tub together.

"Jason," she said later, "it's Sunday and there are still things I have to do before we go home."

"I know, but let's enjoy every moment until we have to leave here," he said in a husky voice, wrapping his arms more tightly around her.

THE GALLERY HAD ONLY three visitors besides Jason and Jennifer. Jennifer stood at the desk with the owner, but her eyes were on Jason. One hand was splayed on his hip, and she remembered the feel of his hands moving over her body, dark against her pale flesh, raising her to quivering peaks of pleasure. She thought of the promises, the words of love spoken in the magic of the night, and her heart beat swiftly.

"Jennifer!"

"Sorry, Leah," she said, turning to the woman behind the desk.

Leah Saenz looked at Jason. "I guess I know why you haven't heard a word I've said."

"I'm sorry." She smiled. "Repeat, please."

"I'll deliver these drawings. I'm sorry about your house and the flood at San Saba. But maybe it wasn't all bad," she said, looking again at Jason.

He approached with his checkbook in hand. "I want to buy a painting."

Jennifer turned to him. "You don't have to do that."

"You think I'm getting it because I feel I have to?"

"No. I don't suppose so," she said, knowing he was doing what he wanted and glad he liked her work.

"Number twenty-three."

"That's one of my favorites," she said, her gaze sliding to the three-by-four painting of the silvery San Saba River cascading around a bend in the mountains in summer, the myriad of brilliant colors caught in the flash of water spilling over the brown rocks.

She gazed into his eyes and for a moment she felt as if they were in their own private world. He looked satisfied, pleased with his purchase, and she felt contentment in return, basking in the love he had showered on her the night before.

They loaded the painting into the Jeep and then they drove to La Fonda to eat chili and blue-corn tortillas in the spacious dining room. When they returned to her house, Jason caught her arm as she stepped out of the Jeep.

"Let me go in first," he said, drawing the pistol.

"Were we followed on the way home?"

"Yes," he answered soberly, "but I didn't make any effort to lose him, and I see no reason to try to lose him when we leave here for San Saba, because he'll know where we're going."

"Jason, I feel like we're going to lead the mob right to my family."

He shook his head, his hand squeezing her shoulder, and in spite of her worries, she felt a certain comfort at his touch. It was as if a dam had broken in her emotions last night, and from that point on, Jason would be part of her heart and, hopefully, part of her life. He gazed down at her in silence. "You're not leading them there. They already know you have that house and they've already been in it. It's just a matter of time until they make another move."

"I feel like a duck on a pond during hunting season."

"It's not that bad, hon. Terrell and I are around, and the FBI are watching. Now wait here." He walked into the house. In spite of his casual attire, he looked formidable with the pistol in his hand. In minutes he motioned to her from the kitchen door, and with a glance over her shoulder, she went inside.

He closed the door, placed the pistol on the counter and turned the key in the lock. He turned around and his gaze met hers, and she could see her own need mirrored in his eyes. As he reached for her, she went into his arms, feeling the solid length of him.

"Jason," she whispered, before his mouth covered hers and he bent over her to kiss her.

"I'd like to have you alone for days," he said. "I don't want to go back to all the interruptions and problems that will separate us. If it weren't for the men who are following us..."

"I'm torn between wanting to stay here forever and an urgent need to get back."

Stroking her cheek, he gazed down at her, his expression serious. "I don't want the boys or Goldie and Osgood in danger, either, but I promise Terrell can take care of them. He won't leave them for a second." Jason brushed the corner of her mouth with a kiss. "This is the way it should be for us, Jennifer," he said in a low voice.

As he kissed her lightly and caressed her, she held him, thinking it was so good with him in every way except one. If only Brett would accept him.

"Jason, we should go," she said, worrying about the boys.

"As much as I don't want to leave here, you're right. One long cold shower and home we go."

Just before they left the kitchen to start home, he drew her close for a long, hungry kiss that left her dazed and breathless and wanting him more than ever. "Let's go," he said when at last he released her.

They climbed into separate vehicles to return to the mountains, and if someone was following them, Jennifer wasn't aware of it. She looked at the familiar landscape, the rugged mountains and the shimmering aspen, and if it hadn't been for the threat hanging over all of them, she would have been bursting with happiness. The weekend had been marvelous and she was in love. After Mark's death, she'd never thought she would fall in love again, but Jason had filled a void in their lives she hadn't even been aware of. She glanced in the rearview mirror and waved at him, and he waved in return. He touched his lips and blew kisses at her and she smiled.

Jason watched her and grinned, wanting her beside him, wanting her again. He would never tire of her silken body, her hot, eager responses that made him shake with desire. He couldn't imagine going back to a life without her or the boys. And he had hopes for Brett. It was easy to understand his fears and worries, and with time, they might regain their old footing.

Jason remembered last night and Jennifer in his arms, and his body responded to his erotic thoughts. He drew a deep breath and glanced at the rearview mirror, his gaze sweeping the long rolling ribbon of road behind them. They would wind up into the mountains soon. The tail had followed them from Santa Fe, turning off about twenty miles out of the city. Jason imagined that when he and Jennifer left the highway for the mountain home, someone would be watching them. The Feds had a man posted to observe the house, though, so Jennifer and the boys should be safe even when he and Terrell couldn't be there.

Jason wondered how many thugs were after Goldie, or whether it was the sole job of the man who'd been in the restaurant. Whoever it was would probably go to the house in the daytime—assuming they didn't know about the constant surveillance. Why strike at night when a ranger was ensconced there? He didn't think it would be much longer before they made a move, and he wondered why they had waited this long. Were they expecting Goldie to leave? That hardly seemed likely. Were they hoping for Rat to show? A possibility. Or were they waiting for something or someone else before they took any further action?

Whatever the reason, they were out there, following Jennifer, watching the houses. He didn't imagine these were men of great patience. What would they do when they learned the money had been turned over to the police? Jason prayed they were under arrest when they made that discovery.

He thought about the future and Jennifer. Would she and the boys be willing to live at San Saba year-round? He suspected Will and Kyle would welcome it, now that they were learning to enjoy the outdoors. He thought about Will, who was not quite a boy, but not yet a man. He was far more responsible than Jennifer had realized. Even so, it was probably only natural for her to still treat him as her little boy.

Tonight Jason was going to try to put another call through to his parents to tell them more about Jennifer and her family. He grinned as he drove, imagining his mother and his dad finally absorbing the fact that he had fallen in love. He thought about the women his mother had wanted him to date, socially prominent, eminently acceptable. His parents were in for a mild shock.

Jennifer rounded a bend in the winding road, and Jason lost sight of her. For a few seconds he felt a sense of panic. His foot pressed the accelerator and he sped around the curve to catch a glimpse of the red rental car as it disappeared around another turn. As Jason rounded the bend, he noticed a car pulled off on the side of the road, a fishing rod fastened to the overhead carrier. The driver was a man in a brown sweatshirt. He glanced at Jason and then back to something in the car.

Jason passed him, sweeping around the next curve in pursuit of Jennifer, but his thoughts were on the man in the car. It wasn't the man from the restaurant in Santa Fe, yet Jason had the feeling that the man wasn't a fisherman, though he couldn't say why. "Getting paranoid," he said aloud, but it paid to be careful. Suddenly he braked and made a sweeping U-turn. He would catch up with Jennifer in a minute.

Jason retraced his route, roaring around the turns, until he reached the spot where the car had been. Green aspen leaves glistened in the afternoon sun and the grass beneath them was smashed flat, but there was no sign of the car.

Jason made another U-turn and raced after Jennifer, feeling a tight knot in his stomach until he caught up with her red car. He whipped past her, deciding he would let her follow. The man in the car could phone ahead to his partner to say that she was headed home. Jason would never know for sure, but he would wager a week's salary that the man had been waiting for them. He reached for his phone to call Dan Garcia.

Twenty minutes later he wound down the mountainside to the valley road. Glancing again in the rearview mirror, he confirmed that Jennifer was behind him. No other car was in sight.

As he neared the gravel driveway to her house, he noticed a sign fluttering from a tree. Jason slowed to read the word MOM, and an arrow was drawn underneath, pointing away from the road. He noticed a set of tracks where someone had driven across the yard. There was a huge puddle of water in the road ahead. Where had that come from? There hadn't been any more rain. Deciding the Jeep could ford a puddle, he drove ahead.

As soon as he hit the puddle, the Jeep sank.

CHAPTER TWELVE

JASON SWORE AND TWISTED around to grab the painting and hold it high. Water gushed in from all sides of what was clearly a deep pit.

In the rearview mirror he saw Jennifer get out and run toward him. "Damnation!" he swore. If he opened the door, the Jeep would completely fill with water. He wriggled through the window, swung his legs out and dropped to the ground. He vanished from sight.

"Jason!"

Eyes blazing with anger, Jason climbed out of the pit. He was muddy, soaked to his hips, and covered with leaves and twigs. "They're at it again!"

"How do you know the boys—" She bit off the statement. "What about the painting?"

"It's in plastic and I've got it propped on top of the seats."

"Jason, there's a sign in the tree that directs us *that* way."

"I know there's a damned sign in the tree. Jennifer, why would they do this? They are pit diggers! They can't resist." He clamped his jaw tightly. He looked at her, then said, "Don't you dare laugh."

She turned away quickly. "Jason, there's another sign on the front door."

"I'll go see what it says." He strode across the yard, his temper frayed, mud squishing in his boots with every step. He paused to see another sign that read MOM with an arrow pointing around the side of the house.

Jennifer drove slowly past the pit while Jason strode around the corner of the house. Suddenly something hit his ankles and he pitched forward, landing on his hands and face.

"Jason!" she yelled, and got out of the car, rushing to him.

"Watch out!" he snapped, getting up.

Jennifer saw the thin wire fastened to a stake by the house and strung to a tree in the yard.

"They've got the whole place booby-trapped!"

"Why don't you wait here."

"I can cope with this!" he growled, and turned. She shrieked and he ducked before hitting another wire that was neck high. "Someone could get badly hurt. This is terribly dangerous for Osgood."

"I know that—I'll deal with them," she said, wondering what had gotten into the boys. She could see the fury in Jason's eyes and wished he could get into his Jeep and go, except his Jeep was stuck in a pit. "Jason, I'll get them to dig your Jeep out, and you can get home before dark."

He turned to give her a steely glance. "You think this doesn't shorten someone's fuse? Pits and holes and wires? How your father has lasted this long, I don't know!"

"He manages quite well," she said, lifting her chin, reminding Jason of Osgood. Definitely a family trait.

She followed him around the corner and saw another sign: "Mom. We'll be right back. We set up traps to protect the house from burglars. Don't try to get inside. Just wait. We won't be gone long. Will."

She looked up at him. "That's why they did this."

The sound of a car engine caught their attention, and they both turned and looked up the curving mountain road.

"Here they come," he said.

"Jason Hollenbeck, you leave them to me. They were only trying to help, and if you had followed their signs, you wouldn't be in this mess."

She thought she saw a flicker of amusement in his eyes. "They're all yours, sweetie. Every ornery inch of them."

"This wasn't ornery."

"No. They were protecting the place. I got the message."

They watched Terrell drive past and stop near the back of the house. The dogs bounded out, barking and wagging their tails, then the boys spilled out, followed by Goldie, Terrell and Osgood, who all carried boxes.

"Wow!" Terrell said, studying Jason. All of them stopped to stare at him, the boys looking from him to the Jeep.

"We put up a sign," Will said.

"Mr. Hollenbeck, you drove your Jeep into our pit," Kyle said, covering his mouth, his eyes sparkling.

"Didn't you see the sign that said to turn?" Brett asked.

"I didn't think it was important," Jason replied evenly.

Osgood laughed and ducked his head. "You went sailing right into it!" He chuckled and shook his head. "I told the boys no one would drive into the puddle when there's a big sign warning them not to, but that just goes to show you."

"Dad, let's get the pizza in the house," Jennifer said, watching Terrell and Goldie as they went inside.

Osgood shook his head, still chuckling as he headed for the kitchen. The boys ran ahead of him, Will bursting out in a guffaw. Jennifer looked at Jason and shrugged.

"Your father has a warped sense of humor."

"At least he has one."

Again she saw a flicker of a smile as Jason looked over at her. "Your father has a warped sense of humor and the most delightful daughter on earth. You might as well go ahead and laugh. The rest of them are splitting their sides."

"You forgive them?"

"It was all for a good cause. Those boys are naturals when it comes to booby traps."

"I don't know that I trust you."

He looked at her and smiled the kind of smile that made her melt. She smiled back at him. "We'd better go in or the pizza will be gone. What should we do? Hose you off?"

"That's not a bad idea. I'd better eat out here in the sunshine."

"We'll all come out and join you." They looked at each other a moment and laughed.

"Come here, darlin', and give me a hug," he teased, holding out his arms. She backed away.

"Never! Sorry. Wait until you're a little less muddy, Hollenbeck."

He grinned and they headed toward the back door.

"As soon as we eat, the boys can help you dig out the Jeep."

Terrell came out and stood with his fists on his hips, a frown creasing his brow. "I agreed to take them for pizza. Now I'd better stay and help get you out."

"I'll get the pizza," Jennifer said, hurrying past him.

Jason looked at his friend. "Have you patched things up with Goldie?"

"No. I intended to leave as soon as you got back. You are one hell of a mess. Why didn't you follow the sign?"

"Terrell..."

Terrell threw up his hands. "Okay, okay. Let's go eat."

THE NEXT DAY Jennifer was brushing her hair while Will stretched out on the bed and studied her. "Mom, are you and Jason getting married?"

"What would you think if we did?"

He sat up. "I think it would be great!" He frowned. "We wouldn't have to live all the time in the patrol cabin, would we?"

"I just wanted to know what you thought about it. We're not planning a wedding."

"Not yet!" he said, grinning and flopping back down on the bed. "Wow, that would be fun. Jason's okay. Are you going to meet his family? Is his dad a ranger, too?"

"No. His father didn't want him to be a park ranger."

"No kidding? What did he want?"

"His father wanted Jason in business with him. He wanted him to major in business."

"Jeez. Too bad. I'd like to be a ranger, Mom."

"You would?" she asked, looking at him in the mirror.

"Yeah. It's neat," he said, rolling back and putting his feet over his head. "Jason said he would take me with him to work again next week if you say it's okay." He tumbled off the bed.

"It's a very lonely job."

"Lonely? All he needs is a television. He gets to do all kinds of neat things. Live on the San Saba all the time and work outdoors and fish and hunt. That's what I want to do." Will stood on his head, his elbows balancing him.

Jennifer studied her son and realized yet again what an impact Jason had had on her family. Will was won over, and Kyle would be easy, but Brett had barely acknowledged Jason this morning.

"Jennifer—" Goldie paused in the doorway. "Oh, I didn't know you and Will were talking."

"We're not," Will said, dropping to his feet and standing up. "It's almost time for a rerun of *L.A. Law*."

Once he'd left, Goldie glanced around and closed the door. "Jenny, Terrell called and we're going out Friday night."

"That's marvelous!" she exclaimed, feeling a rush of happiness for Goldie. "I knew it was just a matter of time."

"He still sounded very cool and very polite. But he said we needed to talk and he wanted to see me and take me somewhere where it would be just the two of us. There's not much privacy around here." She threw out her arms and her eyes sparkled. "I'm so happy! Jennifer, I love Terrell. I mean, I really love him. It's different this time."

"I hope so, Goldie," Jennifer said, praying it was true because she knew someday Rat Tabor would return.

Goldie's smile vanished. "I hope Terrell gets over his anger, because he isn't the same as he was."

"He will. If he's asked you out so you can talk things over, he wants to work things out between you. And if you're really through with Rat, then Terrell will probably put aside his hurt."

"Oh, I hope! He said maybe we could sort out our feelings better if we had a little space, a little absence from each other, but between now and Friday night isn't too big an absence. He's the nicest man I've ever known. Even this weekend when I knew he was angry, he was still considerate and helpful. Sometimes I think he forgets about his anger."

"Just give him time. When you've finally made a break with Rat, things will improve with Terrell."

"I may never see or hear from Rat again!"

"Yes, you will. That much I can promise you, Goldie." Unless he isn't alive, she thought, but she wouldn't say that to Goldie. "You know he'll come for the money."

"Well, I have some things to say to him if he does! Jennifer, Friday night, can I wear your blue dress? The slinky one?"

She laughed and waved her hand toward the closet. "Help yourself."

"I'll get it later," Goldie said, glancing at her watch. "I told Brett and Kyle I'd play croquet with them, so I better go."

She left the room and Jennifer turned to study her reflection. She felt an undercurrent of eager anticipation. Jason should be off duty now and she expected him at any moment. She still felt wrapped in euphoria from their magical weekend.

"Mom! Jason's here!" Will called.

"Coming, Will," she shouted back over the dogs barking. She glanced one more time at her reflection, and then rushed for the stairs. When she walked into the living room, Jason was talking to Osgood and idly scratching Priss's head.

"Hi," she said, entering the room, and he turned to look at her, his gaze seeming to envelop her in a warmth that shut out the rest of the world for a moment.

"Hi. Everything okay?"

"It's fine. There's a croquet game going outside...."

"I know," he said easily. "They've already told me to get both of you to come and play. Osgood?"

"I suppose it'll make the boys happy," he said, getting up and heading toward the door.

"We'll be there in a minute," Jason told him, crossing the room to put his arms around Jennifer's waist. "It seems like a year since I last saw you," he said softly. "I wish we could be alone."

"I know, but that isn't to be until maybe after midnight."

He bent down to kiss her, wrapping his arms more tightly around her, holding her close. Her hands rested on his strong arms, and she revelled in his solid warmth. Finally he released her, his eyes filled with passion as he gazed down at her. "I'm astounded no one has called us."

"They will. Let's go join them." He locked his fingers through hers, and she knew the boys would notice, but Brett was going to have to get accustomed to Jason, because he was becoming a part of their lives.

They played croquet and later ate ice cream on the patio, and all evening she was conscious of Jason beside her, his deep voice, his easy laughter. Finally all the family went to bed and just the two of them sat on the patio. The stars shone brightly in the black sky and Priss lay beside them, her nose between her paws, her eyes alert. Jason stood up and reached down for Jennifer's hand. "Let's take a walk."

"You think that's safe?" she asked, glancing at the dark slope of the mountain, thick with trees.

"We won't go out of sight of the house, and you said we can rely on Priss to bark. And now there's a Federal agent up on the mountainside who keeps a daily watch on your place."

"Someone is watching us *here?*"

"That should be reassuring," Jason said, amusement in his voice.

For a moment Jennifer felt as if she had lost all the privacy she enjoyed at her mountain home. When would this all be over?

Jason seemed to sense her thoughts. "Well, *I* feel better knowing he's there when I have to be at work during the day."

"And when you're not, you're walking around here with a pistol. Sometimes you worry me. I was married to one man who was never afraid to take risks. It scares me to think I've lost my heart to another."

He looked at her, pausing a moment to tilt her face up and brush her lips lightly with his. "I like that part about losing your heart," he said softly. They started walking toward the trees again. "But don't worry. I'm not at all like Mark."

"You're very much the same about some things, and it does scare me. I know you won't hesitate to use that gun."

"Neither would any ranger with the park department," he said dryly. "But Jennifer, I only take *necessary* risks."

She thought about that, then looked at Jason. "Maybe so, but sometimes I think I'd be happier with a bookworm who's afraid of his own shadow."

"Sorry about that," he said lightly. "It seems your heart disagrees. And I can tell you right now, you're raising at least two boys who are going to be the same type of man. Will is brave and loves the outdoors and he likes to do challenging things. Brett does, too. Kyle's still young, but I'd say a kid who would ride an inner tube in a freezing, swift-running creek is not going to be the hand-wringing type."

"You're probably right, and I suppose I'll spend all my life worrying about them."

He squeezed her. "You really wouldn't want any of us to be cowards, would you?"

"That's what you think!" she snapped, and he grinned. They walked in an easy silence, their footsteps making faint swishing noises. The night was cool and smelled of spruce and the moon was bright. Jennifer wished she could forget the danger and enjoy the evening as she once would have been able to. "Do you think he's watching us now?"

"Probably, but in ten more yards we'll be in the shadows of trees and he can't see us." He turned her to face him and stroked her hair away from her face. "This weekend was perfect," he said, sliding his arms around her waist.

"It was for me," she replied, gazing up at him. His face was shadowed now, and she couldn't see his eyes clearly. He leaned over to kiss her, his tongue thrusting over hers, and she wrapped her arms around his neck and kissed him in return, wanting his kisses and wanting his love.

"Jennifer," Jason said softly when he released her, "I've been thinking about us. I've never felt this way about a woman before. I know what I want just like I knew what I wanted when I decided to be a ranger." He tilted her chin up. "I want to marry you."

The words spun in the air and her heart pounded. Her first reaction was a great rush of joy. She wanted to pull him close and shout yes. "Jason!" she exclaimed, standing on tiptoe to kiss him while he held her tightly. She leaned back, studying him, touching his cheek, knowing her life was happier since he had become part of it.

He brushed his lips across hers and then raised his head. "I want the boys to be part of my life, too, Jennifer. I know I haven't won Brett's friendship, but he's just scared about losing his dad and now losing part of you, too."

Even though her heart beat with joy, she was accustomed to thinking about her family, and she knew she had to be careful. The future of the boys and Osgood was at stake, as well.

"I'm glad you like the boys, but there are so many things we have to discuss. I have to consider the boys' feelings."

"You mean you have to consider Brett. I don't think Kyle and Will would object."

"I know they won't. They follow you like the Pied Piper. But I do have to consider Brett. And where would we live? Would you quit your job and move to Santa Fe?"

He shook his head, and she felt a sense of foreboding. "I love my career, Jennifer. I don't have to live in the patrol cabin, though. Married rangers live in housing provided by the park, or we can live here or build our own house. The park doesn't care about that. I live at the patrol cabin because I want to and because it's available. But I do know I want to stay a ranger for now.''

''We can't move out here, Jason,'' she said, feeling torn between wanting to accept his proposal and worrying about their conflicting needs. ''The boys have to go to school.''

''There's a consolidated school in Rimrock. They can get a good education there and we can go into town some of the time. You wouldn't have to give up your home there or we could get another house in Santa Fe. You've already decided to quit teaching.''

Disturbed, she moved away from him. ''That's an enormous change for all of us. The boys have always gone to school in Santa Fe. I have my work.'' She thought about the impending upheaval in their lives.

''You can draw out here and take your work to the gallery in Santa Fe. You're already working that way in the summers now.''

''No,'' she said, turning to look at him again, ''it won't really interfere with my work. It's the boys I'm concerned about, especially Brett. I'll have to talk to them and give it some thought. Have you ever considered changing your career? To work in Santa Fe? Terrell told Goldie he was thinking about getting a job with the park department in one of its offices.''

''I thought about it and rejected the idea. I don't want an office job. If I do that, I might as well go into my father's business and that's not what I want.''

''And I have to think about the boys and their friends and their education.''

''They're still young and in their formative years. Your boys are more adaptable than you think.''

"That's an enormous change," she said, wondering if Jason really knew what a disruption such a move would be in the boys' lives. "I don't know that I want them in the consolidated school. Santa Fe schools offer so much that they can't get in Rimrock."

"On the other hand, they'd really get to know the outdoors and they'd have a decent education. Living here, you wouldn't have to worry about a lot of the problems you'll encounter with them growing up in a busy city."

What he said was true, but it would mean a drastic change in their lives and she had to think it over. She moved away, rubbing her forehead. He reached out to draw her to him.

"I need you, Jennifer," he said softly. "I think Brett will come around."

"Maybe none of them will when I talk about changing schools."

"You talk to them and let them start thinking about it," he said quietly. "Jennifer, my life seemed complete, until we met, but now I can't imagine it without you."

"I'll talk to the boys about moving and about our marrying, but you think about switching jobs, too. You're asking the four of us to make the biggest changes. Dad, too, because he goes where I go."

"You know Osgood is happy anywhere. The boys will be, too, for that matter. I'll give it some more thought, though," he promised. "And you think about a honeymoon. You said you've always dreamed of the Louvre and Paris."

She tilted her head, running her hand across his chest and touching his jaw. "I think I'd prefer something simpler where the whole family could be part of it."

"Not for the first week," Jason said gruffly, his hand sliding over her hip while his arm tightened around her waist.

"How about somewhere west, something you'd like, too—the Grand Canyon?"

"I'd love it, but you'd give up Paris for the Grand Canyon?"

"Yes, I would, because I think it would be less complicated right now."

"Okay, maybe a few days in Phoenix in a suite where we can't be disturbed, and then on to the Grand Canyon. Then we can fly the family to meet us. How about taking them all to Disneyland before we come home?"

"Bribery! You *do* know how to win the boys over! They would agree to all this in a minute if they thought we could go to Disneyland."

He laughed and shook his head. "No. As much as I'd like to use that, I don't want you to tell them until after they've accepted me. I want to be accepted on my own merits, not because I'll get everyone tickets to Disneyland."

"I agree, but that would be a wonderful honeymoon," she said, wondering if they would ever find a compromise to suit everyone.

"As good as Paris, Jennifer?" he asked quietly. "Here's your chance."

"No, right now the Grand Canyon and Disneyland sound better. But before we get to that, there are so many other things to worry about, Jason. We can't marry and leave with this threat hanging over us. I don't know what I'll do if we're still in this danger when school starts."

He nodded, gazing down at her, and then his lips found hers, and for a few minutes she stopped worrying about the future and gave herself completely to the miraculous passion they shared.

As they walked back to the house, he kept his arm around her. "Much as I want you with me, until we have things settled, I think it would be less complicated for the family if you stayed on the sofa the way you have been," she said.

"I intended to stay there," he answered, "though I'd rather be with you. I'll be better protection for all of you if I'm downstairs and can hear what's going on. I'm keeping the ferocious guard dog with me, too."

She smiled. "You can have all four if you want—well, maybe not General."

"No, thanks. One should do, and I don't care to share my bed with four dogs."

At the house, he held open the back door. "I'm telling you good-night here, because I want to look around the grounds."

"Be careful."

"I'll have a dog to guard me." He disappeared into the shadows with Priss trotting after him. Jennifer stared into the darkness, then at the mountain behind the house. She closed the door and went inside, alternately feeling a wild excitement at the thought of marrying Jason and then sobering, because she didn't see how they could overcome the obstacles.

The next morning after Jason left for work, she talked to her father, sitting beside him while he repaired a small stepladder for his dog act.

"Dad, Jason has asked me to marry him."

Osgood's gaze shifted to her and he set down the ladder. "Honey, I think that's grand! I'm so glad to hear that."

"I haven't said yes, because I want to talk to the boys and there are things we have to work out."

"I know you're worrying about Brett, but he'll grow to love Jason. Jason is good with the boys. Jenny, they've changed for the better since he's been around. They've learned new things and have new interests. Even Brett."

"I know. He's a good influence, but Brett still may not accept this at all. And Jason wants to keep his job as a ranger. That means we would have to live here and the boys go to school in Rimrock."

"They might like that. They're too young to care a whole lot. After the first few hours they would have new friends and be just as happy."

"I don't know," she said, amazed at her father's reaction. "What about you?"

His blue eyes twinkled. "I'd be the happiest to see you two married. Jason's been good for you, too."

She smiled and nodded. "I'll finish the dishes. I have to go to Santa Fe to pick up the new Bronco and turn in the rental car. That was the dealership who called a few minutes ago, so when Jason comes by for lunch, tell him where I've gone. I'll talk to the boys before I go."

"Honey, work things out with Jason. He's a good man." Osgood gave her hand a squeeze.

She hugged him and left to clean the kitchen. After the boys had eaten, while Will was gathering up fishing poles, she called them to come and sit down at the kitchen table.

"I want to talk to all three of you about something important." Kyle fidgeted and held a can filled with dirt. She suspected it held earthworms to take fishing. "Jason has asked me to marry him."

"Wow!" Will exclaimed. "That'll be great!"

"Hey!" Kyle grinned. "Jason will be our dad?"

"No, he won't!" Brett burst out. He glared at her, his face red. "I don't want Jason for my dad. He isn't our dad!"

"No, he's not," she said quietly. "You have a father and that will never change. No one will ever take his place. That was forever." She spoke directly to Brett, hurting for him. "Nothing will change that, but Jason wants to be part of our family now and he wants us to be a family to him."

"I think it's great," Will said. "Jason's neat. Lighten up, Brett."

"What do you know?" he snapped back, his scowl deepening as his fists clenched.

"Boys!" she said, raising her voice. "Just calm down."

"When are you getting married?" Kyle asked. "Saturday?"

"No. There's no date set yet, because I had to talk to you guys and talk to Granddad and we have to work everything out. I haven't said yes. It may mean that we'll live here and you'll go to school in Rimrock."

"I don't want to do that!" Brett protested.

"It might be fun to live here all year," Will said. "We'd get to ski."

Kyle nodded and Jennifer knew he was too young to care. She was amazed at Will's easy capitulation, and she looked at him closely. "You really wouldn't mind living here all year and going to school in Rimrock?"

He shrugged. "I like it here. It might be fun. And school might not be as hard."

"Don't count on that," she said. Brett was staring at the floor, his knuckles white. Kyle wiggled on the chair.

"Can I go outside now?" he asked.

"Sure," she said. "We can talk some more later."

"It's great, Mom," Will said, standing up and leaving with Kyle, and Jennifer thought how easily they had accepted her news.

"I don't want him to be part of our family," Brett said belligerently.

"If I marry him, I'd like all of you to be happy about it and to want Jason to be in our family," she said quietly.

"Please don't, Mom," he begged.

"Brett, I'm giving it a lot of thought, but you might try to give Jason a chance. Will and Kyle both like him, and he knows he'll never take your father's place."

"That's what he's trying to do."

"You know that's not true—at least in your heart you do."

"You haven't said you will yet?" he asked hopefully, and she shook her head.

"No, and I'm not going to marry Jason until everyone is happy about it."

"I'll never be happy about it. I don't want you to—*ever.*" He gazed at her, unshed tears in his eyes, and she reached out to hug him.

"Brett, just try to give Jason a chance to be friends. Do that for me, because I love Jason and I want him to be part of our family. Will you do that?"

"Okay," he said, turning away abruptly. "I want to go outside." She nodded and watched him run outside, calling to Will. She ran her hand across her eyes. Brett was not likely to be won over any time soon, and her heart ached for him.

She stood up and went to her room to braid her hair and gather her things to go to Santa Fe. Osgood would tell Jason where she had gone, and she would be back shortly after noon.

In Santa Fe she stopped at the house to get her mail, turned in the rental car, picked up the new Bronco and stopped for groceries in Rimrock. It was two in the afternoon when she finally wound her way back along the mountain road. Her gaze swept the tree-covered slope and she wondered where the agent was stationed. She turned onto the driveway and slowed. Parked ahead was a shiny red Corvette. Whose? Jennifer's heart plunged. It had to be Rat Tabor.

Cold fear uncoiled in the pit of her stomach as she entered the house. She glanced toward the side of the mountain. Did the agent watching the house know it was Rat inside? Had anyone followed him? He would want the money, and Jennifer had never seen Goldie cross him. She suspected beneath his superficial charm lay a mean streak. She set down the groceries and walked into the living room.

"Look who's here," Goldie said. Bright spots of color glowed in her otherwise pale cheeks.

"Jennifer," Rat said, crossing the room to her. Jennifer had forgotten how handsome he was. In spite of what she knew about him, Rat had a sexy aura that made her want to smooth her hair and smile in return. With wavy brown hair, thickly lashed blue eyes and a dimple in his cheek, he was male perfection. The tight jeans and knit shirt he wore accentuated his powerful muscles.

"Hello, Rat," she said cautiously. Any reservation on her part was ignored as he pulled her against his big body, hugging her with his strong arms. Then he ran his eye over her.

"You get more beautiful every time I see you."

"Thank you," she said quietly, deciding the first chance she got she would call Jason.

"I've been away too long." His expression was solemn. "I came back as soon as I could, only to find my little girl is dating someone else." He turned to Goldie. "Or she says she is." He walked toward Goldie. "But I'm going to try to do something about that. I came here with marriage on my mind." He bent over Goldie and took her hand.

Goldie pulled her hand away from his. "I need to talk to you, Rat, and not about Terrell."

"I have to put away the groceries," Jennifer announced briskly, hoping to break the spell he was weaving and to leave Goldie some privacy.

"I'll help," he said instantly, but made no move to leave Goldie.

Instead of going to the kitchen, Jennifer went upstairs to her room. She closed the door and sat down on the bed to call Jason. As soon as Della answered, Jennifer spoke softly into the phone.

"Della, would you please page Jason and tell him Rat Tabor is here?"

"Yes, I will. I think he's at the dam, because the engineers wanted to talk to the rangers, but I'll get a message to him as soon as possible."

"If you can't get Jason, would you page Terrell?"

"Same deal. He's gone, too, but I'll try."

"Thanks, it's important," she said, replacing the receiver and staring at it. Should she call Dan Garcia? She glanced toward the window and crossed over to it, looking at the mountain and wondering about the agent watching the house. They should be safe.

The boys and Osgood and the dogs were all gone, and she wondered if Rat had sent them out so he could be alone with Goldie. She went downstairs to carry the rest of the groceries from the truck to the kitchen. When she finished, she called down the hall, "Goldie, can you come here a minute?"

After a few minutes Goldie appeared, her face flushed.

"Is Rat staying for dinner?" Jennifer asked softly. Rat followed Goldie into the kitchen. He draped a muscled arm over her shoulder.

"My little doll baby here tells me you folks were in a flood."

"That's right," Jennifer said evenly. "That's when Goldie met Terrell Skinner."

"Well, she may have a surprise for Mr. Skinner if I have any say-so," Rat said, sliding his hand possessively down over Goldie's hip. There was a clatter at the back door and Will, Kyle, Osgood and the dogs spilled into the room.

The dogs barked and growled at Rat, who rolled his eyes at them. "Snappy little monsters, aren't they? Hello, boys...Mr. MacFee." He shook hands with Osgood and ignored the boys. "Goldie and I were just going for a walk."

"Rat, I should—"

"I know you should help Jennifer, but she has two helpers here now, doesn't she, boys?" They gave him a look he ignored, and he went on blithely. "So let's take a walk and look at the mountains. I haven't been in the mountains in years."

As they went outside, Jennifer watched them through the window. Goldie said something to Rat and came running back to the house. The moment she stepped into the kitchen, she closed the door and leaned against it.

"Jenny, I haven't told him about the money yet. That's what I'm going to do now."

"The sooner you do, the sooner Rat will be gone and out of your life. At some point we'll have to call the police, you know. I already called the park and asked for Jason. He was out, and so was Terrell. I left a message that Rat was here."

"Oh Lordy, Jenny. Suppose Terrell comes now?"

"I'd be glad to see him. Don't go too far from the house, Goldie. I don't think Rat will be so cheerful when he discovers you gave the money to Sheriff Garcia."

"Well, he shouldn't have given it to me in the first place. I better go. We'll be back soon." She opened the door and hurried to catch up with Rat, who smiled and put his arm around her.

Jennifer glanced at the phone and hoped Della had reached Jason or Terrell. She was uncertain how Rat would react when he discovered what Goldie had done.

When she looked out the window again, Goldie was talking in earnest to Rat, and then they disappeared from her sight.

"Mom! Mom!"

Her breath caught. There was no mistaking the worry in Will's tone. Drying her hands, she ran out of the kitchen toward the stairs. As she rushed into the hall, she saw Will bounding down the stairs with Kyle trailing behind. He was waving a piece of paper in his hand and Kyle's eyes were as round as saucers. She wondered what had happened.

Osgood and the dogs were in the living room, but suddenly the dogs rushed past her, barking wildly as they ran toward the back door. Rat and Goldie were probably returning.

"Mom!" Will exclaimed. "Brett has run away from home!"

CHAPTER THIRTEEN

"OH, NO!" HER HEART sank and she felt as if an icy wave had washed over her. "Will, Brett shouldn't be out anywhere alone! Rat is here and someone could have followed him."

"Gee, he was with us, and then he said he was going back to the house, so we said okay. We weren't far and I saw him cross the porch. I figured he was here with Aunt Goldie." Will sounded stricken. "I didn't mean to lose him."

"It's not your fault, Will. I've just got to figure out what to do."

Osgood whistled and the dogs raced to the living room, but they immediately ran back to the kitchen, barking wildly.

Jennifer took the note from Will's hands, oblivious to the racket the dogs were making. She unfolded a dirt-smudged piece of paper.

Mom: Everyone wants you to marry Jason. I don't, and I don't fit in with all of you guys anymore, so I am leaving and you and Jason can get married.

Brett

P.S. Don't worry about me. I will be all right.

"Oh, no," she said, trying to control the fear that gripped her. "Will, I'm going to call Sheriff Garcia. Then I'm calling the park to tell Della to notify the rangers to watch for him.'' He could have headed to the highway, where someone might have picked him up in a car. She forced herself to quell her rising panic. She started to turn away and then paused. "When was the last time either of you saw him?"

Will and Kyle looked at each other, and Kyle shrugged. "I suppose about lunchtime,'' Will said. "Jason wasn't here today. After lunch Granddad went with us to the mountain.''

Noon. She glanced at her watch. It was now almost three in the afternoon. Her head spun wildly, and she fought for control. "You get Granddad and we'll decide where to start looking,'' she said, hoping she sounded calm. The sound of barking distracted her.

"Will, what are the dogs barking at? Where's Granddad?''

Osgood appeared in the living room doorway. "Someone call me?''

"Dad, Brett has run away from home. I'm calling the police and the park rangers. Would you go with Will and Kyle to look for him?''

"Lordy. He can't be far. He was here at lunchtime.'' He whistled to the dogs, and General came bounding in and then returned to the kitchen.

"What on earth's the matter with those dogs?'' Jennifer said as she hurried after General. When she entered the kitchen she saw figures out on the patio and knew Goldie and Rat were back. "Shush!'' she ordered the dogs. "Dad, will you call the dogs?''

He whistled, and they all turned to run down the hall except General, who had to give a few more barks before he left. She marveled at the way Osgood could get them to obey him. She picked up the phone and started to punch in the numbers to the Rimrock police department.

The back door opened, and Goldie walked in. All color was gone from her face and her eyes were filled with fear. Rat came next, his jaw clamped shut, his cheek scraped and his mouth bloody.

Jennifer stiffened and she looked beyond him. Following Rat with an automatic rifle in his hand was a tall, blond man. Behind him were two more men, each holding pistols, one of them the dark-haired man she had seen in the restaurant. The first man waved his rifle. "Hang up!"

She felt terrified, her first thought about the boys. "No," she whispered.

The blond man yanked the receiver from her hand and slammed it down. "Don't move except to turn around and put your hands on top of your head," he ordered, his gaze raking over her.

"Please leave my family alone."

"Shut up, lady. Let's go into the front room and have a talk."

Jennifer walked into the hallway, where Osgood and the boys were standing. "Dad, some men are here—"

"Shut up!" one of the men snapped, a burly fellow who looked as if he had been put together with bags of cement. His neck was thick, his head almost square.

The dogs barked and growled.

"Shut them up!"

Osgood blinked, then frowned. "Sic 'em, boys!" he yelled, and the dogs raced at the men. Goldie screamed as Osgood threw a vase at them. A shot was fired. Will bounded up the stairs, taking them three at a time, while the stocky man ran after him.

"Will!" Jennifer cried, afraid the man would shoot. She flung herself at the dark-haired man, and his gun discharged, shattering one of the bulbs in the light fixture. Jennifer scrambled toward his rifle, but the man recovered his balance and sent her sprawling across the floor. When she got up, he was pointing the rifle at her, and his partner was marching Will down the stairs.

"Get in there," the tall blond man said, motioning toward the living room with the barrel of his rifle. He appeared to be the one giving the orders.

They filed into the living room, and he shoved Will down. "You kids sit on the floor. You," he said, motioning to Jennifer, "sit down there with them."

Another man shoved Goldie and Rat onto the sofa, and Osgood sat on a chair.

One look at Will's round eyes and Kyle's pale face and Jennifer felt sick with fear. "They're just children."

"Shut up!" The heavyset man swung his arm and struck Jennifer across the face.

The boys and Osgood started to shout and Goldie screamed.

"*Shut up!*" The leader fired into the air, and everyone became quiet. Goldie was crying softly and Rat's face was drawn. The boys looked angry now rather than frightened.

"I gave the money to Bobby," Rat said.

"We know you didn't—he said you gave it to her," the blond man said, pointing at Goldie. "Now where is it?" His long, narrow face was taut with anger, scored by a fierce-looking scar that ran from his temple to his chin. He glared at each of them. "We'll find out. You might as well save yourselves time and pain. We get the money, and we go."

Rat flinched, and Jennifer suspected they would never leave him alive—maybe not any of them. The three men were making no effort to hide their identities. She thought about the agent on the mountainside staking out the house. If only she could stall these thugs—anything to gain time. At the thought of time, she felt another wave of panic. Where on earth was Brett by now? Was he safe? He was still just a little boy. She prayed he was all right. She had never felt so helpless to protect her children. Time—that was all she had on her side. She had to try to gain some time.

Suddenly the burly fellow hit Rat, a quick slap and backhand that made two sharp cracks resound throughout the room. "Tell us!"

"I gave it to her!"

Jennifer could have hit Rat herself. So much for loyalty and protecting the one you love. The man was a rat to the core. The thug walked over to Goldie, and Jennifer drew a deep breath. Now was the time to tell these men the police had the money, but she was afraid they wouldn't believe it. And if they ever were convinced the money was gone, there was no telling what they would do.

"No one can hear you scream," the thug snarled.

Kyle started crying and Jennifer bit her lip, terrified for all of them. The man flipped out a switchblade. The shiny metal caught the light as he moved closer to Goldie, whose eyes were huge in her ashen face.

"No! I don't have it."

"Tell us where the money is hidden and we'll let all of you go," he said. He moved the blade beneath her chin and looked at Rat. "Tell us where it is or she gets cut."

"It's buried in the mountainside," Jennifer blurted out, knowing it was a ridiculous thing to say, yet if it gained them even a few extra minutes, it might make a difference. If only Della had given Jason the message about Rat. Her mind raced. These guys would never believe that she had hidden the money all by herself, and Goldie's nerves weren't up to carrying off the bluff. "Dad and I hid it," she added, wanting to get the men out of the house, away from the boys.

Goldie was crying now, and appeared to be on the verge of fainting. Any hope, no matter how faint, was better than sitting here and being killed.

The man walked over to Jennifer to jerk up her chin. "That's absurd." He struck her, a sharp blow that sent Will lunging at him. He knocked Will down and the boy went sprawling across the floor.

"Stop that!" Jennifer cried. "I didn't want all that money in the house, so Dad and I took it out to the mountain and buried it! Search the house all you want if you don't believe me."

The men looked at each other. The heavyset crook shook his head, studying Jennifer. "I don't believe it. Why go dig a hole in the side of the mountain where anyone could find it and take it?"

"I can believe it," the dark-haired man said. "Look at this bunch—dizzy broads and kids. They wouldn't know much better."

The leader of the group studied her closely. She knew it would be bad for her when he found out she was lying, but she prayed that help would have come by then. His watery blue eyes scrutinized her, and she stared back at him, feeling a rising fury. Her cheeks hurt and she hated him for striking Will.

"All right," he said. "We take her and the old man. Chim—" he nodded to his thickset partner "—you stay here and watch this bunch. We'll take Rat with us."

She saw Rat's expression and felt a wave of nausea. They would probably shoot him before they returned to the house. At the moment she didn't think any of them had a good chance of surviving unless they could do something to draw attention to their predicament. Or unless Jason or Terrell received her message.

As they left the room, she looked at Will, whose eyes were burning with anger. "Do exactly what they tell you, Will." He nodded, and she prayed that he wouldn't try something on his own again.

"We'll have to have shovels," Osgood said.

"Get them."

"They're outside against the back of the house."

Her mind raced for something to use as a weapon. As they went outside, she tried desperately to determine what to do once the men discovered there was no money on the mountain. The moments were ticking by, and she didn't have an alternate scheme. Where was the man who was supposed to be watching their house?

"Up this way," Osgood said, pointing up the mountain behind the house.

"Get the shovels," the blond man ordered.

Jennifer picked up one and Rat took the other as Osgood led the way. Behind Osgood and Rat walked the blond man with the rifle. Jennifer followed him, and the dark-haired man brought up the rear of the strange procession. In minutes she realized Osgood was going much slower then he needed to. He wheezed and puffed, and she guessed he was stalling for more time. The only sound was the tramp of grass underfoot and Osgood's wheezing. Shadows lengthened slightly, but it would be hours until dark.

"I gotta stop for air," Osgood said, puffing, and they all halted. Jennifer looked down through the trees at the house. Other than the extra cars behind the house, everything looked just as it had every other day. Her gaze swept the mountains and the river in the valley. Where was Brett?

"Get moving, lady," the dark-haired man behind her said, and the leader turned around.

"If you're wondering about the guy standing watch, we've taken care of him."

Jennifer's heart plummeted. They were on their own now unless Della had given the message about Rat to Jason or Terrell. If they weren't forewarned, they would be taken prisoner along with the rest of them when they came to the house.

Worries swirled in her head while she tried to think of some way to get help or attract attention. If she could make one of the men fire again, out here high on the mountain, the sound might carry and echo.

They continued the climb up the mountainside she knew as well as the yard around the house. She and the boys had hiked up here countless times. Osgood puffed and wheezed and had to stop several times, but all they were gaining was empty time. She heard a car engine in the distance, too far to be of any help.

They approached a straight drop, and she gauged her chances with the man behind her. He could easily shoot her if she didn't do what he ordered. Yet she had to try something.

She waited until his attention was on his footing. Flinging herself back against him, she hit his arm. It was like coming up against a stone wall. She tried to grab the pistol. It discharged, the shot echoing in the mountains. As he lunged forward to keep from going over the side of the path, she wrestled away the pistol. Squeezing the trigger, she fired several shots then lowered the weapon and aimed it at him.

"Drop the gun," the man with the rifle said coldly, "or your dad goes."

He held the rifle against Osgood's throat and she gave up, tossing the pistol down. The dark-haired man yanked it up and grabbed her hair, shoving her to the ground. "You do that again and you get the bullet. Now get going!"

Dazed, Jennifer stumbled to her feet and trudged behind her father. He veered away from the steep drop, stopping a few minutes later. "I think it's right here."

"Then dig. All three of you."

"There are only two shovels," Rat said, waving one.

"Rat and I'll dig. Let my dad sit down."

They dug through green grass and then damp ground, and Jennifer wondered how big a hole they would have to make before the men knew it was a hoax. She had never been so terrified in her life, and concern for the boys was uppermost in her mind. Any minute now the men would discover the truth, and she was certain they would kill them all.

Blindly she dug, the muscles in her arms aching, her face hurting, and a cold terror for the boys squeezing her heart.

"I think you're lying," the man with the rifle said, pointing it at Osgood. "There's no money buried here or anywhere else around here. Stop playing games, because you'll get hurt badly." He moved closer to Osgood. "The truth now. Where is the money?"

"I think it's right here," Osgood said with a shrug. The man swung around to Jennifer.

"You know where it is and you're going to tell us."

"It's here," she bluffed. "I swear. Give us another ten minutes."

She kept digging, glancing once into Rat's eyes. He looked frightened, too, and she knew this was their last chance. In desperation she struck her shovel across Rat's. "There, I hit the box," she exclaimed.

"J.L.—" the dark-haired man called. Jennifer spun around, swinging the shovel, knowing she might get shot, but it was the only chance they would have.

"Dad!" she cried, hitting the leader's hand and knocking away the rifle as Rat dived at the other thug. She scrambled after the rifle.

"Stop right there," came a deep voice. The cocking of a rifle followed, and Jason stepped out from behind a spruce.

CHAPTER FOURTEEN

"GET YOUR HANDS HIGH!" Jason ordered, training his rifle on the tall blond man. "Looks like we might not have been needed after all," he said, glancing at the rifle in Jennifer's hand. "Good going, Jen."

Terrell held a gun on Rat and the dark-haired man, and both raised their hands and stood up.

"Thank God," Rat said. "You rangers came—"

Terrell tucked his pistol into his belt and walked toward Rat. "I'm Terrell Skinner," he said, and hauled back his fist and slammed it into Rat's jaw. Rat went staggering backward, but Jennifer didn't wait to see what happened. She turned to Jason.

"Jason—the boys?"

"They're all right." Peering at her, he frowned. "Those bastards hit you!"

She grabbed his arm. "Jason, Brett has run away!"

"Oh, hell! How long has he been gone?"

"Since noon. I want to see the boys," she said, suddenly feeling weak. "These men knew about the agent who was watching the house."

"Garcia will send someone looking for him. The Feds will take care of it."

"Is the money in the hole?" the blond man asked, grating the words, his eyes cold with anger.

Jennifer faced him, lifting her chin. "We turned the money over to the sheriff long ago." She turned back to Jason. "I have to get back to the boys."

"Will has a gun on the guy—"

"Will?" she gasped, unable to imagine her little boy holding a gun on a thug. "Oh, no!"

"He's doing fine, and we had to see about you and Osgood. I called Sheriff Garcia and the highway patrol on our way here and another ranger is on the way."

"Jason," she said again, more urgently, "I want to see my boys." As he nodded, she turned and rushed down the mountain. Her heart pounded with fear and she felt an overwhelming need to see for herself that the boys were all right and to start a search for Brett. She was oblivious to the bushes scratching her and branches hitting her. Gasping for breath, she rushed into the house. "Will!"

"In here, Mom," he said, sounding calm and collected.

She rushed into the living room. A ranger held a gun pointed at the third man. Both boys were safe, and Goldie sat huddled on the sofa crying softly while Kyle patted her shoulder. Kyle ran to Jennifer and she scooped him up, not caring that she could barely lift him.

"I'm Jennifer Ruark," she said, holding out her hand to the ranger. He clasped it firmly.

"I'm Ranger Baker. The highway patrol should be here any minute and Sheriff Garcia is on his way. You have some brave boys," he said, glancing at Will.

"Mom, how's Granddad?" Will asked.

"He's fine. He's with Terrell and Jason."

Will came over to hug her, and she set down Kyle and squeezed them both. "What happened, Will?"

"Will got the guy's gun, and Jason and Terrell busted in here," Kyle said. "And *blam—*" he swung his fists "*—that crook was out!*"

"You got his gun?" she asked in amazement, noticing for the first time the man's bruised jaw and swollen lip.

"Kyle told him he had to go to the bathroom and he distracted him, so that helped," Will said, grinning at Kyle.

"We told Jason and Terrell where we thought you had gone, and they went to find you," Kyle added.

"Mom, what about Brett?" Worry filled Will's eyes and she suspected he was anxious to get back out and look for his brother.

"We'll start a search now," she said, glancing at the ranger. "My son is missing."

"One of these guys has him?"

"No. He ran away from home this afternoon," she said, suddenly wishing Jason was there with his quiet strength, yet knowing it was her love for Jason that had caused Brett to run away. "We found a note from him right before these men broke into the house."

The ranger pulled out his radio. "Give me a description and I'll have it sent to all the rangers. Do you think your son might still be in the park?"

"I don't know," she said, looking at Will, who shrugged.

"Jennifer," Goldie said, "where's Terrell?"

"Fighting with Rat," she said dryly, and Goldie jumped up to run out of the room toward the kitchen. In seconds the back door slammed. Sirens sounded, their wails a welcome relief, and soon the house was filled with uniformed men. Finally Jason, Osgood, Terrell and their captives appeared. Rat stood in handcuffs, his jaw swollen, while Terrell and Goldie embraced at the back of the patio.

Jason pulled Jennifer aside. "I talked to Della, and the department is organizing a search in the park. Garcia will handle the area out of the park. We'll divide the park into sections and assign a search party to each area. We've done this before, honey. He isn't the first kid to wander off."

"He may not even be in the park," she said. "Jason, let me go with you."

"Sure. Let me talk to Garcia a minute and check with the office and then we'll go."

"I'll tell Will and change into jeans."

"Tell your dad and Will if they find him to call this number—and tell Della," Jason said, taking out a pen and notepad to write down the number. He tore off the small slip of paper and handed it to her.

After talking to the boys and Osgood and changing her clothes, she waited at the kitchen door while Jason spoke with Sheriff Garcia. Then, as he started down the hall, he paused to talk to Will. She looked at them together. Will seemed to have grown, his head coming to Jason's shoulder, and Jason was listening carefully to what Will was saying. She loved Jason, and the boys needed him whether Brett realized it or not. Jason turned and strode toward her, taking her arm.

"I always knew you could use a gun if you had to," he said, giving her arm a squeeze.

"We were reaching the end of the line with those guys. I told them that Dad and I buried the money on the mountain."

"Good thinking. The minute Della told me about Rat, I got Terrell and we came on the run. These guys were careless enough to park in the driveway. I guess they thought they could come in during the afternoon, get the money and go. They bound and gagged our lookout but he's okay.'' He looked at Jennifer questioningly for a minute. ''Why didn't you call the sheriff as soon as Rat showed up? You risked being charged with aiding a criminal.''

Jennifer didn't answer right away. When she did, she sounded almost sheepish. ''I know... you're right. I guess that even though I know Rat's a crook, and I've tried everything to get Goldie to leave him, he's like a familiar fixture. I wanted to give Goldie a chance to talk to him first—and then I would have called. Thank God you got my message.''

Jason pulled her into his arms. ''Well, it's over now and you're safe. Once we find Brett, we can put this all behind us.''

As she looked at the patrol cars surrounding her house, their bright lights flashing, she wondered whether her life would ever be the same again. And she knew that until she found her son, her heart would never know a moment's peace.

BRETT WIPED THE TEARS off his cheeks as he scrambled over the rocks. Mount Rainy was the highest peak in the park, and he and Will had planned for years to climb it, but Mom would never let them. Now, before he left San Saba, he was going to climb Mount Rainy all alone. He felt the folded square of red silk in his pocket. It was an old scarf of Mom's that she said she didn't want, and he and Will had kept it for two years, because when they got to the top of Mount Rainy, they were going to put it there as their flag.

Several yards up the mountain, he spotted a branch that looked suitable and stuck it into his backpack to serve as a staff for the flag.

He thought about putting up the red silk. When would Will notice it? The peak could be seen on the drive into the park and from lots of other places in the park. When Will saw the red scarf, he would know that Brett had climbed the mountain all alone.

Wind whistled through the spruce, and Brett moved to the edge of a precipice and looked down at the park spread below him, the San Saba a silvery ribbon in the valley far below. "Wow!" he said softly. He had never climbed this high before in his life.

He sat on a log and pulled a candy bar from his backpack. As he unwrapped it, he glanced up the slope of the mountain. Not far away the trees ended, and he would be in the hot sun. He thought of his dad, remembering how he would swing him up high or carry him on his shoulders. He missed his father and wanted him back. He wiped his eyes again. He didn't want another father. Not Jason or anyone else. A slight twinge of guilt came with the thought, because he had taken one of Jason's fishing rods that he had left at the house. Brett knew he could survive in the park by fishing now that he knew how to clean and cook what he caught on a campfire. And he had the money from his piggy bank. Mom had replaced what the thieves had taken, and he had exactly twenty-three dollars and forty-two cents. That should last him a long time.

He stood up and began to climb, listening to the soft whisper of the wind through the trees. Raising his voice, he started to sing. He heard barking in the distance and stopped suddenly, drawing a sharp breath. He knew there could be wild animals about. His heart pounded with fear. He looked for a tree to climb—the tall, straight aspens weren't promising, but he could get up into a spruce. The barking continued and he realized it was a dog.

As he started climbing again, he listened to the high, shrill yips. It sounded like one of Granddad's dogs. If the dogs had followed him, everyone would know where he was! Disgusted, he turned to look behind him. He thought he'd gotten out of the house while the dogs were off with Granddad.

He hurried along, glancing back over his shoulder as the barking grew louder. The aspens thinned, and then he was in the sunlight on the rocky slope. The dog still followed him, so finally he stopped and waited. A small animal broke out of the trees and ran toward him.

"Oats!" Brett shook off his backpack, his heart pounding with joy as he ran to meet the dog. Oats jumped into his arms and Brett hugged the wriggling animal. His ribs showed and his short hair was covered with burrs. He licked Brett's face and Brett squeezed him hard.

"Hey, Oats! Where've you been? Hey, fella! We've all been looking for you. Is Granddad gonna be happy now!"

He suddenly remembered that he was running away from home. He set Oats on the ground and rummaged in the backpack to pull out a small sack. He reached inside for a plastic-wrapped package and peeled off a slice of cold ham for Oats, who gobbled it eagerly.

"Hey, boy, where did you go? Looks like you haven't had much to eat." Brett squatted beside the dog to pet him. "I'm leaving home." Running a hand through his curly red hair, Brett frowned and looked back down the mountain. He should take Oats home, but if he did, he would have to stay himself. If he didn't, he would have to keep Oats with him, and running away from home might be more complicated with a dog. He frowned, stroking Oats and wondering what to do.

If he ran away, he could write to his family and tell them he had Oats. He pulled on his backpack and gazed out at the park beyond. He would climb to the top and camp out tonight, then decide whether he would go on or turn around. If he went home, he could tell them he climbed to the top of Mount Rainy all by himself, besides finding Oats. "Come on, boy. You'll have to keep up, and don't go near the edge."

He looked at the steeper slope ahead. Grass was sparse because of massive boulders thrusting out of the ground, and it was bound to be heavy going. He swung down the pack and plopped it on the ground. He would get it on the way down. He patted the silk scarf in his pocket and pushed the stick for it beneath his belt at the back. With his hands free, he started to climb.

In thirty minutes he was nearing the top. Wind whistled and buffeted him across the peak, and at times he had to squeeze through a narrow space between the rugged outcroppings. Once, he hung over a drop that went straight down to the valley floor. His palms were sweaty and he cast worried glances at Oats.

Climbing and slipping over the rocks, he finally stepped out on the sharply pointed peak. Far below him hawks soared in lazy circles.

"Wow! We did it, Oats! Way to go! We climbed to the top of Mount Rainy! Just me and you. Wow! Will is gonna turn green." Brett looked all around and for the first time noticed the white thunderheads and blue-gray storm clouds building in the sky behind the next range of peaks. "We better get back down," he said.

The slope looked steeper than it had when he was climbing up, and he swallowed hard. He glanced again at the storm clouds and pulled out the red scarf and the stick. He found some loose stones and a crack in a boulder, where he put up his banner, bracing it with the stones.

When he looked up again, the dark clouds were closer, moving toward him and covering the park.

"Let's go, Oats," he said, searching for another way down. But the other side of the peak had steep drops, so he'd have to go back the way he had come. The jagged outcroppings looked ominous now, and in some places if he slipped, he would drop halfway to the valley. He checked the progress of the clouds again and suddenly wished Will was with him. He didn't want to climb down, but he had no choice.

"You stay with me, Oats," he said, truly frightened. Cautiously he began his descent. His foot dislodged a rock, and he watched as it hit a ledge, bounced and then fell into endless space.

A rumble of thunder sounded and Brett's lower lip quivered. "I wish we hadn't done this," he told Oats, who was following close at his heels. Once Oats stopped and barked, and Brett had to reach back and lift the dog down beside him.

"Come on, you have to keep up. You climbed up here without me carrying you," he said, beginning to panic because it was going to rain soon. He scooted along and then came to one of the narrow ledges that wound around a rocky wall.

He stopped and stared at it, suddenly remembering Jason's quiet demeanor whenever the boys were in trouble. Brett bit his lip and leaned against the rocks, dreading to step onto the ledge but knowing that he had to remain calm, like Jason. Oats sat at his feet and wagged his tail. "You'll have to be real careful," he said in his best adult manner, but suddenly he was a little boy again.

"Mom!" he called, feeling helpless and alone. He took a deep breath and began to edge forward, hugging the wall, not daring to look into the open space on his left, feeling air currents change as the storm approached. He put one foot in front of the other, inching along, crying quietly and wishing he were home. When he got off the mountain he was going to take Oats home. He stepped on a rock, slipped and threw himself back against the rocky wall. With a thud he sat down hard. Oats jumped into his lap and he held the dog close and started to cry again.

"Mom!" Tears flowed down his cheeks and he stared into space, too scared to go any farther. He huddled on the narrow ledge and watched the storm approach.

CHAPTER FIFTEEN

JASON PARKED THE JEEP and picked up his phone. Jennifer heard his part of the conversation and realized he was talking to Will. As soon as he hung up, she looked at him questioningly.

"Will thinks he might try to climb Mount Rainy. They had a scarf that you gave them a long time ago and they always wanted to climb the mountain and put the scarf at the top—sort of like conquering Everest. Will said the scarf is gone."

"Jason, Mount Rainy is the tallest peak in this area and people don't often climb it because it's too difficult," she said, becoming even more worried.

"At least it gives us a place to start looking and it's in my part of the park." The Jeep whined as he wound up the steep mountain road again, and he glanced at his watch.

"Aren't you headed the wrong way?"

"I'll have to turn around and go back, but in a few minutes we're going to reach a scenic viewpoint—"

"Jason, I don't give a damn about a scenic view!"

He went on calmly, "I can see Mount Rainy from there. We'll get a clear look at one side."

"Sorry I snapped at you," she said, feeling terrible. "My nerves are on edge. I should have known you weren't taking me to look at the scenery."

He caught her hand in his and gave it a squeeze. "Don't apologize. You can snap and yell all you want."

They turned a bend and the mountain dropped away on one side, leaving them a panoramic view of the park, including Mount Rainy.

"Damn!" he said, picking up his binoculars for a better look at the fluttering scrap of red at the top of the mountain. "He made it up there all by himself."

"Oh Lord, Jason!" she gasped. "Do you see him?"

"No, but this is the steep side. He couldn't get up or down on this side." Jason swept the area and then handed her the glasses. She saw the familiar red scarf waving in the breeze, and she felt a suffocating panic. The mountain looked so forbidding and far too steep for a little boy to climb.

She handed the glasses back to Jason and he looked again, taking his time. He hadn't mentioned the storm clouds to her; he didn't want to add to her worries. He could only hope Brett got off the rocky peak before the storm hit. Rain would make climbing more hazardous, and lightning was the biggest threat of all. Will had said Brett had taken his backpack, and Jason knew it was partly constructed with aluminum tubing. If he was still at the top, he would be a walking lightning rod when the storm came. Jason put down the binoculars and shifted gears, backing carefully until he could turn around and then pressing the accelerator as hard as he dared, knowing they were in a race against the storm.

He picked up the phone to call Della and tell her what he'd discovered. "Let Garcia know he's probably on Rainy, will you?" Jason asked her.

"Yes. He'll pass the word. We'll get rangers in that area. You think he's still up on the mountain?"

Jason glanced at his watch. "He made it to the top. I don't see any way he could have got all the way down again this quickly. He's probably still near the top."

"Okay. We'll send help on the way."

"Thanks." He replaced the phone and gave Jennifer's shoulder a squeeze. She looked as pale as snow, her face rigid with fear. Jason turned back to concentrate on the road as he sped toward Mount Rainy.

"I think he would have come up on the mountain from your place. My guess is, he's gone up on the south side. The west is too steep and he'd have to go a long way around to the east, and I don't think he had enough time to do that."

He glanced at the storm clouds and gripped the steering wheel. There was a lot of territory to be covered on the south side. He prayed they'd find him before the storm hit.

After what felt like an eternity, Jason finally stopped the Jeep and climbed out, looking at the south slope with a feeling of hopelessness. Knowing where to start was impossible. He'd just have to take his chances. "I'm going up," he said, taking a coil of rope out of the back of the Jeep and stuffing leather gloves into his hip pocket.

He looked up at the slope and then returned to the Jeep to call Della. "I'm on the road at point south ten," he said. "I'm going up Mount Rainy from here. When the others get here, scatter them out, but cover the south side, because I don't think he could get up any other way."

"Will do. Good luck, Jason. Help is already on the way and I've talked to Terrell. He's headed in your direction."

"Thank God. We're going to need everyone."

"You have a storm coming, Jason, so be careful."

"I've been watching," he said, glancing at Jennifer and looking into her worried green eyes. He hung up and pocketed the keys to the Jeep.

"Jason, I'm coming, too, but if I slow you down, go on without me."

He nodded and led the way. "Jennifer, every once in a while, let's call him. Sound will carry pretty far."

"Now?" When he nodded his head, she shouted, "Brett! Brett!"

There was only silence, and they continued to climb. In minutes he was wet with perspiration. He glanced down to see Jennifer only yards behind him. He cupped his hands to his mouth. "Brett! Brett!"

He waited, listening, but there was no response. Shortly he heard the drone of an engine and looked down to see a cloud of dust spinning into the air as another ranger arrived farther to the southeast. "Here comes the troops," he said, pointing.

The trees became thicker until they couldn't see what was ahead or behind. He stopped again. "Brett!" he shouted, but the only reply was the wind whistling through the spruce trees.

The next time he stopped, he gazed at the darkening sky. "Brett!" he called again.

"Jason—" Jennifer said, biting her lip.

"This is a big mountain. Just because he doesn't answer doesn't mean anything."

They climbed steadily higher. The sun was hidden by clouds now and the air became cooler. Ahead, the trees thinned and Jason hurried into the open. A blast of cool wind hit him as he gazed up the mountain at the rocky slope and shouted again. "Brett! Brett!" In the distance he heard a dog bark, and he could have sworn it came from higher up. "Jennifer, call him."

"Brett! Brett!" Her cry was whipped away by the wind, but Jason heard another bark. This time Jennifer heard it, too.

"He didn't take any of the dogs with him, did he?"

"No. They were all at home. Jason, it's going to storm," she said, sounding stricken. He wanted to stop to comfort her, but he knew they had to keep moving.

"We need to hurry. The dog could be a stray, but it's a peculiar place for a dog to be." Jason strode along, thinking about the dog. "Call again."

"Brett!" This time there was no mistaking the barking. Suddenly she gripped Jason's arm. "Jason!" He looked at her wide eyes.

"What is it?"

"Suppose it's Oats?"

"Let's go," he said, turning toward the sound of the barking as the first drops of rain hit him.

Jason stretched out his legs, scrambling over rocks and finally turning to her. "Jennifer, from here on we're in the open and lightning will be a danger. Wait for me."

She shook her head. "My son may be up there. No."

He nodded, knowing it was useless to waste time arguing. "Call again."

"Brett! Brett! Oats!"

The barking became louder and Jason headed toward it. The sky darkened and suddenly rain poured over them, icy and stinging, its hiss drowning out all other sounds.

"Dammit," Jason swore under his breath. Suddenly he saw something dashing out of the rain toward them.

"Oats!" Jennifer cried, kneeling down to catch the little dog up in her arms. It wriggled and whined while she hugged him. She looked at Jason, her eyes round with fear. "Jason, it's Oats. Do you suppose he's been with Brett?"

"He must have. They couldn't both be on the same mountaintop and not find each other. Let's go. If you put him down, would he lead you back to Brett?"

"I doubt it. I think he'll stay with me, but I'll try," she said, setting the dog down. He ran around her feet and then sat down, wagging his tail.

"Leave him on the ground. He may run off in a minute if he can get back to Brett. And keep calling your son. The dog heard us, so Brett should, too. Just keep walking in the direction Oats came from."

They moved ahead, cold rain washing over them, Oats trotting beside Jennifer. She spotted the backpack and grabbed Jason's arm. "Look!" She ran to pick up the pack. "Jason, why would he leave this?"

"He may not have wanted to carry all that weight to the top. He knew he was coming back down. He must be farther up."

They began climbing again. Suddenly the dog ran ahead, scrambling over rocks. When Oats stopped barking and looked back at them, Jason's heart leapt with hope.

"Let's follow him! Keep calling, Jen."

"Brett!"

Oats dashed ahead and Jason picked his way over the rocks, losing sight of the dog and then seeing him perched on an outcrop.

Jason climbed the rock and drew a deep breath. He turned to look back down at Jennifer, who had paused at the base of the steep incline. "Stay where you are," he called, motioning to her. He could make out the small figure huddled on the narrow ledge. One wrong move and Brett would go over the edge. Jason leaned over to look down, but rain obscured the valley below. He noted the high rocky wall behind Brett and then slid back down to Jennifer.

"I see him, Jen, but it will be hard to reach him. I'm going to put this rope around my waist." Finding a jutting slab of rock, he looped the rope around it and tied a knot, yanking it tight and tying the other end around his waist. "You stay here and hold this rope on the rock."

"Jason, the way you have it tied on, the rope can't come off that rock. There's something you don't want me to see."

"He's in a dangerous spot," Jason admitted, pulling on his leather gloves. "You keep Oats here, and make sure that rope doesn't slip."

She scooped up Oats and held him close. "Should I call to Brett?"

"Wait until I'm in his sight. He has to be scared out of his wits, and we don't want to startle him."

Jason turned away to climb over the rock and she followed. When he reached the top, he gave in and offered her a hand up. Terror made her freeze in her tracks, her ears ringing as she looked at Brett huddled on a ledge only inches wide. She bit back a cry as she watched Jason begin to climb down. "Brett!" he called in a calm voice.

"Jason!"

"Son, don't move. Just stay where you are and I'll come get you," Jason said evenly.

Jennifer realized Brett hadn't seen her yet and she waited in silence, knowing any sudden movement could send him over the edge. Oats wriggled and whimpered, wanting down, and she tightened her grip on him as she watched Jason move carefully onto the ledge. Her heart pounded wildly as she looked at Brett and heard his sobs between the gusts of wind.

"We saw your flag and knew you'd reached the top of the mountain," Jason said as he eased his way toward Brett. Suddenly Jennifer noticed that his rope was growing taut. She glanced back at the line. The rope wasn't going to be long enough for him to reach Brett!

She didn't know whether to call to him or wait and let him discover it himself. Deciding she didn't want to risk startling Brett, she bit her lip and kept quiet. Jason inched along the ledge and some of his words were whipped away by the wind and rain. Then the rain slackened off as suddenly as it had started, and she could see better.

"Son, just sit real still until I can reach you. Is this how you got up to the top? Did you climb along here?"

"Yes, sir, but it didn't look as scary when I was going up."

"It never does," Jason said. "That was some climb you made."

"Yes, sir, but I'm scared, Jason. I don't want to be here."

"I'm going to get you off. Brett, listen to me. You got up there just fine and we'll get you down. Don't think about the mountain. Think about what you'd like to eat when you get home tonight. Are you hungry?"

"No, sir. I brought some candy bars and some junk from the refrigerator. I found Oats, but I don't know where he went."

"He's all right," Jason said, stopping and tugging on the rope. Then, to Jennifer's horror, he began to take it off. He lowered it to the ledge. "Brett, very carefully now, stand up. Don't look up or down. You keep your eyes on me, do you hear?"

"Yes, sir."

Jennifer held her breath, her hands gripping Oats while she watched Jason battle for her son's life. She felt so helpless. All she could do was pray.

"Give me your hand and stand up carefully, leaning back against the rock," Jason said, and Jennifer saw Brett reach out. A second later, Jason's hand closed over his. "That's it, Brett. Now move along toward me and we'll get off this ledge."

"I can't move," he cried, and hot tears filled Jennifer's eyes.

"Please, Brett, do what he says," she whispered, her fingernails biting into her palms.

"Sure you can. Just lean against the rock and inch toward me. That's it. Good job, Brett. Keep moving and keep your eyes on me. Don't look away from me. Just watch me. Now wait a minute." Very carefully, still holding Brett's hand, Jason bent his knees and caught up the rope, dropping it over his head and under one arm. "Now let's keep going. I have a rope around me now, and we're anchored to a big rock. That's it. Just a little more." They reached the rock where Jennifer was standing, and Jason motioned to Brett. "Come closer. I'm going to pick you up and put you up on top of that rock."

"Mom!"

"Do what Jason says," she told him, crying as she spoke. They were almost safe, so close.

"Careful now," Jason said, grasping Brett beneath his arms.

Jennifer set down Oats and reached forward to grab Brett's outstretched arms and pull him onto the rock. Safe!

Jason joined them seconds later. "Let's get off this rock," he said, and they slid and climbed to the ground.

"Mom!" Brett cried, flinging his arms around her. Jennifer hugged him so tightly he yelped, and both of them shed tears of joy. She looked over his head at Jason, who was coiling the rope. Brett followed her gaze, wiped his eyes on his sleeve and walked over to Jason. "Thank you, Jason."

Jason turned to him, pulling him close, and Brett impulsively wrapped his arms around Jason.

"I'm glad you're safe. Now you can put your name on the list of people who've climbed Mount Rainy," Jason said, smiling.

Brett clung to him tightly. "Thank you for coming to get me. I don't ever want to climb up there again."

"We need to let some people know I found you, too," Jason said, taking the radio from his pocket. While he talked, Brett went back to Jennifer.

"Oats came out of the woods."

"I know. That's wonderful. Granddad will be so happy to have him back and to have you back. You're not going to leave again, are you?"

Brett shook his head solemnly. "No, ma'am."

"Let's go," Jason said, draping his arm loosely across Brett's shoulders as they started down the mountain. Before they reached the trees, the rain stopped.

"Look, Mom! Jason!" Brett exclaimed, pointing, and Jennifer turned to see a sweeping arc of colors beyond the mountain behind them.

"See, rainbows," Jason said softly, giving her a squeeze. She looked up at him and smiled, finally feeling the tension go out of her shoulders.

By the time they reached the bottom of the mountain, Brett was running ahead of them with Oats at his heels. Jason carried his fishing rod while Jennifer had the backpack.

"He acts as if nothing was wrong," she said.

"He's a kid, and it's just as well. You wouldn't want him to be traumatized by what happened."

"No, but I think *I'll* have nightmares about it for a long time."

"He's safe, Jennifer, so try to forget the bad moments. He's going to be as proud as a banty rooster about climbing the mountain when he gets back to his brothers. And I'm going to talk to Will, because they may all want to have a crack at it."

"Oh Lord, surely not! I can't imagine Brett would ever want to go up there again."

"He may completely forget how scary it was. I'll talk to them."

"Jason, I don't think he's going to be a problem from now on. He was so thankful to see you."

"I know, hon. He was just scared about losing you and the memory of his dad. It's okay." Jason helped her down the last steep slope and they crossed to the Jeep, where another was parked facing it. Terrell came forward to hug Brett and stoop to pet Oats.

"I hear you climbed all the way to the top," he said to Brett.

"Yes, sir." He gave Jennifer a worried glance. "I don't want to again. Jason got me down. It's scary up there."

"I don't think you should try again. Where did you find the dog?"

"He was on the mountain."

"I guess I'll go back to the house," Terrell said. "You can ride with me," he said to Brett. He looked at Jennifer. "Is that all right?"

"Sure, if he wants to."

"I do," he said. "Okay, Mom? Jason?"

"Yes," Jason said; and she nodded, watching him go, half-afraid to let him out of her sight.

"Jason, I feel as if I'm going to disintegrate. I feel weak all over."

"How about going out with me after dinner? It might do you good to get away for a little while. Terrell will be there with the boys, and by that time everyone will have discussed Brett's adventure and the scene with Rat and his friends.''

"It sounds glorious."

"You have a date."

IT WAS AFTER NINE when everyone was settled and Jennifer and Jason left for Jason's cabin, promising to be back shortly.

On the way there, she leaned her head back against the seat. "What a day! Will and Kyle can't stop talking about the gangsters we had and Brett can't stop talking about the mountain. The dogs are wild to have Oats back and Granddad is delighted. Even Goldie and Terrell are happy."

"I'm glad they seem to be working things out now that Rat's out of the picture."

"Jason, I'll talk to Brett, but he said he wouldn't leave home again, and he's spent half the night following you around with the other boys, so I think that problem is solved."

"I think so, too."

"I talked to them about going to school in Rimrock."

"And what did they say?" He turned to look at her in the half light as he waited for her answer.

"They think it'll be all right."

"So there's nothing standing in our way?" he asked quietly.

"I want to talk to Brett again. I guess I'm the one who'll have to make the biggest adjustment to living out here all the time. You know I love the city."

"You don't have to give up your home there, and we can go to Santa Fe whenever I'm off."

She didn't reply, and he turned to drive across the bridge over the San Saba. "I'll never cross this bridge without remembering the night the dam burst. It changed everything," she said thoughtfully.

"For the better," Jason added, charging up the mountain. In minutes he slowed before the dark patrol cabin and climbed out of the Jeep. When they stepped inside the cabin, he pulled Jennifer into his arms. He lowered his head tantalizingly close and then stopped. "If I kiss you, I'll hurt you."

"You'll hurt me more if you don't."

Needing her badly, he touched her bruised cheek. "I wish I could have had that guy alone for ten minutes." He leaned down and his mouth covered hers. He tried to be gentle until her kisses became more passionate. With his back against the door, he pulled her closer, pressing their bodies together.

He peeled away her T-shirt, jeans and boots, while managing somehow to remove his own shirt. He held her soft warm body against him while his hands caressed her.

"Jason," she whispered, her fingers working on his belt buckle. Eagerness, joy and desire burned in her. He shed his jeans quickly and she pushed down his briefs to free him, moving enticingly against him.

Swinging her into his arms, he carried her to his bed.

"It's been forever," he said softly, drawing her to him to kiss her hard.

LATER SHE LAY IN his arms while he let long strands of her hair slide through his fingers. "Set a wedding date, Jennifer, and make it soon. We'll try to call my folks in a little while. I've already told them I proposed to you."

"I imagine they almost fainted to find out you want to marry a widow with three boys, a deaf father, five dogs and a crazy sister." He chuckled and she turned on her side to raise herself up slightly and look at him. She drew her fingers across his bare chest. "Admit it."

"They were a little surprised." His blue eyes were warm and filled with love, and she leaned forward to kiss him lightly before settling down against his chest and listening to his heart beat.

"Jason, my boys never cease to amaze me. I can't imagine Will getting that thug's gun away from him, and it terrifies me to think of what might have happened."

"No help needed there. It pays to raise hooligans, sweetie. They can take care of themselves in a pinch."

"I don't know if I like that or not."

He laughed softly and stroked her head. "They're bright kids. Brett got himself into trouble because he probably panicked coming back down. He's as happy as a clam about reaching the top, though."

"I doubt if we'll ever hear the end of either adventure for months to come."

"I doubt it, too. And it'll all be in the Rimrock paper, so when they start school, they'll be celebrities."

"You're probably right."

"Jason, when we marry, you'll want a child, won't you?"

"I might. Is that a problem?"

"I'm getting old."

"Oh, sure. Thirty."

She stared at him, her gaze drifting over his broad chest. "I'd like a girl. Think you can do that?"

"What happens if it's a boy?"

"I guess I'll love him like I love the others," she said, rising up again to look into his eyes. He cupped her head with his hand and pulled her down to him.

It was almost midnight when Jason took her home, but lights blazed from every room. "Jason, everyone is up, so let's tell them now."

"Sounds fine to me," he said, reaching over to take her hand and hold it tightly.

"I want just a minute alone with the boys."

"That sounds fine, too, and then I'd like a few minutes with them."

She raised his hand to kiss his fingers, placing it against her cheek. "Jason, I'm so happy!"

"So am I. My life was lonely and I didn't even know it until you and your family became part of it," he said in a husky voice. "I don't ever want to be alone again."

"It's a good thing you feel that way," she said, smiling at him.

He slowed as they walked toward the back door, and Brett and Will came tumbling out.

"Mom! Jason! Did you see us on television?"

"No!" she exclaimed. "We missed it."

"We were on the news tonight!" Will said, grinning. "We taped it so you can see it. I got to tell them how Kyle talked to the guy and I got his gun, and they told all about the money and Sheriff Garcia was on, and so was Terrell."

"Wow! We'll look at the tape in a minute, but right now I want you to get Kyle so I can talk to all three of you."

"Sure." Will looked back and forth between them. "You guys getting married?"

"Hurry up!" She laughed and nodded.

"I'll be in the kitchen," Jason said, moving past Brett. She reached out to pull Brett closer, holding his hands.

"Honey, I want to marry Jason."

He nodded. "Jason's okay, Mom. I sure was glad to see him today."

"You'll be happy to have him part of our family?"

"Yes, I guess so. Seems like we always need him to rescue one of us."

She reached out to hug him, tears stinging her eyes. "Brett, Daddy would want us all to do this. Jason will be good for our family and Dad would want us to be happy."

"Okay," he said, wriggling, and she released him as Will and Kyle came out.

"I just wanted to tell the three of you that Jason and I are going to get married."

"That's great, Mom," Will said.

"It's okay," Brett agreed as his brothers stared at him.

Kyle nodded. "That's great. Did you see us on television?"

"No, but I will," she answered, smiling. "Now wait a minute before you go running off. Jason wants to talk to you, too. Just stay right here and let me get him." She went into the kitchen. "You've been approved and now it's your turn."

"That's good news," he said, brushing her cheek with a kiss as he passed her to go outside.

She stood at the window and glanced out to see him pull the three of them close while he talked to them. "Oh, Mark, I have to go on," she whispered, thinking about her husband and about Jason, knowing this was so right for her and for the boys. Jason would be good with them. She wiped her eyes and turned away, switching off the light and waiting for all of them to return. The boys burst into the kitchen.

"Hey, you're not cooking in the dark again, are you?" Will asked, flipping the switch. "That's weird.

Come see the video—it's neat. Chase and Bob called from Santa Fe and said they saw us tonight!''

"Great," she said, as Jason slipped his arm around her waist and they followed the boys into the living room, where Terrell and Goldie sat with Osgood, who held Oats in his lap.

"You'll have to see the news," Goldie said. Terrell's arm was around her and she looked more like herself again.

"We're going to, but first," Jennifer said, looking up at Jason, "we want to tell you something. We're getting married."

Goldie shrieked and jumped up to hug Jennifer while Terrell crossed the room to shake hands with Jason.

Terrell looked over at her. "I'm glad. That guy needs a family. You'll be great for him—all of you."

She laughed as Jason draped his arm across her shoulders. "I agree. Now let's look at that video."

THREE NIGHTS LATER Jennifer placed a large pan of lasagna on the table. Jason had arrived after work, and Terrell and Goldie had driven back from Rimrock, where Goldie had spent much of the afternoon talking to Sheriff Garcia again. As soon as everyone was served, Goldie looked across the table at Jennifer. Her eyes sparkled as she glanced up at Terrell and placed her hand on his arm.

"I know all of you want to hear what happened in Rimrock today, but we have some other news first."

Terrell grinned and turned to look at her.

"We have to tell everyone," she said, linking her arm through Terrell's. "You two aren't the only ones getting married. Terrell has asked me to marry him."

"That's wonderful!" Jennifer exclaimed, getting up to hug her sister while Kyle rolled his eyes.

"You're going to be our uncle?" Will asked.

"I suppose I am," Terrell said, grinning at Jason.

"Wow! That's neat," Brett said. "Our family will be bigger."

Talk centered on weddings for the next few minutes until finally Goldie drew a deep breath. "Now I'd better tell you the rest of the news. There will be a trial, and I'll have to testify," she said somberly. "I may have to testify in California, too, because that's where the money was stolen." She looked at Jennifer. "I'm going to have to tell the court that Rat gave me the money."

"Can you do that?" Jennifer asked quietly.

Goldie nodded. "He shouldn't have put me in danger like that. I shouldn't have taken it or come here or..."

"It's all right now, Goldie," Jennifer said.

"Besides, you wouldn't have met Terrell if you hadn't," Kyle added, and they all laughed.

Jason caught Jennifer's eye and winked at her, and she longed to be alone with him, wanting to be in his arms. For a moment she forgot all the others as they gazed at each other and silently communicated their love.

CHAPTER SIXTEEN

THE FIRST SATURDAY in August, Jennifer stood near the altar as Goldie repeated her vows. Then, in the same chapel thirty minutes later, Jennifer walked down the aisle on Osgood's arm. She wore a calf-length turquoise silk dress, and around her neck was a diamond pendant from Jason.

She looked proudly at the man she was about to marry, then at her family, and tears sprang into her eyes.

After they repeated their vows, Jason kissed her, and she felt a wild mixture of emotions—joy, amazement, longing. Dazed, she joined the others in the church parlor for the reception. A band played and she danced with Jason while Terrell danced with Goldie.

Finally it was time for them to leave. As they told Jason's parents goodbye, Jill Hollenbeck brushed Jennifer's cheek with a kiss.

"Welcome to the family. I think you'll be a good influence on our son."

"Thank you," Jennifer said, as Jason leaned forward to kiss his mother. Next she gave her sister a tight squeeze. "I'm so happy for you, Goldie."

Goldie's eyes sparkled. "I've never been this happy, Jennifer. And I'm happy for you and Jason, too. The boys seem to adore Jason and they like having Terrell for an uncle."

Jennifer laughed, turning to look for her sons. They stood at the table eating chocolate cake and she went over to hug them, Jason suddenly appearing at her side. "Now, fellows, please be good and take care of Grand-dad."

"We will," they chorused with wide, innocent eyes.

Jason leaned close to them. "Will, you get everyone to the airport on time. I'm counting on you."

"Yes, sir. Granddad is keeping the plane tickets and we'll meet you in L.A. next Saturday at ten o'clock in the morning."

"And then we get to go to Disneyland!" Kyle said, his eyes sparkling with excitement, a tiny blob of chocolate on his chin.

Jennifer kissed them goodbye, and Jason gave them each a squeeze, then took her arm to find Osgood.

"Dad, we're going."

"Yes, the boys are growing."

"Dad!" she exclaimed loudly, and pointed to her ear.

"Oh." He touched his hearing aid. "Too much noise in here and too many widows. I've never talked to so many women in one hour in my life."

"We're going now, Dad. You have our itinerary. We're flying to Phoenix and we'll be there for three days, and then we're going to the Grand Canyon. We'll meet you Saturday morning in Los Angeles. Get everyone to the plane on time."

"Don't give it a thought." He squinted at Jason. "You take care of my girl."

"I'll do that," he said, sliding his arm around her shoulders. She hugged and kissed Osgood and then Jason urged her toward the door.

"They're leaving!" Will called, and the guests rushed to follow them. They were pelted with birdseed as they hurried to the waiting limo, but when they saw it, they stopped in dismay.

"No!" Jason said, looking around. The boys grinned and ducked, edging back out of sight except for Will, who snapped Jason's picture. "Jennifer..."

She stared at the limo. It sat up on concrete blocks, the back wheels not touching the ground. "The boys can't lift a limo!"

"Your boys would find a way. Terrell! Give me a hand."

Other men came forward and Jennifer searched the crowd. None of the boys was in sight, but Osgood stood grinning at her. With the help of their guests, Jason and Terrell lifted the limo, and the driver shoved away the blocks.

"Now, love, before your boys can do one more thing..." Jason opened the door and Jennifer slid inside. As soon as they pulled away from the church, Jason closed the divider between the front and back seats. "The driver will let us know when we're near Albuquerque and the airport. Until then, come here."

They flew to Phoenix, and as soon as the door closed behind them in the hotel suite, Jason wrapped her in his arms. "Alone at last, Mrs. Hollenbeck."

"Yes, sir."

"I can't believe it," he said. "No interruptions for one whole week."

She wound her fingers in his thick black hair, and his gaze heated as he tightened his arms, holding her against his chest.

"Jason," she said, pushing his jacket away. It fell on the floor as he reached for her buttons. The turquoise silk drifted down in a whisper around her ankles and he inhaled sharply as he pressed her to him. "My love," he whispered, his mouth covering hers while his hands caressed her, brushing her hips and peeling away the bits of lacy underwear.

Her heart pounded with excitement and desire as she clung to him, molding her body against the lean strength of his. Joyfully she held him, overwhelmed with love.

"Jason," she whispered, "I can't believe how lucky I am."

"Not half as lucky as I am," he said in a husky voice, leaning forward to kiss her. She felt she would melt with happiness, because now the Ruark circle of love had expanded to include Jason.

HARLEQUIN SUPERROMANCE®

HARLEQUIN SUPERROMANCE WANTS TO INTRODUCE YOU TO A DARING NEW CONCEPT IN ROMANCE...

WOMEN WHO DARE!
Bright, bold, beautiful...
Brave and caring, strong and passionate...
They're women who know their own minds
and will dare anything...for love!

One title per month in 1993, written by popular Superromance authors, will highlight our special heroines as they face unusual, challenging and sometimes dangerous situations.

It takes real courage to mend a broken heart in #566 COURAGE, MY LOVE by Lynn Leslie

Available in October wherever Harlequin Superromance novels are sold.

If you missed any of the Women Who Dare titles and would like to order them, send your name, address, zip or postal code, along with a check or money order for $3.39 for #533, #537, #541, #545 and #549, or $3.50 for #553, #554, #558 and #562, for each book ordered, plus 75¢ (1.00 in Canada) postage and handling, payable to Harlequin Reader Service, to:

In the U.S.	In Canada
3010 Walden Ave.	P. O. Box 609
P. O. Box 1325	Fort Erie, Ontario
Buffalo, NY 14269-1325	L2A 5X3

Please specify book title(s) with order.
Canadian residents add applicable federal and provincial taxes.

WWD-0

MEN MADE IN AMERICA

Fifty red-blooded, white-hot, true-blue hunks from every State in the Union!

Beginning in May, look for MEN MADE IN AMERICA! Written by some of our most popular authors, these stories feature fifty of the strongest, sexiest men, each from a different state in the union!

Two titles available every other month at your favorite retail outlet.

In September, look for:

DECEPTIONS by Annette Broadrick (California)
STORMWALKER by Dallas Schulze (Colorado)

In November, look for:

STRAIGHT FROM THE HEART by Barbara Delinsky (Connecticut)
AUTHOR'S CHOICE by Elizabeth August (Delaware)

You won't be able to resist MEN MADE IN AMERICA!

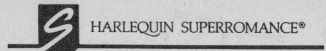

THE MONTH OF
LIVING DANGEROUSLY

**LIVE ON THE EDGE WITH SUPERROMANCE
AS OUR HEROINES BATTLE
THE ELEMENTS AND THE ENEMY**

Windstorm by Connie Bennett pits woman against nature as Teddi O'Brian sets her sights on a tornado chaser.

In Sara Orwig's *The Mad, the Bad & the Dangerous,* Jennifer Ruark outruns a flood in the San Saba Valley.

Wildfire by Lynn Erickson is a real trial by fire as Piper Hillyard learns to tell the good guys from the bad.

In Marisa Carroll's *Hawk's Lair,* Sara Riley tracks subterranean treasure—and a pirate—in the Costa Rican rain forest.

Learn why Superromance heroines are more than just the women next door, and join us for some adventurous reading this September!

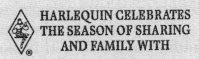